NIMBUS

NIMBUS

BY
JAN ELDREDGE

ILLUSTRATIONS BY
DEVIN ELLE KURTZ

SCHOLASTIC

Published in the UK by Scholastic, 2023
1 London Bridge, London, SE1 9BG
Scholastic Ireland, 89E Lagan Road, Dublin Industrial Estate,
Glasnevin, Dublin, D11 HP5F

First published in the US by Balzer + Bray, an imprint of
HarperCollins Publishers, 2023

Text © Jan Eldredge, 2023
Illustrations © Devin Elle Kurtz, 2023

The right of Jan Eldredge and Devin Elle Kurtz to be identified
as the author and illustrator of this work has been asserted by them
under the Copyright, Designs and Patents Act 1988.

Typography by Andrea Vandergrift
ScoutAutomatedPrintCode

ISBN 978 1407 18103 5

A CIP catalogue record for this book is available from the British Library.

Printed and bound in Great Britain by Clays Ltd, Elcograf S.p.A
Paper made from wood grown in sustainable forests
and other controlled sources.

1 3 5 7 9 10 8 6 4 2

www.scholastic.co.uk

For Mom and Dad

✦ ✦ ✦

+ + +

Ah! Cats are a mysterious kind of folk. There is more passing in their minds than we are aware of. It comes no doubt from their being so familiar with warlocks and witches.

—Sir Walter Scott (1771–1832) to Washington Irving (1783–1859)

+ + +

CHAPTER 1

There was something inside the room that made Nim uneasy—something very old, something very wicked.

With ears perked and whiskers at attention, she prowled into the dimly lit room that Fletcher's father used as his home office. A streetlight's beam shone through the half-opened window blinds, but she didn't need it. She could see perfectly well in the darkness. All cats could.

She drew to a stop and her fur bristled.

"Something's definitely in here," she whispered. "Something that shouldn't be."

Sweeping her gaze around, she spied the tip of one of Fletcher's handmade arrows hanging over the edge of his father's large desk. It was the one Fletcher made from the old gray arrowhead he found in the woods—his most prized possession. Nim frowned, wondering if she should return it to Fletcher's room where it belonged.

But the old arrowhead wasn't the problem. She turned her attention to the towering shelf along the wall, running her eyes over the rows of vintage horror comics and up to the top ledge where Fletcher's father kept his figurines of classic movie monsters.

She didn't understand why Fletcher's father loved old scary movies or why he loved his job as a Saturday night TV horror host more than he loved his job as a weekday weatherman. But in her eleven months of life, she'd come to realize there were a lot of things she didn't understand.

Narrowing her eyes, she scowled at the monster models: Dracula, with the huge white fangs hanging from his mouth; the Wolf Man's pointy ears and dark, hairy arms and feet; the Mummy's unraveling bandages; and the webbed and clawed hands of the Creature from the Black Lagoon. Fletcher didn't like the monster models. She didn't like them either.

She lifted her nose and sniffed, detecting a wispy thread of mustiness. She stepped closer to the shelf and the unpleasant smell grew stronger. Her ears perked higher as she followed the trail, tracking it along the top of the shelf to the sand-colored jar with a stone stopper wedged in its mouth. Spiky black claw marks were painted on its surface, along with an elongated animal skull filled with jagged teeth, saber-like canines, and huge empty eye sockets. A shiver rippled her fur. The old jar made her uneasy and so did its twin sitting upstairs on Fletcher's bookshelf. They'd given her the jitters from the first moment she saw them.

With the fur on her neck prickling, she sniffed deeper, this time perceiving the scents of something ancient and cruel. She twitched her tail nervously, hoping the old jars would stay put where they were, far up and out of reach. What she wished even more was that they'd never been brought into the house in the first place. She stood glaring at the hateful thing when a sharp *clank* sounded in the kitchen, startling her. She whirled around, and with a soft snarl rumbling in her throat, she crept into the dark hallway to inspect the noise.

An aroma of steaming vanilla, along with a few herbs she couldn't name, seeped up her nose, and her pounding heart slowed. "Aunt Caroline," she growled. It was just Fletcher's aunt making a cup of tea; she'd come to stay with them during Fletcher's spring break while his father was away at the Florida Weather Forecasters' Convention.

Nim supposed it was a nice thing for the woman to do, but really, Fletcher was *her* friend, and it was *her* job to protect him. She frowned, remembering that Aunt Caroline would be taking him out for a picnic tomorrow with fresh lemonade and sandwiches cut into little triangles. Nim peeked at the front door. Her shoulders slumped, and she took a step back.

There was nothing good outside, and she always worried for Fletcher when he left the house.

She had just turned to make her way up to his room to continue her nightly inspections when the sight of another black cat drew a hiss from her mouth and made the fur rise on her back. But it was nothing more than her own reflection peering out from the tall mirror on the wall, only a young black cat with an old, injured foreleg. Embarrassed, she glanced around, pleased no one else had witnessed her foolishness. "Stop being such a scaredy-cat," she scolded herself.

She padded her way up the staircase, and when she slipped through the half-opened door into Fletcher's room, her spirits lifted.

He was sitting up in bed, dressed in his pajamas with the wizard hats and wands on them. The light of the nearby lamp gleamed off the lenses of his round eyeglasses, and tufts of his fair hair stuck up like chicken feathers. He needed grooming.

"Where did I put those pliers?" he muttered as he patted the top of the starry-patterned bedspread. He leaned over and rummaged through the drawer of his bedside table. "Ah, here they are!"

Nim glanced around Fletcher's domain, comforted by the tug of her bright green collar, the one Fletcher had chosen because it matched the color of her eyes. And he was the one who'd attached the identification tag to it, the small gold disk engraved with the family's phone number and the name he'd given her when they first met: Nimbus.

She smiled as she began her nightly patrol of the room, carefully inspecting everything to make sure no insects or lizards had invaded. She passed the rumpled socks and T-shirts strewn across the floor. They smelled like Fletcher, like the pages of a well-read book, along with tree bark, chocolate, and oak leaves.

She strode to the tall bookcase and sniffed at the magical fantasy titles lining its lower shelf. She rubbed her cheek against *The Hobbit*, Fletcher's favorite and the story he'd read to her when she was recovering from her injuries.

Up on the bed, Fletcher huffed with annoyance, then frowned at an item lying on his lap. Using the pliers, he tried to pry something from it. He was always working on projects and studying interesting objects. And not for the first time, Nim wondered if there was anyone else in the world as smart and curious and talented as him. Her heart swelled with pride. He especially liked things that he found in nature. His favorite discovery was the old gray arrowhead. She glanced up at the empty spot on the wall above his bed, the place where his prized arrow usually hung. "Aunt Caroline," she growled again. The woman had taken it to the antique fair that morning to have it appraised, then forgot to return it to his room. Nim didn't appreciate such careless treatment of Fletcher's belongings.

Swishing her tail, she continued her inspection, strolling past Fletcher's desk with the drawers hanging half-open. She glanced under the bed, peered into shadows, and studied the nightstand with the big jar of arrows sitting on top of it. Fletcher had made the weapons himself, carving those arrowheads from stones. Another surge of pride filled her heart. Then she stopped and pricked her ears, sensing an unwelcome presence nearby.

Rumbling a low growl, she climbed onto Fletcher's desk and wound her way around his laptop and the small piles of rocks and feathers sitting there. She pushed down a slat of the window blinds, peered at the backyard below, then bent her ears in annoyance. The stray had returned—the silvery-gray tabby that had started hanging around a few weeks ago. She wished it would go away. What if Fletcher were to suddenly grow tired of her? What if he wanted a cat to join him on his explorations in the woods and decided to replace her with the stray? The cat was wild, though, a skittish thing, always hurrying away whenever Fletcher set out food and water for it. Nim didn't begrudge the cat such necessities, she just wished it'd find a new home. A nice home like hers, with a nice human like hers, just not her home and her human.

She climbed down from the desk and peered up at Fletcher, propped against the pillow in his big bed, which always made him look so small and thin. She jumped up to join him, but when she stepped closer, she froze. A wispy odor of mustiness bloomed in her nose. Her fur bushed, and she drew her lips back in a silent snarl.

CHAPTER 2

The second old jar lay on Fletcher's lap. He was so focused on it that he hadn't noticed Nim hop onto the bed.

She frowned with disapproval. It was Aunt Caroline who'd brought the horrible things into the house. She'd bought them at the antique fair that morning as gifts. One for Fletcher's father and one for Fletcher.

Fletcher wiped his forehead on the sleeve of his wizard pajamas. Then he set the pliers on the bedside table and turned his attention to a book lying open beside him.

Nim walked across the bedspread and right up to him, her nostrils flaring at the scent of the jar. It smelled just like the other one downstairs, and now that she was closer, the odors of panic and fear radiated from it like drafts of cold air. It bothered her that she hadn't detected the smells as soon as she'd entered the room. She butted her head against Fletcher's arm, trying to nudge his hand away from the awful thing.

He glanced up, and a crooked smile lit his face. "Hey there, Nim." She meowed a greeting in return as he scratched her head. "I've been doing some research on this jar," he said. "I know it doesn't look very ancient because it's still in great shape, but I'm wondering if it might actually be older than Aunt Caroline or the antiques dealer thought it was." His eyes widened. "I'm thinking it might even be from the Mycenaean period! Wouldn't that be amazing?"

Nim loved that Fletcher always talked to her. And while she couldn't respond with words that he understood, she could still communicate her feelings. She smiled in reply, not because she was happy about the old jar, but because she liked to see Fletcher happy.

"See?" He tapped the page of the opened book. "Here are some examples of Mycenaean pottery for rituals. Except for the weird symbols painted on this one, they look very similar."

Nim peered at the pictures, running her gaze over the different statues and vases, the buildings with tall white columns, and the people dressed in clothes that looked like sheets they'd tied around themselves.

"It's possible it could've been used in a magical ritual."

Fletcher shook the jar. "It sounds like there's some sort of grainy particles inside. Maybe it's dried-up magic that's kept this old thing in such good shape!" His eyebrows rose with excitement behind his eyeglasses. "Don't you want me to open it and see what's inside?"

Nim fixed her gaze on his face, bent her ears back, and yowled as loudly as she could.

Fletcher smiled. "Don't worry, girl, I've been trying for a while now to get this stopper out, and it won't budge. See?" He tugged at the top, but it didn't move. "If there's anything mystical inside this old thing, I guess it's stuck there."

Fear crept through Nim's veins. If the jars had contained magic inside them, it couldn't have been the good kind—not with such ominous smells still coming from them.

"Most people don't believe in magic," Fletcher continued as he ran his thumb along the strange claw marks painted on the artifact. "They don't believe in the existence of secret laws and powers within nature. But I know it's real."

It surprised Nim that most people didn't think there was magic in the world. Maybe they just couldn't see things as well as cats could. She still didn't want Fletcher to open the jar, though. She sat down and scowled at him.

He ruffled the top of her head. Then he pushed his

glasses up onto his nose, returned his attention to the artifact, and jiggled the stone stopper again. When it didn't loosen, he turned back to the book and flipped through its pages.

Still scowling, and with anxiety nibbling her nerves, Nim rose onto her hind legs. She rubbed her cheek against the side of his face, mingling her scent with his, creating the reassuring smell that always comforted her.

The stopper wasn't going to come out, and she was glad. Though she was sorry to see Fletcher disappointed. Leaving him to continue his research on the ugly old jar, she hopped down to the floor and went to her small bed in the corner. She preferred it to Fletcher's big bed, not only because it gave her a better view of the room and any intruders that might try to enter, but because Fletcher had made it just for her. And while it was nothing more than an old flat pillow stuffed inside a piece of green fabric and sewn together with crooked black stitches, she thought it was beautiful.

With a sigh of contentment, Nim rested her head on her paws. Other than the troubling clay jars, all was right in her world. She purred softly, and her eyes drifted shut.

"Fletcher?" Aunt Caroline called from the hallway.

Nim's whiskers drooped, and her eyes opened. All was right in her world except for Aunt Caroline, with her sensible haircut and sensible shoes, always wearing a cardigan sweater no matter the temperature.

The bedroom door swung open, and the woman entered with a laundry basket tucked beneath her arm and her phone held to her ear. "Hold on just a second, Patrick." She cast a puzzled look at Fletcher, then glanced around the room. "Who were you talking to?" she whispered.

"Nim," he replied as he flipped through more pages of the book.

She arched an eyebrow, then handed him the phone. "It's your father, calling all the way from Tampa. He wants to tell you good night."

"Tampa's only an hour's drive away," Fletcher pointed out as he took the phone. "Hi, Dad." He nodded. "Yes." He nodded again. "Yes." He paused. "Yes, I will. Okay . . . okay. Good night to you too. Bye." He disconnected the call and returned the phone to his aunt.

Aunt Caroline bit her lip, her face furrowing with concern. "Fletcher, I think you need some real friends . . . people friends. You should join a sports team, spend more time outdoors with other kids and not so much time in your room or out alone in the woods collecting . . . things." She motioned toward the piles of stones and feathers sitting on his desk, the items that he used to make his arrows.

Nim huffed. As far as she was concerned, Fletcher

already spent too much time outside without her, exploring the nearby wooded area looking for old arrowheads and interesting rocks.

Wrinkling his brow, Fletcher stared up at his aunt. "But spending time in nature is a good thing. Researchers have discovered that admiring plants and listening to the sounds of wildlife reduces stress."

"I just think you'd be a lot happier if you mingled with other kids." His aunt gave him a forced smile.

While Nim knew Aunt Caroline was genuinely fond of Fletcher, she didn't like her trying to change him. And she most definitely didn't like the woman implying she wasn't a real friend for him.

Aunt Caroline sniffed the air, then grimaced at the sight of Fletcher's clothes strewn across the floor. "It smells a bit stuffy in here."

Nim watched sulkily as she marched across the room, raised the blinds, and opened the window. "There," she said, looking satisfied. "Fresh air is good for you, especially on such a lovely spring evening." An enormous ghostly-green moth fluttered up to the opening, and she flapped her hand at it. "Shoo!" she cried, sending it fluttering away.

"It's just a luna moth." Fletcher shook his head at her foolishness. "They don't bite. They don't even have mouths." Then his eyes brightened. "Some people believe seeing one is a sign that a big change is about to happen in their life."

"Whatever it is, it doesn't belong in the house," Aunt Caroline replied.

But to Nim, the moth was quite pretty, like a beautiful leaf with wings.

Leaning closer to the open window, Aunt Caroline inhaled the outside air. "Ah, just smell that night-blooming jasmine!" A sudden breeze blew in, bringing with it a scattering of oak leaves and depositing them on the sill. "Messy things," she grumbled, and swept them back out.

As Fletcher returned his attention to twisting and jiggling the jar's stopper, Aunt Caroline glanced at her watch. "It's getting late. Time for lights out." She plucked his sixth-grade geography textbook from the floor and set it on his desk. Then she gathered his dirty clothes, dropped them into the laundry basket, and tucked it under her arm. "Good night, Fletcher dear," she called over her shoulder as she headed to the door.

"Good night, Aunt Caroline." He took off his glasses and set them on his bedside table, along with the book and the old jar. "Don't forget to tell Nim good night too," he said, fluffing his pillow.

Aunt Caroline paused, and in a sugary-coated voice she cooed, "Good night, little Nim."

Nim's face warmed with shame. Maybe she'd been wrong. Maybe Aunt Caroline wasn't so bad. Maybe they could even become friends. She lifted her head and gave a hopeful thump of her tail.

Aunt Caroline stepped into the hallway, but when she pulled the door shut, she narrowed her eyes and frowned down at Nim.

Nim's hopefulness withered; she'd seen that expression of dislike before, right before she'd come to live with Fletcher.

As Aunt Caroline's footsteps receded down the staircase, a soft *click* sounded from Fletcher's bed, then he set a flashlight on the side table. Sitting up, he pulled on his glasses, and by the weak glow of the flashlight's yellow beam, he took the jar and went back to work on it. "Why won't you open?" He grabbed a large rock from his nightstand and tapped it against the stopper. "Open already!" he muttered.

Nim rested her head on her paws, watching him with worried eyes, wishing he'd leave the stinky jar alone.

"Hey! I've loosened it!" He grinned triumphantly as he pulled the stopper free.

The temperature in the room plummeted.

An ancient and malicious stench mushroomed in the air. Mingled within it swirled the potent smells of panic and fear. Not even the night breeze coming through the open window could erase the foul odors.

Nim sprang to her feet, her hackles rising.

Wrinkling his nose as a sooty fog seeped from the old vessel, Fletcher frantically waved his hand, trying to clear it away, and in the process knocked the flashlight to the floor. It rolled underneath the bed, its tiny ray of light nearly extinguished by the shadows. The grimy mist glided toward him, floating around his head, almost as if it had done so intentionally. Fletcher gasped, and with eyes squeezed shut, he fell back against his pillow. The jar tumbled from his fingers as the smoke drifted away.

For a moment, Nim thought the strange substance would vanish, but it gathered into a dense cloud and hovered above Fletcher's heart.

A growl rumbled deep in her throat. She arched her back and dropped her tail. Her paws remained glued to her bed, though. She had no idea how to fight smoke.

Before her terrified gaze, the shadowy mass grew thicker, lowering itself, morphing and solidifying until, to her confusion, it assumed the form of a small hairy goblin clothed in tattered rags. It crouched upon Fletcher's chest, peering at him through round, glowing yellow eyes. Then it leaned its pointy-eared head close to his, peeled its lips back over its fangs, and snarled.

Fletcher's eyes popped open, and trembling, he stared in horror at the monster.

"Get away from him!" Nim spat, but the unearthly being ignored her. Hissing and unsheathing her claws, she crouched, ready to leap to Fletcher's defense, when the creature placed the tip of its sharp-clawed finger to Fletcher's forehead. Fletcher grew suddenly still, seemingly too terrified to move, like someone trapped in the middle of a terrible nightmare.

With teeth bared and fur bristling, Nim lunged from her bed, but her feet tangled, and she crashed to the floor. The goblin grasped Fletcher's chin with one of its webbed hands, and in a raspy voice, it whispered a string of menacing, ancient-sounding words.

Nim scrambled up as Fletcher's mouth dropped open, and a flickering bead of light, like a firefly or a blinking Christmas tree bulb, floated out.

"No!" she cried. Before she could leap again, the goblin darted its head forward and chomped onto the tiny light.

CHAPTER 3

The horrifying sight struck Nim like lightning, scattering her fear and confusion, jolting her with a surge of energy, and awakening her fierce feline instincts.

Hissing and snarling, she sprang up to Fletcher's bed and onto the goblin's back, driving her nails into its cold, musty-smelling skin.

The creature spun around with a squeal of surprise, its claws raking four gashes across Fletcher's cheek and knocking his eyeglasses askew. It swung its arms over its shoulders, desperate to fling Nim from its back, but she only dug her nails deeper.

Twisting and snapping, they collided into the old jar, sending it rolling off the bed and smashing against the floor.

"Fletcher?" Aunt Caroline called from downstairs.

But Nim hardly heard; her only purpose at that moment was to destroy the monster. She clamped down on the side of its neck, and a vile bitterness flooded her mouth as if she'd just taken a bite from something poisonous. Nausea bloomed throughout her, unfolding like the petals of a deadly flower. The strength left her limbs. Her teeth and claws slipped from the creature, and she fell onto the bed.

She lay on her side, desperate to leap up, struggling to catch her breath. The goblin whirled around on her. Snarling, it glared down with its acid-yellow eyes. It pressed its clawed finger to her forehead, as it had done to Fletcher, and her muscles and limbs grew impossibly heavy.

She tried to climb to her feet but couldn't. Her thundering heart seemed to be the only part of her still moving within her panicked body.

Baring its fangs and snarling, the creature crouched beside her. It drew back a hairy arm, its hand lingering above her as though relishing its victory. Then it swiped down, one of its talons slicing an opening through the flesh on her side.

Fiery pain reawakened her frozen muscles. She lashed out with her paw, slashing her claws through one of the monster's glowing yellow eyes.

The beast screeched and stumbled back, cupping its webbed hands to its face as a burst of white light exploded in Nim's head, blurring her vision.

"Fletcher?" Aunt Caroline's footsteps pounded up the staircase.

Nim thrust out her paw, ready to strike again, but the goblin was shrinking, deflating like a ragged balloon. It dissolved into a cloud of ashy smoke, drifted to the open window, and disappeared into the night.

Nim trembled with relief. She'd done it! She'd killed the monster! Pride and disbelief twined inside her: pride that she'd been so clever and courageous, and disbelief because she'd never killed anything in her life.

Her heart still booming, she climbed to her feet and limped to Fletcher. His eyes were now squeezed shut as he lay gasping. She lowered her face to his and sniffed the four bloody gashes splayed across his cheek. Traces of the creature's damp, moldering stench lingered there.

The bedroom door flew open. The overhead light snapped on. Aunt Caroline stood for a moment with her mouth gaping as her gaze swept past the broken shards on the floor and up to a wheezing Fletcher, fiery-red scratches swelling across his face, and finally landed on Nim leaning over him.

Her face pinching with panic, she hurried across the room and swept Nim away, sending her tumbling to the floor in a pain-filled heap.

"Fletcher?" She sat on the side of the bed, worry rising in her voice. "Fletcher, are you okay?"

He didn't answer. His eyes remained shut, though his breaths were coming easier.

Nim struggled to her feet and limped away, taking shelter behind the wastepaper basket and the crumpled papers littering the floor next to Fletcher's desk.

"Fletcher, what happened?" Aunt Caroline leaned closer, peering worriedly at his cheek. "How'd you get those scratches?"

He peeled his eyes open, lifted a shaky hand, and pointed toward the window above the desk, the one the creature's grimy cloud of smoke had passed through. "It was a monster," he rasped. "With dark hair, claws, fangs, and pointy ears."

Aunt Caroline cast a glare where Nim hunched panting beside the desk. If Nim had possessed enough energy, she would've snarled at the woman, but she was too tired and too sick. Her wounded side shrieked with pain, and warm blood trickled through her fur.

Aunt Caroline removed Fletcher's glasses and smoothed the hair away from his damp forehead. "You're okay now. It was only a nightmare." She cast another glare at Nim.

Fletcher's breathing had grown slow and steady, and Nim knew he'd fallen asleep.

"I'll get some antiseptic for those scratches," Aunt Caroline whispered. She frowned down at the broken jar. "Then I'll clean up this mess." She rose from the bedside and moved across the room toward Nim, scowling.

Nim scrambled back and pressed herself against the wall, but it did no good. Aunt Caroline grasped her by the scruff of her neck and hauled her out. She tried to wiggle free, but every twist sent a rush of agony down her gashed side.

Holding her at arm's length, Aunt Caroline carried Nim down the stairs, muttering how Patrick would never forgive her if he came home to find Fletcher mauled to bits by his own cat.

Summoning what little strength she could, Nim bared her fangs and whispered a hiss.

"Oh, poor Fletcher." Aunt Caroline shook her head sadly as she hauled Nim through the kitchen. Then she frowned. "But I warned Patrick this could happen. I told him he shouldn't allow a cat inside the house. Animals just cannot be trusted; you never know when they'll revert to their feral behaviors."

Nim narrowed her eyes and managed a weak growl.

Aunt Caroline opened the door that led to the garage, continuing her muttering. "I'd heard stories of cats stealing breath from babies, and now I catch you trying to do it to

Fletcher!" She gave a huff of annoyance, then she shook her head. "I told Patrick black cats were unlucky, even evil. And this certainly proves it!"

She dropped Nim into a shallow cardboard box, one that the corner store had delivered groceries in. Nim's injured side throbbed and her head grew woozy.

Then Aunt Caroline strode back into the house and closed the door, leaving Nim alone in the murky garage.

Nim wanted to leap up and run to Fletcher, but she couldn't. She had no strength. A fresh wave of nausea rolled over her, and she wondered if the creature really had poisoned her. She shivered in the darkness, the odors of gasoline, paint, and cardboard filling her nose. Her discomfort didn't matter, though. Fletcher was all that mattered. She needed to get back to him, to make sure he was okay. She tried to rise to her paws, but she sank down instead and into a deep blackness tinged with strange smoky swirls of purple.

The next thing Nim knew, the box that she lay in was rising. She had no idea how long she'd been in the garage. Confusion blurred her mind. Her eyelids were too heavy to lift. She heard the car door open. She felt the box lower onto the seat. The car door closed. Aunt Caroline climbed in on the other side. Nim recognized her by her rose-scented soap and the smell of her nervousness and fear.

It wasn't the first time Nim had been dumped into a cardboard box. And now that her head had cleared a little, she remembered exactly what it meant. Boxes were the places where people put unwanted things before taking them away. Panic spread from the top of her ears to the tip of her tail. She had to climb out. She had to get back to Fletcher.

"Fletcher needs real friends, not a cat," Aunt Caroline mumbled to herself. "It's what's best for him." Her voice dropped, the anger dissipating and a thread of uncertainty creeping in. "It's the right thing to do."

The garage door rose with a rickety rolling rumble, and the car backed out.

Nim lifted her head and tried to stand, but her legs buckled beneath her.

The car drove away, and blackness swallowed her once again.

CHAPTER 4

Nim slept, yet the smell of the cardboard box swelled in her nose, and the sound of the car's tires hummed in her ears. A part of her knew she was traveling far away from home, and far away from Fletcher. She tried to force herself awake, but like a falling leaf she drifted downward, into an even deeper slumber where she dreamed.

A woman stood in the shadows. A bat, or maybe a large black moth, flew back and forth behind her. She appeared to be a bit older than Aunt Caroline, with streaks of gray shooting through her black hair. A purple mist lapped at the hem of her long lavender gown. She looked like one of the ladies in the Greek history book Fletcher had been studying.

"Can you help me escape?" Nim asked her, remembering the last time she'd been trapped in a cardboard box and how awful it'd been.

The woman fixed her dark eyes on her and spoke, though her voice sounded distant and muffled.

Nim shook her head. "I can't hear you. What are you saying?"

The woman faded away, and Nim found herself walking along a road. She could see the forms of people, animals, and objects up ahead, but they were so very blurry. Hoping to clear her vision, she squeezed her eyes shut. When she opened them, though, she found herself on the sidewalk in the middle of a busy downtown. In front of her sat a tall cardboard box. She stepped up to it, rose on her hind legs, and peered in.

Inside the box was herself as a kitten, along with her five siblings.

Nim watched, unable to look away as events from her past played out like the scenes in a TV show. And as she watched them, she remembered.

The box's sides had towered above them, far too high to climb over. And at only five weeks old, she and her siblings were too small to do anything other than cry out for their momma. People passed by, back and forth, most of them with their phones held to their ears or their eyes glued to the screens. Car horns and bus horns honked. Too many smells filled the air. Some of the people stopped and peered into the box. Some of them reached in and petted her siblings, cooing and speaking to them in high, singsong voices. Her past-self tried to bump her head against their palms or rub against the backs of their hands, but they always ignored her and petted her brothers and sisters instead.

Sometimes, though, a child would reach for her, but someone else would always caution them:

"No. You don't want that one. Black cats are unlucky."

"They're evil."

"Don't touch it! It could be a witch or the devil in disguise."

Until that day, she hadn't known such things about black cats. But she had been pretty sure she wasn't a witch or the devil, and that she wasn't evil either. Could she really be unlucky, though?

One by one, her siblings were lifted out and taken away, hugged to the chests of the smiling people, until she was left alone in the big, tall box.

Day turned to evening. Evening turned to night.

Nim remembered how her stomach had rumbled with hunger. How she mewed loudly, calling for her momma, or anyone, but no one came.

The kitten-Nim tried scrabbling up and out of the box,

over and over again, until she exhausted herself. Then she curled into a ball in the corner and cried.

Overhead, swollen black clouds rolled across the night sky. The rain came down, pelting her with cold, wet drops. Thunder and lightning followed.

Rain drenched her and she shivered. She flinched at every thunderclap and bright flash.

The box finally became so soggy that its sides wilted, and she was able to sink her claws in and climb out. She had been afraid and alone. Everything looked so big, and she'd felt so small.

Her past-self raced away, unsure where to go, searching for comfort to calm her terror. The pounding rain blurred her vision and she dashed into the street.

With a roar, a monstrous car came speeding around the corner. Its white headlights lit the world around her. She heard her body thump and crunch as she bounced off one of the automobile's big tires. She flew up in the air and fell back down, crashing and tumbling beneath a bush on the side of the road.

The car sped on, its red taillights shrinking and disappearing in the distance as her pain grew. And while the cold rain pattered down, one truth had glowed bright in her mind: she really was unlucky.

Throughout the night, she drifted in and out of wakefulness. Then the sun rose, its bright rays piercing the lingering storm clouds.

People walked past. She tried to cry out for help, but only the softest squeak escaped her dry throat. If anyone noticed her, they didn't stop. She closed her eyes, deciding she would struggle no more.

Footsteps approached. Someone knelt beside her. He spoke, and his voice pulled her up from the darkness. She opened her mouth, and with the last of her will she gave a weak cry, pried open one of her eyes, and squinted up at the small, skinny boy wearing round eyeglasses. "Hello," he said. He reached out with one finger and stroked the top of her head.

The boy's father knelt beside him. "I think her leg's broken," he said.

"We can get it fixed," the boy replied.

His father shook his head sadly. "She might have other internal injuries, Fletcher. She might not survive."

"She'll survive," Fletcher said. "I won't let her die."

His father gave a sigh of resignation. Fletcher slid his hands beneath her and gently lifted, careful not to wobble her twisted leg.

She was frightened, but she had no strength for fighting.

Fletcher held her on his lap inside the warm car as his father drove them away. She peered up, hardly able to keep her eyes open. Outside, the sky had again grown heavy with rain clouds. Fletcher stroked her nose. "Don't worry. I'll take care of you," he said.

She believed him, and her fear began to fade.

"Now, to give you a name." He looked out the car window and up at the drizzly, gray sky. "Nimbus," he said.

His father arched an eyebrow. "As in cumulonimbus or nimbostratus?"

"No. Just Nimbus," Fletcher replied. "As in the Latin word for black rain cloud."

That day, a veterinarian named Dr. Glass operated on her. Dr. Glass told Fletcher and his father it was fortunate they'd found the kitten when they did. Nimbus was lucky to be alive.

That night, she slept on a stack of old towels and ended up soiling them because she'd been too weak to make her way to the litter box. She'd feared Fletcher would be angry with her, but he stroked her head instead, murmuring that she would soon be well enough to walk on her own. He carried her to the litter box when she needed it, administered her medicine, and changed her bandages, apologizing when she cried out in pain.

As she recovered, he read to her from his favorite

book, *The Hobbit*, where the courageous little Bilbo faced a fierce dragon and the clever old Gandalf kept a band of trolls arguing until daybreak arrived and turned them to stone. Fletcher told her he was practicing his speaking voice because his father needed an assistant on his Saturday night horror TV show. But she knew he'd done it because the sound of his voice comforted her. She knew he didn't really care much for horror movies and that he actually had no interest in being on his father's show.

Under Fletcher's care, she grew stronger, and she felt loved. She didn't need anyone else, and she didn't need to be anyplace else. He was her one true friend. With him, she'd never again be abandoned. Contentment filled her with warmth. She had everything she wanted. She was the luckiest cat in the world.

Aunt Caroline's car came to a stop and Nim awoke.

Her side blared with pain. Sickness billowed inside her stomach and head.

She peeled her eyes open.

It was dark outside, and she was very far from home, and very far from Fletcher.

Maybe she wasn't so lucky after all.

CHAPTER 5

The car door opened.

Aunt Caroline lifted the cardboard box off the seat, murmuring nervously to herself as she carried it away, "I'll just tell Fletcher and Patrick I don't know where the cat wandered off to." She knelt in the early morning darkness and set the box on the ground. Then she wiped her perspiring forehead on the sleeve of her cardigan sweater.

Panic clawed at Nim. She needed to return to Fletcher. She tried to stand, but her injured side burned as though someone had swiped it with a fiery torch.

Aunt Caroline squinted at her. "Oh! You're hurt!" She bit her lip as if she might be rethinking her actions. Nim grew momentarily hopeful, until Aunt Caroline shook her head. "You'll be just fine." She started to rise, then stopped.

"Though I better take this. Just in case someone tries to return you." She removed Nim's collar and flung it away. Casting another look down at Nim as she stood, she pursed her lips. "I always pass this way on my drive to the city. I've seen a few houses scattered about. Maybe you can find a home at one of those."

Nim seethed with anger and fear. She wanted to lash out, but all she could do was rumble a feeble growl.

"You'll be just fine," Aunt Caroline repeated. She paused and gave a heavy sigh. "This really is for the best." Then she turned and walked away.

But Nim knew she wouldn't be fine. She wouldn't be fine at all.

Aunt Caroline climbed into her car and drove off.

"Fletcher," Nim whispered, her heart breaking. Exhaustion pressed down on her like a powerful hand. She dropped her head onto her paws, hating her helplessness. At least Fletcher was safe; she had killed the goblin.

Then dreamless sleep overtook her.

Nim was awakened by a poke to her shoulder and a faint whiff of artificial cheese flavoring.

"Hey, are you alive?" a squeaky voice asked.

She opened her eyes.

A gray rat was sitting up inside the box and staring at

her. In one of his pink paws he clutched a half-eaten puffy Cheez Doodle.

Nim shrank back. She tried to focus her vision as her mind spun with confusion, but no matter how hard she blinked, the bizarre image remained. The rat was wearing a little sweater. One he'd apparently made by gnawing the appropriate holes in an old woolly sock.

"Oh! You are alive!" He shoved the rest of the Cheez Doodle into his mouth. As he crunched and chewed, orange crumbs rained onto the front of his sweater.

Nim narrowed her eyes at the strange rodent. She attempted a threatening snarl but managed to produce only a pathetic gurgle. With an overpowering need to get home to Fletcher, she ignored him and scrambled onto her shaky legs, cautiously peering over the side of the box.

The blue-gray tinge of dawn was spreading across the horizon. All around her loomed mountains of broken furniture, torn mattresses, paint cans, and discarded tree branches. Rats scuttled everywhere. Most of them went about their business of gnawing, foraging, and eating, while a group of younger ones played in the distance, tugging on a piece of twine, chewing on a pencil, and rolling a scuffed-up marble through the dirt. Nearby, though, a crowd of adult rats had gathered. They crouched, gazing at her through their glassy black eyes.

With a huge effort, Nim pulled herself over the edge of the box and dropped to the ground. She hunched with her tail tucked beneath her, trying to catch her breath. The rat scrambled out after her, sat up again, and spread his arms wide. "Welcome to the dump!"

Nim lifted her nose and sniffed the air, grimacing at the sour, moldy stench of rot and decay. This place was nothing like home. Instead of comfortable beds and shelves filled with books, it was cluttered with mangled lawn chairs and broken televisions. A rusted washing machine leaned nearby. Shriveled brown produce overflowed from boxes. An avalanche of apple cores, chicken bones, and half-emptied yogurt cups spilled out of busted black trash bags. And she was now a part of it all, abandoned among jumbles of unwanted things. For the second time that day, she truly wondered if the superstitions about black cats were true. Maybe her bad luck had finally caught up with her.

"Well." The rat cleared his throat. "Technically, it's not really a dump, it's just a place where people in the country-side ditch their big junky items instead of paying someone to haul them away. And they drop off other things too!" His eyes sparkled. "Like boxes of fashion magazines and celebrity gossip tabloids."

Ignoring the jabbering rat and her own self-sorry thoughts, Nim climbed to her feet. *Fletcher needs me*, she reminded herself. She turned away, focusing on detecting the direction that led to home.

The rat scuttled around to face her. "You can also find an abundance of food here, and all sorts of surprises. Like you, for instance. I've never found a cat in a box before." He leaned closer. "By the way, just let me know if you'd ever like an outfit of your own. I have a keen eye for fashion, you know. I designed this sweater myself." With his tiny pink paws, he tugged on the holey piece of sock. "My name's Rhett, by the way. My dad, who has no imagination, wanted to name me Rat. But my mom wanted something with a little more flair. So, they compromised and settled on Rhett." He shrugged. "I would've preferred something more regal and majestic like Alfric, Frederick, or Rex." He closed his eyes, then tilted his head up and to the side. "But what's in a name?" He thrust an arm out. "'That which we call a rose by any other name would smell as sweet.'" After a short pause, he opened his eyes and grinned. "That's a line from *Romeo and Juliet*. I saw it acted out on a show called *Great Theatrical Performances*. I just love TV, don't you?"

Nim frowned and turned away from him again. She needed to focus on what she was doing. She gazed all around, morning's gray light revealing that the dump had once been a huge front lawn. The now lumpy, grassless stretch of land led up to an abandoned Victorian mansion, three stories tall and fronted with decorative railings on the wide wraparound porch. The roof had caved in on one side, exposing a jumble of blackened beams like giant charred bones. Scorch marks ran in streaks from the shattered windows like a lady's smudged makeup. The whole place whispered of sadness and broken dreams.

An image of the broken clay jar suddenly sprang from her memory. Her stomach twisted at the thought of its twin in Fletcher's father's office. If someone released another goblin, she wouldn't be there to protect Fletcher. Her panic surged, but she forced herself to remain calm. *Be courageous like Bilbo*, she thought. *Be clever like Gandalf.* All she had to do was locate the way to the city, then set off toward it.

Observing her worried glances, Rhett nodded at the ruins of the house. "That's the old Whittaker mansion, but no one lives there anymore. That's why people ignore the private property notice and dump their unwanted stuff here." He pointed up at a tall post nearby with a faded metal sign bolted to it. "Lucky for us," he added with a grin.

Nim wished he'd stop talking or, better yet, go away. She sniffed the air, trying to smell beyond the stink of the dump, trying to determine the direction that led to the city.

Rhett indicated a round hole in the ground near the signpost. "That's our main burrow. Lots of us rats live there. It's filled with bunches of tunnels and chambers. It even has a treasure room where our most valuable heir-looms are—"

"Say no more!" a large rat ordered as he scurried through the growing gathering of rodents. He rose on his muscular back legs, glaring and twitching his whiskers at Rhett. "You know the law of the colony. This cat, this *predator*, is not welcome here. By order of the sovereign!"

Rhett placed his paws on his hips. "Well, there's no need to be so persnickety, Thorn." He turned to Nim and whispered, "Thorn's the sovereign's second-in-command. Cinder, Bristle, and Raider are part of the guard too. Cinder's all right, but Bristle's a bit of a snitchy tattletale, and Raider poops when he gets nervous or frightened."

"Is it a big cat?" an old rat with milky-white eyes called from the crowd.

Nim took a step back as Thorn glowered at her. "It's not fully grown," he replied. "Probably hasn't seen its first full year of life yet, but it's still dangerous."

"Thorn's right!" one of the rats piped up. "If it stays here, it'll want to eat us."

"I agree," another one called. "Dusty just birthed a new litter. Cats love to eat rat pups."

Nim bent her ears back, her stomach roiling at the thought of eating a rat.

"Let's kill it now while it's weak!" one cried out. "Best not to take chances."

"Right you are," another added, sitting up and crossing her arms over her chest. "It's kill or be killed, that's what I always say."

"Oh, have a heart for the poor thing," another one chimed in.

Others also called out, recommending kindness, but Nim didn't care what they thought. She needed to get home to Fletcher. She tried to walk away, but her legs were as weak as wet paper straws, and she crumpled to the ground.

A rat from the crowd scuttled over and peered at her, sniffing with his pink nose. Then he called over his shoulder to the others, "No need to fret! It's nearly dead anyway."

"And then we can eat it!" another one shouted.

Rhett drew up beside Nim. "Pay no attention to Skittles," he murmured. He lowered his voice to a whisper. "He eats *roadkill*." He gave a small shudder. "So disgusting!"

By then, the group had wandered off to gnaw on broken chair legs and browned apple cores again.

Rhett wrinkled his brow and peered closer at Nim. "Are you really going to die?"

"Not today," she muttered. She forced herself up onto her paws, swaying as she tried to regain her balance.

The sky had grown more light than dark, and all the rats were now scurrying away, disappearing into the junky depths of the dump or down into the nearby burrow. The blind rat clamped his mouth onto the tail of another and let it guide him away.

"Either die or leave," the big rat named Thorn said to Nim. "But you cannot live here." He dropped onto his four paws and followed the others.

"Don't mind them," Rhett said, tugging the sock sweater down over his belly. "It's just that we have rules to protect the colony. It's nothing personal. Dogs, snakes, hawks, and owls are our predators too."

Nim wasn't offended. She had no intention of staying. She'd taken a few wobbly steps when another distressing thought hit her. What if Fletcher believed the goblin had frightened her away? What if he believed she'd abandoned him? "No," she whispered with a shake of her head. She would *never* abandon Fletcher.

Ignoring the throbbing pain, she limped off. She picked her way over the ruins of the old lawn, past a lopsided sofa with its stuffing spilling out, then skirted around broken dishes and more bags and boxes overflowing with unwanted items.

Rhett scampered alongside her. "Hey, are you hungry? I have a ketchup packet and some moldy string cheese stashed away. I also have a jelly jar with some little gobs still at the bottom, though you'd have to be careful trying to get to it. Snickers got his head stuck in an olive jar once. He went around like that for days before Cinder and Raider managed to remove it."

Nim turned to him with what she hoped was a threatening glare, wishing he'd go away.

He gasped. "Did you know you have two different-colored eyes? One is the most striking shade of yellow I've ever seen. Like banana yellow." He furrowed his brow. "Or maybe it's more of a mustard yellow."

"Both of my eyes are green." Nim scowled at him. "Green, just like my collar." She touched a paw to her neck, then gasped at the memory of Aunt Caroline throwing her collar away. She cast a wild glance at the heaps of junk all around her. She'd never find it in all of this. And besides, there was no time. She needed to get home.

"Hold on," Rhett said. He scurried away, rummaged through a nearby pile of dirt-crusted shoes and purses, and returned with half of a makeup compact gripped in his mouth. He held it up to her. "See?"

Nim peered into its cracked mirrored surface. One green eye and one yellow eye stared back at her. "But how can this be?" she whispered. Maybe her battle with the goblin really had poisoned her!

"Perhaps you're going blind like old Scampers," Rhett offered as he tossed the mirror aside.

It doesn't matter, Nim thought. Fletcher wouldn't care that one of her eyes was yellow instead of green. The only thing that mattered was getting back to him.

Finally, she reached the edge of the property. A dirt road ran from the abandoned mansion to an old two-lane highway she was certain would lead to the city.

She'd found her path home.

CHAPTER 6

Nim sat for a moment, hoping to regain her strength. The thought of soon being home sent her brain buzzing and the world spinning. She squeezed her eyes shut, willing the dizziness to go away.

"These things are always falling over," Rhett muttered.

Nim peeled her eyes open, watching blearily as the rat gripped a garden stake. A word she couldn't read had been scratched across its rectangular surface.

He rammed the stake into the ground, then pointed at the tiny sign. "This is a boundary marker to let any inter-lopers know the dump and the old Whittaker place are rat territories. The dirt road is a neutral zone. It's all a bit silly, though, if you ask me."

"I didn't ask," Nim muttered, relieved that the dizziness was subsiding.

"Our rat ancestors made the boundary rule ten years ago," he explained anyway, "and every generation has followed it since." He dropped his voice to a whisper. "The colony has a lot of silly rules."

Nim didn't want to be rude, but the rats and their territories were of no interest to her. She limped onward, out of the dump and onto the dirt road.

"Hey, where are you going?" Rhett asked, scuttling after her.

"Home."

"Oh." He nodded. "Where's your home?"

"In the city."

He whistled in awe. "It's a long way from here to the city. Good luck getting there."

Nim stumbled but regained her footing, and Rhett shook his head sadly. "I don't think you're going to make it in your condition. You'll probably die out there on the side of the highway, and the Florida turkey vultures will eat you. And if they don't, Skittles will."

The rising sun had already painted pink swaths across the blue-gray sky. Daylight was quickly dawning. Not wanting to waste any more time, she tried to hurry her steps, but her heavy paws tangled together and she fell. Her wounded side pulsed with pain as she lay motionless with her face pressed to the dirt.

"Oh, dear!" Rhett skittered closer. "Are you dead?"

"I'm not dead," she muttered. She slowly forced herself onto her feet, too weak to shake the dust from her coat. She glanced down at her side, wincing at the gaping laceration beneath her disheveled fur.

"Oh, you're in bad shape." Rhett shook his head again. "You really need to get well before you set off for the city. Hey, maybe the old lady can fix you up!"

"The old lady?"

"Yes. The one who lives in the gardener's cottage over there." He pointed across the dirt road, toward the big grassy field beyond it. A small gray house with a brown roof and a stone chimney sat at the rear of the property.

"That's where I watch TV, but only through the window." He lowered his voice. "I have to sneak over so no one in the colony sees me when they're foraging at night. We rats are nocturnal, you know." He lifted a tiny pink finger. "Not that that's a bad thing. Being out in the dark is the only way to appreciate the beauty of the stars and the moon." Clasping his paws together, he gazed longingly up at the sky, as though it were still black instead of pink, blue, and gray. "'Take him and cut him out in little stars, and he will make the face of heaven so fine that all the world will be in love with night and pay no worship to the garish sun.'" He peered at Nim as though waiting for a response. But she only wrinkled her brow in puzzlement. "That's another line from *Romeo and Juliet*," he said.

Ignoring him, Nim peered at the little house, lifting one paw as she often did when she was confused or indecisive. She didn't want to delay heading home for even a second longer, but perhaps the goblin wound did need some medical treatment. Going to the old woman would be risky, though. People could be mean. Other dangers might be waiting there too. Maybe it was best to just continue her journey home.

She was headed toward the highway again when sharp pains lanced her side. She staggered to a halt. At this rate, it'd take years to reach the city. Reluctantly, she turned to Rhett. "Why would the old lady want to help me?"

"Oh, she takes in all kinds of unwanted cats." He motioned up the highway. "There's another old lady nearby who takes in stray dogs."

Nim bristled. "I'm not *unwanted*. I have a home, and Fletcher loves me. I have a collar and tag that proves it." She gave him a glare for added emphasis.

"Uh, you're not wearing a collar and tag."

Nim scowled. "That's because Aunt Caroline threw them into the dump."

"Oh, I see," he replied. Though to Nim, it didn't look like he saw at all. She glanced toward the small gray house, then down at her blood-matted fur. With a sigh of frustration, she set off toward the field.

Rhett hurried alongside her. "So, what'd you do to get dumped? Let me guess. Someone in the family is allergic to cats, or did you claw the furniture?"

Nim didn't answer. She limped her way through the blades of green grass and past clumps of sweet-smelling pink wildflowers, her thoughts turning to Fletcher. He would have liked the flowers. He probably even knew what they were called.

"Oh, I know!" Rhett exclaimed. "Your people moved away and they didn't want to take you with them."

Nim came to a stop and curled her lip. "It was Fletcher's aunt who brought me here. She said I hurt Fletcher, that I tried to steal his breath while he was sleeping."

Rhett's eyes bugged out. "Did you really do that?"

"Of course not! That's just a ridiculous myth about cats! It was something else that attacked Fletcher."

"What was it?" His whiskers were standing straight at attention.

Nim shook her head. "It was a goblin with dark hair, pointy ears, fangs, and claws."

He arched an eyebrow. "Uh, you do realize you just

described yourself. Are you sure you didn't do it?"

Nim scowled. "I defended Fletcher! I fought the creature and destroyed it!"

Rhett whistled. "Wow! But why did Fletcher let his aunt take you away, then?"

"He didn't let her!" Nim replied, bristling at the rat's insinuation that Fletcher was a coward. "He didn't know Aunt Caroline was doing it. If he had, he would have stopped her."

"Sure. Sure. No doubt." Rhett nodded. "But Aunt Caroline obviously doesn't want you there. Next time she might do something more drastic, if you know what I mean." He paused long enough to slash one finger across his throat.

Nim remembered Aunt Caroline's fear and anger, and a shiver rippled her fur.

She didn't know how she was going to stay safe from Aunt Caroline when she got home, and she didn't know how she was going to let Fletcher know what the woman had done, but she'd figure something out. The most important thing was getting back to Fletcher and protecting him.

CHAPTER 7

The morning sun climbed steadily as Nim made her way to the little house with the brown roof.

Rhett scampered alongside her. "Hey, by the way, what's your name?"

"Nimbus."

"Nimbus," he repeated, as though trying it on for size.

Nim stopped to rest for a moment, unable to keep from panting. She was thirsty and tired. And the wound hurt.

Rhett stopped too.

He smoothed his whiskers. "You know, Nimbus, you and I have a lot in common. I also feel a calling to go to the big city. I want to become an actor—a superstar! One day I want to see my face on the cover of *Rat Fancy Magazine*."

Doing her best to ignore his ramblings, Nim padded

onward, and he dashed after her.

"Some of the colony members say rats like me will never get their picture on the front of a magazine." He huffed in exasperation. "But just because my coat doesn't have any fawn-colored splotches doesn't mean I can't be fancy too! I think I'm just as handsome as any of those pedigree pets." He paused for a second. "You know what the real difference is between those fancy rats and us dump rats?"

Nim didn't answer.

"I'll tell you! Whether a rat is considered to be a pet or a pest depends on if there's a human who loves it."

Nim didn't want to hear any more. She was tired and grumpy, and she just wanted to go home. "I can make it to the house on my own. You can stop following me now and go back to your rat territory."

"And another thing—" He gasped and came to a sudden stop. "There you are!"

Despite herself, Nim turned to see what had caught his attention.

He reached into a clump of wildflowers and drew out a tall plastic black cap, the kind that belonged on top of a mouthwash bottle. He sat up on his haunches, dusted it against the front of his sock sweater, then tugged it onto his head. "It's my top hat. It went missing last week." He turned side to side. "Don't I look dashing? Maybe a bit like a famous actor?" He held his paws up and gazed dreamily into the distance. "I can picture it so well, the bright lights and cameras, mountains of fan mail arriving every day." He gave his top hat a small pat. "When I couldn't find it in my stash of fashion accessories, I thought a scrounger had stolen it for sure, but I guess it just fell off my head when I was passing through the field."

"A scrounger?" Nim asked, then immediately regretted it.

"The scroungers are a family of rats who live in the colony. They come from a long line of thieving rodents." He frowned. "They get fixated on a certain type of item and that's what they go after, stealing things from the other colony members: buttons, coins, keys. . . . To be fair, though, lots of rats collect things." He motioned to his plastic top hat. "I scavenge items I can turn into accessories. And Tibby and Ricket collect game pieces, you know, like dice and little plastic pegs, sometimes even old playing cards. But we find our stuff fair and square."

"Oh. Okay." Nim nodded. "Well, goodbye, then. Thanks for your help." She turned away. The little house wasn't far off now, but with each step closer, her anxiousness rose. Would the old woman help her? Or would she chase her away?

Rhett continued on beside her. "One time I found some

doll clothes in the dump." He sighed wistfully. "But I gave them to a rat who'd just given birth to a large litter. She shredded them for nesting material."

By then, they'd reached the cottage's flower-filled front yard. To Nim's surprise, the wooden house wasn't gray, but rather a sun-bleached blue with a rusted tin roof, and the whole thing looked a bit rickety.

"Well, here we are!" Rhett announced. "The old lady will get you fixed up."

"Are you sure it's safe?" Nim gave a nervous lick of her lips.

He shrugged. "I suppose it's possible she takes in unwanted cats to fatten them up and eat them." He placed a finger to his chin. "Now that I think about it, I know she's taken stray cats inside, but I've never seen them come out again."

The front door creaked open. A figure loomed in the shadows and stared down at them.

Nim gulped.

"Well, good luck." Rhett pushed his bottlecap hat lower onto his head and skittered away.

An old woman with a long gray braid hanging down her back moved out of the house and into the morning sunlight. Clothed in a mauve housedress, a gray multipock-eted apron, and a pair of green rubber gardening boots, she didn't look much like an eater of cats.

As she slowly descended the steps, Nim crouched and tucked her tail beneath her, willing herself to stay put because she needed help. But when the woman drew closer, fear overtook her. She attempted to bolt away and tumbled face-first into the dirt.

A shadow fell over her. Nim peered up. The unsmiling woman stared down at her with pale blue eyes in a wrinkled, tanned face.

Nim tried to scramble up again, but her legs wouldn't obey.

The old lady leaned forward, a silver owl amulet swinging from a chain around her neck, and scooped up Nim.

She twisted and snarled, but it was useless.

As they climbed the steps, Nim glanced toward the dump, cursing the treacherous rat that had led her to her doom.

CHAPTER 8

The old lady carried Nim through a small living room, past a faded green sofa, a wooden rocking chair, an old-fashioned TV, and an iron cauldron hanging inside the empty fireplace. Nim cried out, but the woman's hold was too firm to squirm out of.

They came to a stop in the adjoining dining area, where a cluttered wooden table stood with a single chair tucked beneath it. The spicy aroma of herbs filled Nim's nose, clinging to the roof of her mouth. She darted her wide eyes all around. Leafy green bundles hung from the low ceiling's rafters. Baskets, sharp knives, and pointy scissors dangled from hooks on the walls. A fresh wave of terror rushed over her, and she yowled and thrashed, doing her best to claw at her enemy.

The old woman clamped her beneath her arm, then strode to a nearby cupboard and pulled out a tiny brown bottle from an assortment of other brown bottles. In an instant, she was seated on the chair with Nim on her lap.

Moving with the skilled hands of a doctor—or maybe a butcher—she pried Nim's mouth open, squeezed a few drops of cold, bitter liquid into her throat, and forced her to swallow it down.

Nim knew she was being poisoned. She growled from deep in her chest. It was the last bit of fight she could offer as her strength slipped away. She grew as limp and as floppy as a dead fish.

The woman swept away a pile of ferns, roots, and bark and laid Nim on the table. Numbness weighed down her muscles and bones, as well as her jittery fear.

As Nim's vision grew blurry, the old lady leaned closer, studying the gash the goblin had inflicted. She scrunched her gray eyebrows. "It appears you've tangled with quite a vicious creature, one not of this world." She stroked her chin, lost in her thoughts for a moment. Then she gave a heavy sigh. "I think a dose of hawthorn should set you right." She moved her gaze to Nim's face and paused. "One green eye and one rather intriguing yellow one." She peered closer at Nim, a half-hopeful expression filling her face. "Is it you?" she whispered. "Have you finally returned?" She stared for a moment longer, then slowly shook her head in disappointment. "No. I don't think so."

The words made no sense to Nim, and as the woman turned to rummage inside the cupboard, Nim swept her gaze past a bookshelf and a couple of side tables to a broom leaning in the corner of the adjoining living room. Despite a stack of cardboard boxes—one sitting open in the middle of the floor—the place looked tidy enough.

With her hands full, the old woman returned to the table and set out more brown bottles, a curved needle, and a spool of thick blue thread.

Exhaustion tugged at Nim and she gave a wide yawn. As her half-lidded eyes drifted shut, the woman squirted another dose of liquid into her mouth, but Nim hardly noticed as she fell into a deep sleep once again.

Nim dreamed she was walking in a shadowy, unfamiliar world. A starless purple sky hung overhead, lit only by a white crescent moon.

She strolled up a long dirt road bordered by endless grassy fields. Yet, something about the place wasn't quite right. And it was strangely quiet. There were no sounds of cars rumbling in the distance, not even the chirp of a bird or an insect. She felt different too. She glanced down at her side and was surprised to see the goblin-inflicted wound had vanished.

Soon she arrived at a point where the road split into three directions. She wondered if one of the routes would lead her home.

On the path straight ahead, colors and shapes shifted and morphed in the distance, like the images inside a kaleidoscope. Far up the road leading to her left, people and animals appeared as blurry figures, as though she were peering at them through a smudged window. And when she looked to her right, her fur stood on end. Swollen dark clouds roiled in the distance, zigzags of lightning leaping out from them. Wisps of white fog grasped the roadway below like ghostly hands.

Nim glanced over her shoulder, considering heading back in the direction she'd come from, but when she turned back again, a dark-haired woman stood at the intersection.

With a hiss of surprise, Nim leaped back. There was something not quite right about the woman dressed in the long lavender gown, yet Nim was certain she'd seen her before. A tall, pointy-eared black dog sat regally at her side, its amber eyes fixed on Nim.

Nim wasn't nearly as frightened of the dog as she was of the woman. Perhaps it was her unsmiling face and stony eyes that she found so unnerving. "Who are you?" Nim asked with a small, squeaky voice.

The woman studied her for a long moment before finally answering. "Those who dwelled in ancient times addressed me as the Nameless One. Others have known me as Queen of the Moonlight; Lady of Nightmares and Dreams; or the Goddess of Boundaries, Crossroads, and Magic. But most acknowledge me as Hecate."

"Heckity?" Nim tilted her head, unsure she'd heard her correctly.

The woman nodded. "Yes, or Heh-kah-tay if you wish. How it's pronounced is not of importance."

Nim suddenly recognized her from a dream early that morning. Her fear intensified, but her instincts told her it'd be foolish to flee, the way that running from an undisciplined dog would only make it chase after you. "What is this place?" she whispered.

"You've come to your crossroads in the dream realm, one of numerous realms beyond the physical world." The woman rested one hand on the head of the dog at her side, motioning around with her other. "Anything you've ever experienced, every fragment of information you've acquired, it all resides here. The older you grow, the larger this world expands."

"This is all in my mind?" Nim asked, feeling slightly confused.

"In a way."

Nim twitched her ears. "But it feels too real to be just an ordinary dream."

"Dreams aren't ordinary," the lady replied. "They're often messages from your dream guide, offering you direction and inspiration."

"I have a dream guide?"

"All living beings have dream guides. And I am yours."

"You are?" Nim lifted her paw, puzzled.

The lady nodded. "I've been with you since you were born."

Nim shook her head, uncertain. "But I've never seen you before today."

"Dreamers seldom see their crossroads or their dream guides in their true form. They are there nonetheless, standing behind the backdrop of each dream's scenery."

"I don't understand what's happening," Nim replied.

"You have acquired a unique ability, Nimbus. With it, you can see and traverse the dream realm at will. Most dreamers have no control over their destinations here."

"But I don't even want to *be* here," Nim protested. "All I want is to go home."

A wave of whispers and murmurs raced up the road behind her. The sound circled her, spinning like dried leaves in a whirlwind, brushing against her fur. Her heart thundering, she swung her head from side to side searching for the source of the voices, but she was alone.

CHAPTER 9

Nim awoke from the strange dream, not remembering where she was. A strong aroma of herbs tickled her nose, and she was lying on an orange cushion atop a small wooden table. Her perch stood next to a window, and the midafternoon sun illuminated a length of gauze wrapped around her midsection.

She blinked her sleep-bleary eyes as she took in her surroundings, apprehension replacing her confusion. She was still in the old lady's cottage, the one the rat had tricked her into coming to.

She tried to heave herself onto her paws, but the bandage around her middle weighed her down. Beneath the binding, she could feel a tugging sensation holding the edges of her wound together. She could smell the greasy, pungent ointment that'd been slathered all over it. She licked her lips and frowned at the bitter taste coating her mouth, remnants of the vile liquid the scary old woman had forced on her. But none of that mattered. She needed to get home to protect Fletcher. What if another monster were to emerge from the other old jar? She glanced around for a means of escape, but the front door and all the windows were shut.

The murmurs and whispers from the strange dream began again, and her gaze fell on four cats conversing among themselves on the floor. They must have been prisoners too. No doubt being fattened up for the old woman to eat. She pricked her ears, trying to make out what they were saying. Maybe together they could come up with a way to escape.

"No new cats are welcome here," one of them growled. "She must leave immediately."

"She could be the one, though," another replied.

"Do you really think so?" another one asked. "Oh, I hope she is."

"She can't possibly be," the fourth one sneered. "Just look at the state of her."

All four cats turned their gazes toward her.

Nim stared back at the big ginger tabby, the plump calico, the creamy-white-and-tan female, and the gray male with a stripe of white fur curving beneath his nose like a mustache and two white stripes arching above his eyes like bushy eyebrows. She shook her head, trying to clear her vision and hearing. They didn't sound like prisoners at all.

The gray male sauntered over, a small silver charm in the shape of a book jingling on his blue collar. He jumped up to her table, and she hissed and raised a paw in defense. She was too vulnerable in her current condition, too easy a target to be attacked.

He didn't appear offended, though. He sat up straight and thrust out his white chest. "You've been dosed with a potent sedative," he informed her. "It'll take some time for the effects to fully wear off." He lifted his face and sniffed the air. "Your stitches have been coated with hawthorn ointment. A curious choice since it's used to keep evil spirits at bay and heal supernatural ailments." He cocked a white eyebrow. "But perhaps you already know that?"

Nim did not know that, but now that he'd mentioned it, she realized she no longer felt as sick as before. Though she did feel so very heavy and tired.

"I happened to be watching out the front window when you arrived. Very bold of your rodent escort to enter cat territory." He yawned widely. "These borders are all rather nonsensical, though they suit us just fine. We have no desire to venture into the dump."

Nim wasn't interested in hearing about the cat and rat

territories. She tried to rise again without luck.

"We house cats have convened a gathering to decide if we should shun or accept you," the gray-and-white cat continued. "And while the vote was not unanimous, it was agreed you may stay, whoever you might be."

Nim shook her head. "I'm not staying. I have to—"

Paying no attention to her protest, he motioned toward the large-pawed ginger tabby who'd left the gathering and now lay stretched out within a sunbeam on the floor. "The polydactyl is Abraxas, named after the Egyptian sun god or the demon from hell. We're not sure which. By the way, polydactyl means six-toed." He then indicated the plump calico. "That's Fern. And that—" He pointed to the creamy-white cat with the tan-colored face, ears, and tail. "That's Bianca."

Bianca cast her sapphire-blue eyes on Nim for less than a second, then turned her gaze away.

"I'm Rochester," the dignified gray cat said. "Now that we've issued an invitation for you to join us, there are a few ground rules we must cover, such as the location of litter boxes and assorted scratching posts."

Nim tried to object. "But I'm not—"

"Let's start with nap-time etiquette. As you know, cats sleep an average of fifteen to sixteen hours a day. We—"

"I'm not staying here!" Nim blurted. "I have to get back to the city."

"The city?" His whiskers stiffened. "Why, that's a tenday journey by paw for a cat in prime physical condition. And the dangers . . . hunger, thirst, predatory animals, cruel humans, cars."

Nim cringed at the mention of cars. The pain in her old injury seemed to suddenly flare.

Rochester frowned down at her bandaged side. "I'm sorry to say, my dear, but you stand very little chance of making such a trip anytime soon." He hopped off the table and strode to the cardboard box in the middle of the living room.

"I don't care," Nim mumbled, making it halfway up before falling again.

"I suppose you can try to leave if you want to," he added, sitting up straight and tall in the box. "But I suspect it might be a waste of your time and energy attempting to get away from Agatha."

Nim wasn't sure what he meant by that; would the old woman force her to stay? "All I want is to go home," she said, her voice trembling.

From inside his box, Rochester gazed at her sympathetically. "Sometimes the Ways of Magic intervenes and we don't get what we want," he said softly. "Instead, it gives us what we need."

Nim had never heard of the Ways of Magic, but whatever it was, it wasn't going to stop her.

"The poor little thing." The calico named Fern shook her head sadly. "She must have been out on her own for a long time."

Still seated on the floor beside her, Bianca glared at Nim through her icy-blue eyes. "Her human obviously didn't take good care of her. Look at the state she's in—dusty fur and a bloody gash on the side of her belly." She wrinkled her nose and turned her face away.

"Life has no doubt been hard for her," Rochester replied with a shake of his gray head.

"And, so what?" the six-toed tabby growled from his patch of sunlight. "Life's been hard for all of us."

Their comments stung, but Nim didn't have time to linger on them. Gathering what confidence she could, she glanced at each of the four house cats. "If you could just show me how to get out of here, I'll be on my way."

Fern waved a paw toward the back of the house. "There's a cat flap in the kitchen door, but we hardly ever use it. We seldom leave. And why would we? There's not much outside except rat territory."

Bianca cut her eyes toward Nim with a sneer. "Agatha's a witch, you know."

Nim's heart jolted. Her eyes widened with fear as she cast another glance at the broom in the corner and the cauldron hanging inside the cold fireplace.

"And what does that matter?" Fern replied. "Agatha's good to us."

Rochester nodded. "Even her name indicates her goodness. In Greek, the name Agatha means kind."

"If you say so." Bianca smirked. She sauntered away with her fluffy tan tail held in the air, a silver snowflake charm jingling on her collar. She jumped onto the old green sofa and curled up on one end.

"I do say so," Rochester replied, turning his mustached face toward Nim. "Not all witches are evil, you know. It's been a few wicked ones that have ruined the reputation for the rest of their magical kinfolk."

With a great deal of determination, Nim finally pulled herself up to her feet. She stood wobbling on her unreliable legs.

"Oh goodness, no." Fern waved a paw to dismiss the notion. "Agatha's not wicked at all, she's just a recluse."

"A recluse?" Nim asked, her voice cracking in fright. A recluse was a venomous spider. She'd seen pictures of them in Fletcher's books about arachnids and insects. Her fur prickled at the thought of the witch woman turning into a giant brown spider.

"Yes. A recluse: someone who doesn't go out into the world very often," Rochester replied. "She seldom leaves the house and gardens, preferring to spend her time creating various salves, poultices, and powders."

"Oh," Nim whispered with relief. She supposed she must be a recluse too. After all, the only thing she wanted was to be home with Fletcher. She took an unsteady step off the orange cushion and set one paw on the tabletop, but her weak legs threatened to give way again. It was the bandage weighing her down. She was sure of it. She stumbled back onto the cushion.

Fern's whiskers perked. "Agatha grows lots of things in her gardens: parsley, cilantro, mint, lungwort, bloodroot, stinking hellebore." Her eyes sparkled. "And lots of catnip! She's a green witch, so she specializes in plants and herbs."

"She also grows the loveliest daisies," Rochester added.

"Blah, blah, blah." Bianca scowled. "If new cat doesn't die from her injuries, your endless babbling will surely bore her to death." She laid her head on her paws and closed her eyes.

Even more determined to free herself from the hateful bandage and the strange household, Nim began gnawing and tugging on the gauze dressing.

"Though, Agatha's ability to choose the perfect protection amulet for anyone may be her most impressive gift," Rochester continued, ignoring Bianca.

"Oh, yes," Fern agreed. "She can make them out of almost anything small and special to the wearer. See?" She lifted her chin, proudly displaying her blue collar and the silver charm dangling from it. "Mine is a rocking chair."

Nim paused, sorrow filling her at the memory of her lost collar and tag—her own symbols of home and family. But she couldn't think about that now. She went back to work on the bandage, and with one final tug, it finally came free.

Her breath caught at the sight of the pale, furless strip of skin and the angry red gouge that'd been stitched together with thick blue thread and covered in ointment.

Rochester arched a white eyebrow. "Considering the extent of your injury, you should really stay here for a while and heal."

The back door creaked open. Footsteps sounded in the kitchen, along with the sound of the old lady humming.

"I can't stay!" Nim blurted. "I have to get home!"

Fern shook her head. "Poor little dear." She waddled to the rocking chair in front of the TV and settled down on its worn cushioned seat.

"She's obviously unlucky," Bianca said from her place

on the sofa. "That's what they say about black cats, you know."

"That's just an antiquated superstition from medieval Europe." Rochester frowned. "Back when people believed witches, or even the devil, could transform into shadowy felines."

Bianca rolled her eyes. "Please spare us the lecture, *Professor* Rochester."

"Our inky friends are no more star-crossed than any of us cats," he continued. "And in some countries, they're even seen as harbingers of good fortune."

"Ugh!" Bianca rolled her eyes again. "Why did we have to get stuck with a former bookstore cat?"

While Nim appreciated Rochester's reassurances, she really was beginning to question her luck. Getting abandoned in a dump only to find herself trapped in the house of a witch with a bunch of unhinged cats were not the most fortuitous events that could have happened to her.

Summoning as much strength as she could, she rose to her feet, grateful when her legs didn't buckle. Leaving the length of bandage behind, she carefully made her way down a nearby chair and stack of boxes onto the floor.

"Look at you!" Fern exclaimed from her place on the rocking chair. "You're quite determined." Her face beamed, before her smile melted into a frown. "But you mustn't overdo it. You've been through a lot."

"She's obviously experienced some misfortune," Abraxas said, his voice gruff and raspy. He climbed from the patch of sunlight and onto his huge, six-toed yellow paws. Then he prowled toward Nim like a tiger, claws clicking beneath him, tail swishing menacingly. "But is she wiser as a result?" He circled her, narrowing his orange eyes, the silver lion charm on his collar gleaming. "Are you a fighter, little cat? One of those strays who intrudes on the territory of others and attempts to take it for herself?"

Nim stumbled back, but he continued his circling and tail swishing. "Do you need to be slapped down?"

"No," Nim murmured, terrified of his sharp teeth and claws.

He loomed over her and growled, low and threateningly, then drew back one of his massive paws with a hiss.

Nim fell onto her non-injured side and raised her own paws in defense. "I don't want any trouble," she squeaked.

He narrowed his eyes again. "Then know your place. And see that you keep to it."

"I . . . I'm not staying," she protested, panting with fear and exhaustion. "I'm leaving. I'm going back to my home."

A clinking noise sounded from the kitchen, as though someone were tapping a spoon against the side of a ceramic bowl.

"Lunchtime!" Fern exclaimed, breaking the tension.

"Come and get it!" Agatha sang out.

Abraxas turned away from Nim, and with shoulders held high, he strode toward the sound of the clinking bowl.

"Don't worry about Abraxas, lovey." Fern gave a sigh and hopped down to the floor. "He's a troubled soul."

Rochester frowned. "Let's just be glad he didn't urinate on the wall in protest."

CHAPTER 10

With tails held high and silver charms swinging from their collars, the other house cats disappeared through the kitchen doorway at the back of the house.

Agatha's voice floated out, "Here you go, my little ones."

The cats yowled and meowed hungrily at her.

"Patience. Patience!" she scolded.

Four bowls clinked against the floor, and the cats began chomping their lunch.

A pang of homesickness struck Nim. She missed the way Fletcher replied when she meowed at him, as though he understood what she was saying. She desperately wanted to begin her journey home, but the old witch might try to stop her.

She folded her ears back, planning her strategy. It was

best to wait until the woman wasn't around, then she'd sneak out through the flap in the back door. She glanced about nervously. Until then, it wasn't safe to remain lying out in the open. She was too vulnerable to being attacked. She hated feeling so helpless. She hadn't been this weak since she'd been a kitten recovering from the car accident. She struggled up, limped to a nearby side table with a landline telephone sitting on top, and slunk into the shadows beneath it.

No sooner had she settled down with her tail wrapped around her when Agatha entered the room, her green gardening boots squeaking as she approached.

Nim's claws gripped the floor in terror. The old woman was coming for her. Torturous images flashed through her mind. What vile-tasting liquids would the witch force her to drink this time? Would she hold her down and cut off more of her fur? She scooted back and pressed herself against the wall.

Agatha stopped before the table with a huff of exasperation. She leaned down, the silver owl amulet swinging from her neck and the smell of fresh herbs wafting off her. In one hand she held a bowl of wet cat food, in her other was a bowl of fresh water. She peered at Nim and frowned. "I see you didn't like your cushion bed." She glanced at the table next to the window and at the cast-off heap of gauze lying there. "Didn't care much for your bandage either, I guess."

Her pulse racing, Nim opened her mouth and gave her a silent hiss.

The woman pursed her lips as she studied Nim. "So, you're determined to leave, are you? I suspected as much." She set the bowls down and pushed them toward Nim. "You'll need to eat and drink first to regain your strength." She stood and wiped her hands on the front of her gray apron.

The food's meaty aroma danced tantalizingly in Nim's nose, and her stomach rumbled. She licked her dry lips, but there was no way she would allow herself to eat or drink. The witch might've added something that would put her into a deep sleep and make her have more strange dreams.

Agatha gathered the discarded bandage and returned to the kitchen just as the four house cats strolled back into the room, each one appearing happy and well-fed.

Abraxas padded toward the side table, and Nim's adrenaline spiked. She bared her fangs and hissed softly.

He paused long enough to cast an orange-eyed glare at her, before lowering himself onto a sliver of sunlight only an arm's length away. He snapped his tail threateningly against the floor. Then he stretched out and rested his head on his massive paws.

Nim gulped, frozen in place. There was no way she

could fight her way past the big tabby. He'd easily tear her to shreds. Then there'd be no chance of her making the long journey by paw. Her heart sank, but there was nothing she could do. She'd have to wait for him to fall asleep and for the old woman to leave the kitchen. Then she would make her escape. Despite her stress, her stomach rumbled again. She cast another glance at the food and water and licked her lips.

From the kitchen came the sound of the refrigerator opening. A plate was set down, and a moment later a microwave oven hummed. Based on the spicy aromas drifting out, Nim guessed the old woman was preparing her own lunch. A minute later, a chair scraped across the floor, and Nim guessed she was sitting down to eat.

By then, Rochester had climbed into his box and Bianca had settled onto the sofa. Clutching a ragged toy squirrel in her jaws, Fern plopped down on the rocking chair's worn cushion, hugging the matted toy to her chest.

Nim cast an anxious glance at the nearby Abraxas. To her relief, his eyelids were slowly drifting shut.

Bianca, who'd been busily grooming her cream-colored fur, paused mid-lick and stared down at Nim. "So, what's your story, unlucky cat? How did you end up in the rats' dump?"

Rochester's white mustache drooped as he frowned at

Bianca from inside his box. "I thought we'd already established that black cats aren't unlucky."

"What?" Bianca blinked her blue eyes innocently. "I'm only joking with her."

"Well, your joke is about as humorous as a hairball." He turned his gaze to Nim. "Though a story before nap time would be most welcomed."

"I don't want to talk about it," Nim murmured, careful to keep her voice low so as not to disturb Abraxas.

"There's no need to be self-conscious," Bianca replied. "We were all abandoned before Agatha took us in." She licked her paw and washed her whiskers.

"Very true," Rochester agreed. "Before my arrival here, I was a shop cat at a small bookstore in the city. It was a lovely place—soft lighting and a couple of comfy reading chairs. Soaring shelves packed with books, books stacked on tables, books displayed in the front window. Ah . . ." He closed his eyes in bliss. "The smell of the books—that fragrance of the written word—I can recall it all even now."

Nim's gaze wandered back to the food and water before her. Her stomach was so empty, and her mouth was so parched.

"I was called Jeffrey back in those days," Rochester continued. "The store's owner, Mr. Hooper, was a kindly but rather eccentric gray-haired, bespectacled gentleman.

A voracious reader—and thus very knowledgeable, as all voracious readers are. He quite enjoyed reading aloud, and I quite enjoyed listening. He was particularly interested in philosophy, ancient religions, and the occult."

Nim hardly heard him, though. Her stomach gurgled loudly. Her nostrils quivered. She lowered her nose to the chunky brown food, gave it a sniff, and her mouth watered at the aromas of chicken and beef.

"It was a satisfying life." Rochester smiled fondly, his light green eyes gazing into the distance. "The store's patrons came from all backgrounds and professions, and most of them liked to chat with Mr. Hooper as much as he liked chatting with them. I quite enjoyed observing their unique mannerisms and learning of their interests. And I was rather helpful, if I do say so myself, guiding customers to the sections they were looking for. If they needed further assistance, I would jump on the shelf and direct them to the specific volume they were in search of. I knew all the titles by heart."

Nim tried to focus on Rochester's words, but her eyes kept drifting back to the full bowls before her. She sniffed again yet detected no suspicious odors. Maybe she would take a very small drink and maybe one tiny bite. She gave a cautious lick of the food. It didn't taste contaminated—it tasted delicious.

Rochester sighed. "When Mr. Hooper died, the land-lord discarded the books he didn't want, as well as me, in a box on the sidewalk."

Unable to hold herself back any longer, Nim wolfed down the food. Then she slurped up as much water as her stomach could hold.

"Those copies of *Jane Eyre* and *Charlotte's Web* on the lower ledge are two of the books Agatha picked from the box when she asked if I, along with another nearby cat, would like to come live with her, Abraxas, and Grimalkin."

Nim glanced up as Rochester motioned toward the shelf across the room. On top of it stood an assortment of candles and candleholders. The rest of its shelves were packed with books. "That's how she came to name me Rochester, after the mysterious and secretive gentleman in *Jane Eyre*."

"And she named me after the kind young girl in *Charlotte's Web*!" Fern piped up.

Rochester nodded. "Agatha likes bestowing her adopted cats with names that she finds in books. Bianca's came from an Italian guidebook. And she chose Abraxas from *The Encyclopedia of Deities and Demons*." He arched an eyebrow at the big ginger tabby. "Abraxas, perhaps you'd like to share a story about your previous name and life?"

"My past is none of her business," Abraxas growled, not

even bothering to open his eyes.

Rochester pursed his lips. "I hardly think such rudeness is warranted."

But Nim was just grateful the big cat's attention wasn't fixed on her. She watched his sides softly rising and falling as sleep overtook him.

Rochester turned his attention back to Nim. "By chance, did the story of my arrival here sound familiar to you?"

Nim shook her head, puzzled that he would wonder such a thing when she'd only just arrived herself.

"Ah, well." He sighed. "Perhaps you'll begin to recall some memories in your coming days here."

"I'm not staying!" Nim shook her head vehemently. "I have to get home to Fletcher. He must be very worried about me by now."

Bianca flicked her fluffy tan tail. "I doubt it. He's probably already replaced you with another pet. Humans are like that."

Nim's whiskers wilted at the thought of the silvery-gray tabby that'd been hanging around the house.

"Pay no mind to Bianca." Fern scowled at the creamy-white cat.

Bianca gave Fern a scowl of her own, then returned to grooming her fur.

Nim yawned. Then she blinked. Her eyelids suddenly

felt as heavy as bricks. So did her head. She yawned again, much wider this time, and her body swayed back and forth like a branch in the breeze.

Rochester squinted across the room at her, then shook his head sympathetically. "It appears Agatha has sedated you again, my dear. You'll have to delay setting off on your journey after all."

"Well, it serves her right," Bianca said. "If she'd just lie still and let Agatha's healing work take place, she wouldn't be in this predicament."

"Oh, hush, Bianca," Fern scolded. "You're becoming as annoying as a flea."

Nim fell onto her side. She tried to get up but managed only to lift her head a whisker's length before it plopped back down again.

"There's no point in fighting it, lovey," Fern said. "Just like you can't fight the Ways of Magic." She gave the ragged toy squirrel a motherly lick, then laid her own head down and draped a paw over her eyes to block the afternoon brightness. "Happy dreams, little one," she murmured.

Nim wasn't sure if she was speaking to her or the toy squirrel. She yawned again as a wave of weariness washed over her. She didn't want to sleep, but her fatigue was too powerful. A tiny flame of anger ignited at the thought of Agatha's trickery. The witch had put something in the food or water, just as she'd suspected. She never should have trusted the old woman.

On the sofa, Bianca curled up and draped her tail over her eyes.

The sound of Agatha's squeaky rubber boots filled the quiet room as she emerged from the kitchen to grab a straw gardening hat off one of the wall hooks. Humming to herself, she exited through the back door.

Outside the window, a cloud drifted by and the nearby patch of sunlight faded to shadow. Abraxas peeled his eyes open and cast a sour look at Nim, as though it were somehow her fault. Then he padded away to a different sunbeam and stretched out in its warm strip of light.

As Nim's eyelids drifted closed, she took a last worried glance at the tabby, hoping he wouldn't attack her while she dozed. As sleep dragged her away, she wondered why he was so mean, what his story was, and why he hadn't wanted to share it.

CHAPTER 11

Nim was surprised to find herself once again in the strange dreamworld, strolling along the road beneath the purple sky and white crescent moon. She glanced at her side, and the goblin-inflicted wound still wasn't there.

As before, she arrived at the crossroads. Silence hung all around. Hecate stood gazing down at her.

Nim drew to a stop, her nervousness sending shivers down her spine. She wanted to tuck her tail and back away, but she forced her feet to stay put. Her instincts warned her the lady was powerful, maybe even dangerous.

"Hello, Nimbus," she said. "I see you are troubled. What is it that you seek here?"

"Oh, I'm not looking for anything here. I just want to go home."

Hecate arched an eyebrow. "Perhaps your newly acquired gift can help you do that."

"Gift?" A soft squeak sounded nearby, momentarily distracting Nim from her puzzlement. A black mouse skittered by, easily within reach of her paws, but she let it pass, ignoring the urge to pounce on it.

Hecate bent forward with her arm extended, and the mouse scurried onto her hand. Then she stood, caressing the small velvety creature as it settled against her palm and curled its black tail around her finger. Twitching its whiskers, it watched Nim with its onyx eyes. "You now possess the gift of dream sight," Hecate said, returning her attention to Nim, "the ability to walk with awareness through the dream realm. It's a rare opportunity granted to very few physical beings."

Nim's paw rose in confusion. "But how did I get such a thing?"

"You took it."

"Me?" Nim shook her head. "I don't understand."

"You took it from a nightmare demon."

Nim's eyes widened. "Nightmare demon?"

"A creature that slinks from this realm and into the physical one, twisting dreams into terrible visions, then feeding off the dreamer's emotions." Hecate cast a glance toward the mist-covered road at Nim's right. "They've been known by many names since the beginning of time: mara, alp, cauchemar, ephialtes. They are inflicters of nightmares and paralysis, and sometimes, stealers of life force."

Understanding suddenly dawned on Nim, and the fur stood up on her back. "The goblin that attacked Fletcher!" She lifted her shoulders proudly. "I fought and killed it."

"Did you?" Hecate asked.

"Yes." Nim peered at the scary, foggy road, but a tiny doubt nibbled her confidence. She swept her gaze away. She had killed the thing. She was sure. It had faded into nothing more than a wisp of smoke and drifted out the window. She drew her shoulders up again and faced Hecate. "I even scratched out its eye."

"A courageous and dangerous thing to do," Hecate observed. "Blinding the creature granted you its dream sight, but biting it could have sickened or killed you. A nightmare demon is a powerful being, though not without weakness."

"So that's why my eye turned yellow!" Nim frowned as Hecate nodded. This was yet another example of her recent bad luck. The thought of possessing the dream sight of such a monster soured her stomach. But at least she'd destroyed the beast and she was glad for that.

Before she could ask how to rid herself of the unwanted ability, the goddess spoke again. "Something is troubling you, though. What is it you seek?"

"All I want is to go home," Nim replied. "I want to get back to Fletcher, and far away from Agatha and her cats."

"Is it really so dreadful there?"

"Yes!" Nim nodded as hard as she could. "Abraxas and Bianca are mean. Abraxas even tried to attack me!"

"Why not discover the solution to the problem?"

"The problem?" Nim once again lifted her paw in confusion.

"When others lash out, it's because they are frightened. What does Abraxas fear?"

Nim couldn't imagine the big tabby being afraid of anything.

"Perhaps you can discover what made him this way by walking in his dream," Hecate offered. "You're free to travel wherever you wish in this realm, even within the dreams of other sleepers."

A sudden idea occurred to Nim, sending her heart leaping with hope. "Can I walk in Fletcher's dreams too?" If she could just speak with him the way she was speaking with Lady Hecate, she could warn him about the other jar. She could tell him she hadn't abandoned him. She could tell him where Aunt Caroline had taken her! Then he would come right away and bring her home.

"Yes," Hecate replied. "You can walk in his dreams too."

Nim stepped happily from paw to paw. Fletcher would be so surprised and pleased to talk with her. She was sure of it. All she had to do was wait until he fell asleep tonight, then . . . Her dancing feet slowed to a stop. She had no idea how to visit someone else in their dreams.

She furrowed her brow. Maybe walking through the grumpy old tabby's dream was a good suggestion after all. If she learned how to do it now, then she'd know what to do tonight. She turned her gaze up to Hecate. "How can I find Abraxas here?" Frowning, she glanced at the three roads. "How do I even find my way around in this place?"

Hecate pointed at the dark, stormy path lying to Nim's right. "That way leads to the place where nightmares dwell."

Nim's fur prickled as she gazed into the distance at the fog-covered road with churning black clouds flinging out zaps of lightning. She twitched her ears, certain she could hear thunder rumbling there too. Her legs trembled. "Please don't make me go that way."

"It's not my purpose to make you go anywhere," Hecate replied. "I serve only as a sort of signpost at the crossroads. It's up to you to choose which path you'll travel."

"Oh." Nim gave a small huff of relief.

Hecate pointed to Nim's left and at all the blurry images located far away. "That route leads to the place where your memories are gathered. All the pieces of your past reside there, even the smallest details you might not recall when you're awake. You may travel to them but can only view them as they occurred."

She motioned behind her to the middle path that lay stretched before Nim, the one with the faraway shapes and colors that seemed to be shifting and morphing before her very eyes. "This road will take you to the place where others dream. There, you may talk to the dreamer, and your presence will alter the course of their dream."

Nim nodded that she understood. "But how can I find Abraxas there?"

"To find another dreamer or to visit one of your memories, simply step onto the appropriate path. Focus on who you want to meet or what moments you wish to visit, much as you did previously when you found yourself in your own early memories. The road will take you there." She lifted a finger of warning. "But know that if a dreamer objects to your presence, they can vanish and hide themselves from you, locking you out of their mind's eye for as long as they wish to."

Nim stared at the middle road and the colorful, mutating shapes in the distance, guessing they were images from others' dreams. "Okay. I'll give it a try." But when she turned to thank the goddess for her help, she was gone.

With a sigh, Nim returned her gaze to the road ahead, picturing the huge ginger cat with the six-toed paws and the angry orange eyes. Her stomach flittered nervously at the thought of talking to him, even in this realm, but she was determined to learn how to walk with others in order to visit Fletcher's dreams that night.

Steadying her nerves, she set off. Except for the kaleidoscope of color up ahead, the road itself was empty, with endless grassy fields running alongside it. As she traveled, it occurred to her she could've tried dream walking with Fern or Rochester, who were much friendlier than Abraxas. She frowned as she thought about it. Maybe Hecate knew something. Maybe sending her to visit Abraxas's dreams would help her in some other way. Then she remembered Hecate's words about discovering the thing Abraxas feared. What if she could help him not be afraid anymore? Then he wouldn't be so grumpy toward the other house cats. It would be something nice she could do for Fern and Rochester before she returned home. She nodded to herself. Yes, that must be why Hecate suggested she seek him out.

As she walked, the air grew warmer and the plum-colored sky spilled into a sapphire-blue one. A scattering of trees rose in the distance. Just up ahead, a furless gray rabbit hopped out of the tall grassy field and hunched on the side of the road. Nim strolled past it, puzzled at the sight of the small elephant-like trunk protruding from where its nose should've been. She strode onward, and a line of cockroaches scuttled across the road, their wings and bodies covered with spotted patterns like those of giraffes.

She took a few steps more and the path suddenly ended, leaving her standing on the edge of a wide grassy savanna dotted with trees that looked like leafy green umbrellas. The sun was a white-hot ball in the endless blue sky. Mice with zebra-striped fur and tan-colored lizards bearing horns and black-and-white facial markings like miniature gazelles lapped water from a nearby stream. And there, hiding in a clump of tall grass, was Abraxas, his eyes and ears fixed on a nearby zebra-striped mouse.

Nim stood as tall as she could. She wanted to turn and tiptoe away from the bully, but she forced her paws forward. Before she could change her mind, she took a deep breath and called out, "Abraxas!"

He slowly turned his head toward her. "What do you want, interloper?" he sneered.

She bent her ears in irritation. "I have a name!"

"I don't care." He turned back to the mouse.

Nim trembled with hurt. Why did he have to be so mean? Then Lady Hecate's words returned to her. *When others lash out, it's because they are frightened.*

Nim glanced around, but she didn't see anything that might scare the big tabby. It must have been something that had already happened. Fletcher once told her that the best way to overcome a fear was to face it. Maybe if she could lead Abraxas to the place where his memories were gathered, he'd stop being frightened. Tensing her muscles, she stepped closer. "Abraxas," she whispered, "I know you're afraid of something."

He swung his head around with a warning growl.

Nim gulped. "I can help you if you'll just follow me."

"I'm not going anywhere with you." He narrowed his eyes. "Leave me."

Then he and the savanna vanished.

The bright sun no longer shone down. The sky hung cloudless, pale, and colorless. There was only a still and heavy silence pressing upon her.

"Abraxas?" She peered all around. But he was nowhere to be seen. Even the road was empty, one direction stretching toward the crossroads, the other toward the distant swirling lights.

Nim had never felt so alone and so far away from anyone or anything.

CHAPTER 12

Embarrassed and disappointed that the dream walk with Abraxas hadn't gone well, Nim hurried away. Her shoulders drooped as she traveled toward her crossroads. She should have tried finding Fern instead. Fern was so much kinder and wouldn't have kicked her out.

As she continued on, musing and pouting, rows of huge oak trees sprang up on the shoulders of the road. A disheveled squirrel skittered along their branches. Others jumped from limb to limb and then to the ground, each one looking as if its fur had been endlessly groomed and gnawed. More squirrels ran down from the leafy treetops and climbed onto tiny rocking chairs lined up alongside the road. They stared at Nim with their round, shiny eyes.

Being surrounded by so many rabid-looking rodents made her uncomfortable. She decided that the next time she saw Lady Hecate, she'd ask her why dreams were so weird and confusing.

She soon came upon Fern sitting in a human-sized rocking chair in the middle of the path; more scruffy squirrels chittered and scampered about on the ground below.

"Hello, Fern!" Nim said, surprised to have found her. "I was just thinking about you." Then she paused, realizing her thoughts had led her right into Fern's dream, just as Hecate had told her they would.

"Hello, little one." Fern smiled down at her and waved a calicoed paw.

"I'm sorry to interrupt you," Nim said, hoping Fern wouldn't think she was intruding, "but I'm practicing dream walking with others."

Fern tilted her head to one side. "Dream walking?"

"Yes." Nim nodded. "I can step into the dreams of others."

To her relief, Fern's eyes brightened with delight. "That's wonderful!"

"I'm practicing so that I can find Fletcher tonight." Nim took a seat on the roadway, sitting up tall and proud.

"What a useful skill to have!" Fern beamed with pride

for her. "What else can you do with it?"

"I can also visit my memories, even the ones I've forgotten."

Fern's shiny eyes widened. "You mean you can go back and see all the places you've been and all the things that you've done?"

"Yes," Nim replied, then paused. Maybe she'd spoken too soon. "Well, I haven't actually tried it yet. I'm not sure what memory I'd want to revisit anyway."

Fern shook her head in admiration. "If I had such an ability, I'd go back and see my kittens."

Nim's ears twitched with surprise. "You had kittens?"

"Oh, yes." Fern nodded proudly. "Three of the most darling things you ever could've seen. Two calicoes and one gray."

An idea began to form in Nim's mind, and her whiskers tingled with excitement. "Maybe I can lead you to a memory of your kittens."

Fern rose to her feet, balancing on the seat of the chair as it rocked back and forth. "Could you really?" She swished her tail happily.

Nim shrugged. "I'm not exactly sure that I can, but I know who might help us." She leaped up to her paws and waved for Fern to follow.

Fern hopped down, and they scampered off, past all the

scruffy squirrels and along the path leading back to Nim's crossroads, where she planned to ask for Hecate's guidance. As they went, Nim wondered if the goddess would tell them how to get to Fern's crossroads and then to the route that would lead to her memories. Would that even be possible? The road suddenly branched off before them, and Nim came to a stop, puzzled for a moment as she glanced around.

They'd reached a crossroads, but it wasn't hers. The sky was a warm pinkish blue instead of purple, and there was no crescent moon, only a scattering of stars faintly twinkling. A shady forest of oaks surrounded the paths, and beams of golden sunlight streaked down through the trees' branches.

"What is this?" Fern asked as she gazed about.

Nim flicked her ears in amusement. It had to be Fern's crossroads. She was sure of it. Once again, her thoughts had easily led her to where she wanted to go. Then she frowned. She'd have to make sure she didn't think of any bad memories while she was here. She didn't want to accidentally end up in some awful time from her past.

Trying to familiarize herself with their surroundings, she looked to the right. The path leading to the nightmare place was crowded with leafless, gnarled trees, their branches twisting in unnatural directions. Giant squirrel-like creatures as big as dinosaurs stomped around in the distance.

"I don't like that place," Fern whispered, her eyes wide as she stared at the crooked trees and monster squirrels.

Nim looked toward the path on the left with its far-off blurry images. She was certain it would lead to the location where Fern's memories were gathered. Colorful shapes twisted and turned in the distance ahead of them; no doubt it was the place where others dream. Nim wondered if that way could take Fern into the minds of her sleeping kittens. "Would you like to try visiting one of your kittens right now as they're dreaming?"

Fern didn't have to think about it. She shook her head. "I'd much rather go back to the time before they began their new lives, back when they were still my young ones."

Nim gave her a nod. "This way, then." She indicated the route to the left, and she instructed Fern to fix her mind on the memory she wanted to visit.

Fern furrowed her brow in concentration; when they passed a pink bowl on the shoulder of the road, she exclaimed, "That's my old food dish!" She pointed ahead. "And look! That's my favorite rug. I used to nap on it in the afternoons." They passed a brush, a stack of canned cat food, and numerous well-chewed, overgroomed, ragged toys. Fern smiled, happy to see the bits and pieces of her past scattered along the way. She sighed contentedly. "I was known as Cally in those days."

Nim was about to ask if it felt strange to lose your old home and name, but her throat grew tight at the thought of such a thing happening to her.

"There it is!" Fern's whiskers perked. "Just up ahead."

A low, sprawling building rose before them. In front of it stood a tall flagpole. Nim squinted, not sure what she was seeing.

The sky shone a morning-time blue as they drew up to the redbrick building with a set of glass doors in the front.

"Where are we?" Nim asked.

Fern smiled, half-happy, half-sad. "It's school."

Nim flicked her ears with confusion. What kinds of memories could Fern have of this place?

"Look." Fern motioned toward a minivan that had pulled up to the front of the building. A man climbed out. He went around to the vehicle's side door and took out a blue plastic storage bin. He lugged it over to the school's entrance, and with a look of guilt, he glanced around. Then he hurried back to the minivan and drove away.

Fern and Nim padded over to the open storage container. When they stood up on their hind legs and peered inside, Nim gasped.

A younger Fern lay inside the box. Mewing and wobbling around her were three kittens. None of them appeared to have heard Nim's gasp or to even see her and Fern peering at them.

"Aren't they darling?" Fern crooned.

"I don't understand." Nim shook her head. "Why did that man leave you and your kittens at a school?"

"With so many people soon to pass by, he thought someone would take us." Fern's shining eyes never left sight of her purring kittens as they tumbled and swatted at one another. She sighed sadly. "He wasn't a very mean man. And though his wife and children loved us well enough, he said they couldn't afford to take care of us."

Nim's heart grew heavy.

A few cars had pulled into the school's nearby parking lot. The Fern inside the bin drew her kittens closer, and she licked the top of each small head. "Now listen carefully, my young ones," she said. "The time has come for you to make your way into the world and live your own lives."

Three sets of eyes blinked up at her in puzzlement.

"The world can be scary and dangerous, so you must be cautious, just as I've taught you to be. However, you must also enjoy as much fun and happiness as you can."

Adults, along with children wearing backpacks, climbed

out of the cars in the parking lot. Nim's heart thudded with nervousness.

"Sad things might happen to you, my kittens," the mother Fern said. "I wish I could prevent them, but I cannot."

People came up the sidewalk, drawing closer to the blue storage container. Nim wanted to scramble away, but she forced herself to stay put, reminding herself this was only a memory that had already happened.

A girl and her mother stopped next to the bin. "Kittens!" the girl cried with excitement. Her mother smiled, and they crouched down and observed Fern's little ones.

Sickness welled within Nim at the memory of her own awful experience inside of a box, the last time she'd seen her own siblings.

The mother Fern gave each kitten another grooming lick to their heads. "Embrace the adventure that is life," she said.

Nim tilted her head to one side, replaying the words in her mind. She nodded to herself, her sadness seeming to grow lighter, and she hoped she would remember Fern's wise advice when she awoke.

Over the next few moments, a blur of teachers, parents, and children reached into the container and took out a kitten. One family told their little calico how they went boating on weekends and that they planned to bring her with them each time. Another family lived on a large farm, and the gray kitten was told he could run free through the fields and catch all the mice he wanted. The other calico was taken away by a small girl who hugged her to her heart, promising to brush her and feed her treats and let her sleep in the bed with her.

Only the momma Fern remained in the box. She smiled sadly as she watched the last of her kittens be carried off. When they were gone, she leaped out of the bin and walked away.

Nim, and the Fern standing beside her, watched until the momma Fern turned and disappeared down the street.

"Fern?" Nim swallowed the lump in her throat. "Weren't you sad to see your kittens leave?"

"Oh, yes." Fern's tail drooped. "But life is always changing, and that's the way it's meant to be. There's a time to raise your kittens, and there's a time to let them go out on their own. I do hope their lives have turned out to be wonderful." She released her hold on the side of the blue container, then she too walked away.

Nim scampered after her, and as the school and the plastic bin faded to nothingness, she caught up with Fern. They walked past nearby apartments and houses, and Nim asked, "How did you end up at Agatha's cottage?"

Fern chuckled. "After my kittens went into the world, I set out to find something to eat. I happened to stroll past a small shop that had just been emptied. It used to be a bookstore, and out front sat a box of leftover books, along with a gray-and-white cat."

Nim's ears perked. "Do you mean Rochester?"

Fern nodded. "I was listening to his life story when Agatha walked by carrying a bag of cat food she'd purchased at a nearby pet store." Fern smiled as she strolled onward. "And so began the next chapter of both our lives with dear Grimalkin and cranky Abraxas."

CHAPTER 13

Nim awoke, wondering where Fern had gone, before remembering she was still in Agatha's cottage underneath the side table where she'd fallen asleep.

Through the window across the room, the sun was inching its way toward evening. Fern was asleep on the rocking chair, curled up with her ratty toy squirrel. Abraxas lay sleeping on the floor, but Rochester and Bianca were up and grooming their fur.

Nim rubbed a paw over her face and blinked her bleary eyes. Did she really dream walk? Had Abraxas kicked her out of his dream, only for her to wander into Fern's and visit a memory of her kittens? The throbbing of her injury and the smell of the hawthorn ointment jolted her fully awake.

"It was just a dream," she whispered, surprised by her disappointment. She looked down at her side. The old woman had rebandaged her while she slept. She flattened her ears in annoyance. Whatever the witch had put in her food made her sleep deeply again and have more of the strange dreams—dreams that felt so very real. She snapped her tail angrily at the thought of having been tricked. She would not make the mistake of eating or drinking anything else the sneaky old woman offered her. She needed to get home. She needed to protect Fletcher in case another nightmare demon escaped from the other old jar, and she needed to leave right now.

The first thing she'd do, though, was remove the scratchy, unbearable binding—again. She set about chewing and tugging on the gauze. She still didn't know what she'd do about Aunt Caroline when she finally reached home, but a long journey lay ahead of her with plenty of time to figure out something. A moment later, she pulled the bandage off and let it drop to the floor. She frowned down at the blue stitches, reminders of how difficult the walk back to the city was going to be. But that didn't matter. She climbed to her feet and lurched out from under the table. She'd made it two steps when her trembling legs gave way and she slumped to the floor.

"No need to worry," Rochester said, sitting up taller

inside his box. "The medicine's sedating effects will wear off soon, and then you'll be able to walk without wobbling."

Nim didn't have time for waiting. She tried to stand again, with similar results.

"You need to rest." Rochester pursed his lips. "You want to remain in good health and not get a fever. You won't like where Agatha puts the thermometer to check your temperature. And if you fuss with those stitches, she'll put a lampshade over your head."

"A lampshade?" Nim furrowed her brow.

"Fern calls them that because they do resemble miniature lampshades." Rochester chuckled to himself. "They're actually referred to as collar cones."

"I don't care about any of that." Nim shook her head with determination. "I need to get home."

Bianca yawned from her spot on the sofa. "Are you sure they want you back? Humans can be very fickle, you know."

Of course Fletcher wanted her home! An image of the stray tabby crept into Nim's mind once again, though. Her stomach twisted at the memories of Fletcher leaving it food and water, trying to befriend it. Would he replace her with that other cat while she was here? She shook the thought away, forcing herself to focus. She gazed around the room, planning her route of escape, but paused at the sight of the sleeping Abraxas. She still couldn't get over the feeling she'd really entered his dream. She shifted her stare to Fern, asleep on the rocking chair. She'd just been walking and talking with Fern. She was sure of it. "Dreams aren't real!" she muttered, shaking her head again as though to clear the idea away once and for all.

"What's that you say?" Rochester leaned forward, his freshly groomed whiskers perking at attention.

The heat of embarrassment rushed up Nim's neck. "It's just that, I've had some dreams lately that felt so real." She lowered her eyes, awkwardly studying her paws. "I went to a place where the sky was purple. I was standing at a crossroads and a woman named Hecate was there, and she was holding a black mouse."

"Ah. Hecate, the ancient Greek goddess possessing the power to conjure up dreams." Rochester nodded sagely. "It makes sense you dreamed of meeting her at a crossroads, as they were locations sacred to her." He gave his ear a casual scratch. "Some believe that dreaming of a crossroads means something is about to change in the dreamer's life."

A low growl sounded across the room. Abraxas climbed to his paws and narrowed his eyes at Nim. "My dreams are my own. Stay out of them, interloper." Then he padded away, swishing his tail behind him as though he were a majestic lion king.

Nim's eyes widened with bewilderment as she watched him go.

On the sofa, Bianca gazed after the big cat too. "What's gotten into him?"

Rochester arched an eyebrow, then shrugged. "Perhaps senility is setting in. At least he's headed to the litter box and hasn't taken to soiling the floor."

Nim's pulse raced with hope. Had Abraxas seen her in his dream just as she'd seen him? What about Fern?

"Fern!" she called, trying to rise, but her numb legs still wouldn't cooperate. "Fern, please wake up! I need to ask you something!"

"Really, new cat." Bianca rolled her eyes. "Why is everyone acting so squirrelly?" She laid her head on her paws and huffed.

"Fern!" Nim called again.

Fern peeled her eyes open. She gave a long, luxurious stretch of her front legs and then her back legs.

Excitement bubbled in Nim's stomach. Could she really walk in others' dreams? Was such a thing even possible? "Fern–" She paused, not sure exactly what to ask.

Fern's gaze settled on Nim. "Oh, hello, lovey." She gave a lick to the tattered toy squirrel lying next to her.

"Fern . . . did you . . . did you have a nice nap?" Nim asked.

"Oh, yes." Fern nodded.

"Did you happen to dream anything interesting?"

Fern paused for a moment that lasted an eternity. Then a smile spread across her face. "I had the loveliest dream."

"Yes?" Nim held her breath.

"I went to see my kittens," Fern said. "And you were there too."

Fern chattered on about the visit, but Nim hardly heard her. She was too overwhelmed with wonder and hope. Her mind turned over with the possibilities. She'd be able to talk to Fletcher and they'd have a real conversation. She'd tell him how Aunt Caroline had taken her away. She'd tell him where she was; he'd come get her at once. She wouldn't have to make the long and dangerous journey by paw after all.

Abraxas, smelling faintly of floral-scented kitty litter, strolled back into the room and plopped down in the center of the floor. He glared at Nim, but she didn't care. "Fern! Rochester! I have something wonderful to tell you!" In her excitement, she'd managed to climb to her feet, and she stood wavering on her legs.

"Oh?" Rochester arched an eyebrow.

Fern sat up on the rocking chair.

"I have the gift of dream sight!" Nim proclaimed, and thrust her chest out.

"Dream sight, you say?" Rochester arched his other eyebrow.

Nim nodded. "I have the ability to walk with awareness through the dream realm. Hecate told me so."

Fern and Rochester exchanged meaningful glances, but what those glances meant, Nim didn't know.

Rochester rubbed a white-gloved paw to his chin. "The ability to walk in others' dreams is a powerful skill, one that only a very special cat would have."

"A truly, very special cat," Fern added with a knowing look.

On the sofa, Bianca huffed in exasperation. "She's not special."

"Perhaps she is. Perhaps she isn't," Rochester replied. "But you must admit this revelation is indeed curious."

Nim didn't understand what they were talking about, but it didn't matter. She lowered herself back to the floor before her trembling legs collapsed again. She smiled, hardly able to contain her happiness. All she had to do was wait a few hours more. Then it would be Fletcher's bedtime. And when he fell asleep, she'd find him in his dreams. Her mind whirled with excitement. It would be hard to wait patiently, but everything was going to work out!

"Tell me more about this curious dream with the goddess Hecate and her black mouse," Rochester said. "Did she by chance reveal anything else interesting about you?"

All eyes fixed on Nim, except for Abraxas, who'd shifted around so that his back was now turned toward her.

"Yes," Nim replied. "Hecate did tell me something else."

Fern's, Rochester's, and even Bianca's ears perked.

"She told me that acquiring the dream sight had turned one of my eyes yellow." Nim lowered her shoulders. She didn't want to talk about the nightmare demon. Thinking about the horrible creature seemed to suck all the happiness from the moment. Nor did she want to admit she'd stolen the dream sight, even though she hadn't meant to.

"Did Hecate say there was anything else that was . . . different about you?" Rochester prodded.

Nim thought for a second, then shook her head, a tinge disappointed. Wasn't being able to dream walk special enough?

Fern sighed sadly.

"I told you," Bianca said.

"That doesn't prove or disprove anything," Rochester replied.

"I can walk in people's dreams too!" Nim added, her

pride flaring again. "I'm going to visit Fletcher tonight when he goes to sleep. Then he'll come and get me. I'll be home soon!"

Fern studied Nim, her whiskers turning down, her face etched with sympathy.

"What?" Nim's stomach clenched. "What's wrong?"

"Nothing's wrong, lovey." Fern smiled, but Nim knew it was a forced one.

CHAPTER 14

"Tell us about the mouse in your dream," Fern said from her seat on the rocking chair. The forced smile remained stretched across her face.

Nim wrinkled her forehead, certain Fern was trying to change the subject.

"Did you see any other mice there? Did you hunt any of them?" Fern's eyes glinted. "Give us all the details of how you stalked it, caught it, and inflicted the killing bite!"

"I've never actually caught a mouse." Nim lowered her eyes, embarrassed. Her voice dropped. "And what's a killing bite?" She didn't think she'd ever done that either. Though she supposed it could be what she'd used on the nightmare demon.

"Oh, you poor dear! Has no one ever taught you?"

Fern shook her head sadly. "Have you not learned the three diversions?"

"The three diversions?" Nim had never heard of them.

"Well, now," Fern replied with an enthusiastic thump of her tail. "There's an art to being a cat, aside from enjoying numerous meals and naps throughout the day, of course. And that art consists of the three diversions: hunting, playing, and watching. If you want to become the type of cat that's feared and respected by rodents and birds, you must learn the appropriate use of your teeth. An expert hunter must know the proper way to inflict the killing bite."

"Could you teach me?" Nim asked, her spirits rising a little. It'd be a most valuable skill to know, and the lesson would be a great way to keep her mind distracted while she waited for Fletcher's bedtime to arrive.

"Yes. I taught each of my kittens how to do it," Fern said with a nod, "and now I will teach you." Gripping the prickly toy squirrel in her mouth, she jumped down and strode toward Nim, the tiny silver rocking chair swaying on her collar.

"Thanks, Fern," Nim replied.

Fern plopped down and dropped her toy. Then she leaned forward and licked the top of Nim's head with her scratchy tongue. "It's the least I can do in return for the lovely visit with my kittens."

Nim glanced up at the window. The sun had set. Gray twilight hung over the world outside. She wished nighttime would hurry and arrive.

Fern nudged her. "Are you paying attention, dear?"

"Yes," Nim said, returning her focus to her teacher.

Fern cupped her paws over the body of the ragged toy squirrel. "Once you have your prey in your clutch, grasp it by the back of the neck, mindful to position your mouth where its skull meets its backbone. Then drive your teeth in and sever the spine! Like this." She sank her fangs into the scruffy gray toy, gave it a small, vicious shake, then released it from her mouth. She glanced at Nim to see if she understood.

Nim nodded.

"After you've killed your prey, you'll want to take a moment to groom yourself in order to calm your excitement and steady the rushing of your blood." Fern licked her paw and drew it across her cheek a few times. Then she pushed the squirrel toward Nim. "Now you try."

Nim bit down on her scruffy victim. "Like this?" she murmured. She hoped Fletcher would be impressed with this new ability too. She was going to have so much to tell him.

On the sofa, Bianca raised her head and glared. "Can you two keep the noise down with your silly lessons? Some of us are trying to sleep." She settled her chin back on her paws and closed her eyes.

Fern released a sigh that was half-annoyed, half-sympathetic. "Poor Bianca," she murmured.

Keeping her jaws clamped on her prey, Nim glanced up, Fern's words pulling her thoughts from Fletcher and home. "What do you mean?" she asked through a mouthful of fake squirrel fur.

"Hers is a story of heartbreak," Fern whispered.

"It is?" Nim replied, her teeth still clenched on her prey.

"Bianca doesn't trust anyone with her affections anymore, and it's turned her rather sour." Fern peered down at Nim and wrinkled her brow. "No, no, no. You must really chomp down! Lock on to it. Deliver enough pressure to sever the spine!" She clacked her teeth as an example.

"But what happened to Bianca?"

Fern shook her head sadly. "She's been given up twice. The first time, she was abandoned by a young woman she loved and trusted more than anything in the world. One day the young woman just gave Bianca away without even a word of goodbye. She'd taken up with a boyfriend who didn't like cats." Fern sighed. "Bianca's human chose the boyfriend over her, and it broke Bianca's heart."

Nim stared across the room at the beautiful, creamy-white cat, surprised that the cool and confident Bianca somehow looked smaller and sadder. Fletcher would *never* do that to her; he would never give her away. Nim was sure of that. Fern softly popped the top of Nim's head with her paw. "Focus, little one."

Nim tried again, this time driving her fangs in with all her might, clamping her jaws in what she imagined to be a grip of death.

"That's very good." Fern nodded approval. "But it's still not enough. You must also apply a rapid side-to-side motion, a chattering movement as if you were watching a brazen bird strutting outside the window."

Trying not to think of Bianca and all the sadness she'd been through, Nim focused her attention on the toy. She sawed her teeth back and forth through its neck, vibrating her jaws up and down. Its cottony innards squished and churned under its grungy fur. If another nightmare demon came anywhere near Fletcher, this was what she would do to it! A wild satisfaction surged through her. A small growl escaped her throat.

Fern's pupils grew large with excitement. "That's it!"

Nim released the shabby squirrel. Then she licked her paw and groomed the side of her face, pleased with herself.

"Well done, little one!" Fern beamed. "Very well done! Just look at you! Going out into the world, learning valuable skills, and starting a new life here at the cottage."

Nim shook her head. "I'm not staying here. Fletcher's coming to get me."

"Oh, lovey." Fern's eyes filled with sadness. "I don't think the Ways of Magic is going to let you leave."

"No." Dread pressed down on Nim. "This Ways of Magic thing, whatever it is, isn't going to keep me here. I'm going home to Fletcher!"

"This *Ways of Magic thing*, as you call it, cannot be so easily defied." Rochester sat up straighter inside his box and pursed his lips. "It's a force that's far bigger and far more powerful than any of us."

Nim shook her head. "Well, I've never heard of it. And I don't believe in it."

"Nonetheless, it still exists," he replied. "Its presence can be felt throughout the world and even the universe, a power that draws things together, creating events that are often explained away as nothing more than coincidental happenings."

"I don't understand what it has to do with me," Nim said, her stomach knotting with fear.

Rochester fixed his gaze on her. "You might not be able to leave here because it's highly likely you are Agatha's familiar."

"Seriously, Rochester, and you too, Fern," Bianca scolded. "Do you really think unlucky cat could be Agatha's assistant? Isn't that a bit cliché? A black cat as the familiar of an old witch?"

Rochester frowned at her, his mustache seeming to droop with disapproval. "It's just as cliché for you to insinuate she's unlucky because of her fur color."

"Oh, go back to sleep, Bianca." Fern snapped her tail against the floor.

Abraxas peered over his shoulder, casting glares at all of them, before returning his head to his paws and resuming his nap.

"I'm leaving. No one can make me stay." Nim glanced from Fern to Rochester, her blood rushing with panic. "Whatever a familiar is, I'm not one of them."

"But being a witch's helper is wonderful!" Fern exclaimed. "My goodness. We all wish we were familiars."

"Indeed we do. Such feline partners are no ordinary cats." Rochester nodded. "They're companions and protectors, assistants in magical work who share a close bond with their witch. They also possess the added advantage of being very long-lived."

Nim refused to believe their words. She didn't want to be Agatha's assistant. Rochester and Fern were wrong, and that was that.

"Agatha's familiar died about eleven months ago. She died of old age. Right there." Fern pointed at the table by the window, with the chair and stack of boxes next to it. "She spent a lot of her last months lying on a purple pillow and looking out at the world. Agatha put the chair and boxes there for Grimalkin to climb up and down." Fern's shoulders slumped, and her words faded to a whisper. "She just didn't have the heart to move them away after Grimalkin died."

"Agatha's been looking for her to return ever since," Rochester added. "She's quite anxious for their reunion."

Nim's eyes bulged. "A cat that's returned from the dead?" She gulped. "A zombie cat?"

"No, no." Rochester chuckled. "A familiar is reborn as a kitten as soon as he or she dies. Though they won't look the same as they did in their previous life, they're still the same soul. For instance, the last incarnation of Grimalkin was a white cat with green eyes. And my understanding is that the first Grimalkin was gray, perhaps with blue eyes, but that was long before our time." He shrugged. "Sometimes it takes a while to reunite with their witch. The familiar might have even grown into adulthood by then."

Nim's skittering heart slowed with relief. "Then I'm not her. I don't remember any of that, or Agatha, or any of you."

"The memories and knowledge from Grimalkin's former days reside deep in her mind and must be sparked into remembrance. If you are her, you simply need to experience something that will ignite that flame. Then it'll all come back to you—Agatha, your duties as her helper, your previous life here." Rochester sighed. "But you'll know soon enough. A witch and familiar are drawn to discover each other, as if pulled together by a magnetic force. It's nearly impossible to repel the Ways of Magic. If you are Agatha's feline partner, you won't be able to leave this place."

"Witch and familiar always find one another," Fern said with a nod.

"I don't want to be Agatha's familiar." Nim's lip trembled.

"Ugh! I can't take any more of this nonsense!" Bianca hopped off the sofa and strolled to the kitchen.

Fern watched her go. "Bianca was very close to Grimalkin," she murmured. "She saw her as a mother figure, and it really broke her heart when Grimalkin left us." She sighed sadly. "When Grimalkin was dying, she told Bianca she'd return, but it's been so long now. Bianca doesn't believe her friend is ever coming back."

From the kitchen came the sound of a spoon clanging against a bowl, accompanied by the sounds of Bianca's hungry yowling. "Come and get it!" Agatha called.

"Dinnertime!" Fern sat up, her eyes brightening.

Rochester stood in his box and stretched.

"Chin up." Fern gave a soft pat to the top of Nim's head. "Once you realize you're with your witch, you'll settle in and be quite happy. You'll see." She smiled encouragingly. "I'll leave baby squirrel here so you can practice killing it." Then she trotted off to the kitchen with Rochester and Abraxas strolling after her.

"They're wrong," Nim muttered. Yet worry gnawed at her insides. The aroma of chicken and beef in hearty gravy wafted into the living room, and hunger also gnawed at her. Her mouth watered, but there was no way she was eating or drinking anything else Agatha offered. Fletcher would be coming for her. She would be home soon. And then she could eat and drink as much as she wanted.

"Psst! Nimbus!" a voice squeaked. "Hey, Nimbus!"

Nim glanced all around, and her ears perked at the sight of a gray rat scuttling out from behind the broom in the corner. "Rhett?" But who else could it be? He was still wearing the piece of sock he called a sweater. "I didn't expect to see you again, especially inside a house full of cats!" Nim smiled, surprised at how happy she was to see him. But her gladness quickly melted to concern. "This is a dangerous place for you."

He rose on his back paws, folded his hands together, and lifted his furry chin. "'Cowards die many times before their deaths; the valiant never taste of death but once.'" He grinned and twitched his whiskers. "It's a line from Shakespeare's *Julius Caesar.*"

"What are you doing here?" Nim whispered, worriedly glancing at the kitchen, where the house cats were still eating.

Rhett dropped down to his four feet, scurried over to the side table, and peered at her with his shiny black eyes. "I just wanted to see how you were getting along. You were in such bad shape this morning." His gaze fell on her sutured wound, and he grimaced. "The old woman's stitchwork is admirable, but"—he shook his head in disapproval—"that particular shade of blue is questionable. It's not the color I would have chosen."

"But how'd you get in here?" Nim asked.

He shrugged. "I'm a rat. There's a small hole in the floor. It wasn't difficult."

"Thanks for coming to check on me, but you really shouldn't be here." Nim paused. "By the way, thanks for helping me back at the dump."

He shrugged again. "It was nothing, no skin off my tail."

"You need to leave, though," she said, "before one of the other cats—"

The sound of squeaking rubber boots approached.

"Go!" Nim whispered.

Agatha strode from the kitchen carrying a bowl of cat food. "I've brought you some dinner," she called to Nim.

Rhett froze as Agatha trudged through the dining room. Nim's heart stopped as she entered the living room.

Agatha switched on the floor lamp and came to a halt. She stared down at the rat, blinking in surprise. After a moment, she slowly leaned forward and set the food before Nim. Then she turned and left the room.

"Run!" Nim hissed at Rhett. The woman could return any moment with a bottle of poison or some other sort of weapon to use against him.

Rhett nodded, his eyes round and glassy, yet he remained rooted to the spot, trembling with fear.

CHAPTER 15

"Rhett, go!" Nim ordered. "Get out of here before Agatha or the house cats come back!"

He swung his head side to side, searching the small living room for the quickest route of escape. Before he could skitter away, though, Agatha was headed back toward them, this time carrying a saucer.

She leaned down, her owl amulet swaying on its chain as she set the dish in front of him. Upon it sat a single saltine cracker. She peered at Rhett. "You're certainly an interesting little fellow." Then she stood.

Rhett gave her a quizzical look, twitching his whiskers.

"Go on. It's okay to eat." She chuckled. "I've always had a soft spot for nature's critters. They all have important parts to play in the way our world runs, now, don't they?"

Her gaze fell on the nearby discarded bandage. With a huff of exasperation, she scooped it up and tucked it into one of the many pockets on her gray apron.

Nim and Rhett watched her, not moving or making a sound.

"Well . . ." She sighed. "Time to get back to work. That vervain isn't going to harvest itself under tonight's full moon." She paused, stroking her chin as she studied Nim. "Perhaps next month, when you've healed, you can help me out? You might enjoy night gardening as much as I do. It's certainly a welcome reprieve from the heat of the day."

Nim watched Agatha grab a garden basket off one of the wall hooks, along with a white-handled knife bearing a crescent-shaped blade, before disappearing into the kitchen. "No TV tonight, my darlings," she called to the cats as they ate their dinner. "I have a long evening ahead of me in the garden." A moment later the back door opened and closed.

Rhett gazed after her. "What a nice lady! Though, I'm sad there won't be any TV shows tonight." He sat up on his back feet and bit into the saltine. "Mmm, fresh! You never find fresh crackers in the dump." He munched for a moment, crumbs raining down on his sock sweater. "Don't get me wrong," he said through his full mouth. "The dump does have its positive qualities, like all the celebrity magazines I can collect and all the items I can forage to create my latest fashion accessories." He swallowed and took another bite. "But you've got it pretty good here. A human bringing you food in a bowl and even an extra plate for your friend!"

Friend? Nim gave him a side-eyed glance. They weren't friends. They'd only just met. Though, now that she thought about it, maybe he wasn't so bad. He'd certainly been very kind to her.

Rhett took another bite of cracker, crunching as his gaze drifted over the lamps and candles and the shelf full of books. "The old lady sure has a lot of treasures," he murmured. "Our burrow has a few too."

A startled gasp sounded nearby and the two of them whirled around.

Bianca stood at the edge of the room, curling her lip as she glared at Rhett. Fern, Abraxas, and Rochester strolled in after her, each of them stopping and staring too.

Rhett gulped. The piece of cracker hung from his paw as he gaped at them.

Nim hunched down, her muscles tightening with fear. There was no way she could defend Rhett against four cats who were bigger and stronger than she was, but if it came down to it, she hoped she would have enough courage to at least try.

The house cats sauntered over and surrounded them, folding their ears back as they stared at Rhett.

"What . . . is . . . this?" Abraxas narrowed his eyes.

"I'd classify it as a *Rattus norvegicus*," Rochester replied. "Also known as a common rat. It's the same one that escorted our new friend over this morning."

"Why . . . is it in our house?" Abraxas snapped his tail threateningly.

"Why is it wearing a piece of dirty sock?" Bianca turned her nose up.

"Oh, the poor little thing," Fern crooned, her pupils growing wide with excitement. "It's just hungry." She smacked her lips as she waddled closer to the trembling Rhett.

Nim's alarm ratcheted up another notch. Fern was going to inflict the killing bite on Rhett. She was sure of it. She couldn't bear to watch. But the plump calico gave him a lick on the head instead, just as a mother cat would do to a kitten. Then she plopped onto her bottom and smiled down at him.

Nim didn't understand Fern's behavior. She furrowed her brow. Perhaps Fern missed her kittens more than she wanted to admit, and maybe the small, defenseless Rhett reminded her of them. At least, Nim hoped that was the case. The fierce hunter's proximity to him made her very uneasy.

"Wasn't it you rats who imposed boundaries between us?" Abraxas sneered at Rhett. "Wasn't it your colony that claimed the dump and the old Whittaker mansion as your own? And now, now you've come here? Encroaching on our territory?"

"I . . ." The bit of cracker wobbled in Rhett's paw. His eyes bulged with fear. "I just came here to talk to my friend, Nimbus."

"And who, pray tell," Abraxas growled, "is Nimbus?"

"Tell them, Nimbus!" Rhett squeaked, never taking his eyes from the huge ginger tabby. "Tell them we're friends."

Nim stood as bravely as she could at Rhett's side.

"Oh." Bianca frowned. "He's referring to the new cat, the unlucky one."

"Stop calling her that, Bianca," Fern chastised.

Tossing her head back, Bianca sauntered over to the sofa, wrapped her fluffy tan tail around her, and curled into a ball.

"Rhett was just leaving," Nim said as steadily as she could.

"Please don't eat me," Rhett begged the house cats.

"Ugh!" Bianca rolled her eyes. "As if!"

Rochester scratched at his neck, jingling the tiny silver book charm on his collar. "Oh, we're far too well-fed to eat rodents." He strolled away to his cardboard box.

"You . . . you're not going to eat me?" Rhett gulped.

"We might not eat you," Abraxas snarled, "but that

doesn't mean we won't kill you."

"No! Please!" Nim stepped between the two of them.

Abraxas frowned at her for a moment, and to her surprise, he didn't snarl. He turned to the other cats. "What say the three of you?"

"I don't care," Bianca replied, "as long as it stays away from me and my food, it can do as it pleases."

"Oh, he's such a darling thing. He should be allowed to visit anytime he wants," Fern said, licking the top of Rhett's head again. Then she padded off to the rocking chair.

Rochester yawned. "I have no objections."

"Very well, then." Abraxas returned his gaze to Rhett. "We won't kill you." He cast another glance at Nim, one that might have contained the tiniest shimmer of curiosity. Then, swishing his tail, he strode toward a patch of lamplight on the floor.

Rhett exhaled a sigh of relief.

"Well, that turned out better than expected." Rochester yawned and turned his gaze on Rhett. "Normally, Abraxas would have knocked you unconscious and swatted you around the room just for fun." He turned his gaze to Nim. "I think Abraxas must be warming up to you."

Rhett took a bite from his cracker. "You certainly live in an interesting place, Nimbus." He shifted his focus from the big tabby to the old television, and his admiration was evident. "None of the old TVs in the dump work," he murmured. "You're so lucky to live here."

"I don't live here," Nim said. "And I'm leaving very soon. Fletcher's coming to get me."

Rhett didn't reply. He swallowed the last bit of cracker, then brushed the crumbs off the front of his sock sweater. "Well, good night, Nimbus. I'm off to the dump. I have a long evening of foraging ahead of me." He gave her a salute with one of his little pink paws, then scurried away.

Rochester watched him go. "Your rat friend is certainly a unique character."

"He's not really my friend," Nim said. "We only just met."

Rochester raked his paw over the sides of his mustached face and groomed his whiskers. "Do you think he'll return soon?"

Nim shrugged. "I don't know." Part of her hoped he wouldn't, for his own safety. Abraxas could still change his mind and decide to kill him.

"I'll keep a watch out." Rochester gazed toward the shadows. "I daresay we'll see him again, dressed in that silly sock and clinging to the baseboards as he scampers into the room."

"Thanks," Nim replied, "but that's not really necessary."

"Watching is certainly not necessary, but I find it most

interesting," Rochester returned. "After all, any sort of thing could happen, and if you're not watching, you might miss it. And really, it's the only way to study those otherworldly creatures that occasionally cross into this realm."

The flesh beneath Nim's fur prickled.

"Cats can see them quite well, you know," Rochester continued, seeming not to notice. "Perhaps that's why the malevolent ones don't like us."

"I saw one last night, and it attacked Fletcher!" Nim blurted. "It was a nightmare demon!"

Rochester raised a white eyebrow. "Is that so? I've never seen one of the fiends myself, but I understand they're most revolting." His mouth turned down in disgust. "Approaching their victims as a seemingly harmless drift of smoke, they quickly transform into a terrifying being and perch upon the chest of the sleeper to feed off their panic and fear, the way mosquitoes feed off blood."

"Yes!" Nim's eyes widened. "That's what it did to Fletcher! But I fought it and destroyed it." She drew her shoulders back proudly.

Rochester looked uncertain. "Are you sure you destroyed it? Such malevolent creatures are not always so easily extinguished."

"Oh yes." She nodded. "It turned into smoke and floated out the window."

He nodded thoughtfully. "Perhaps you did. My understanding is that while the creatures might look horrifying, they aren't physically strong. That's why they immobilize their prey, so they can't wake and fight back." He sighed. "Let's hope for the sake of your friend, Fletcher, that you really did destroy it. They've been known to occasionally revisit a victim and feed off them night after night."

Nim's breath caught. What if she hadn't really killed the demon, though? What if it came back tonight? Apprehension tightened her chest. Fletcher's bedtime couldn't come soon enough. She needed to know he was safe, and she needed to warn him to be careful.

Rochester stretched inside his cardboard box. "I confess, I find myself a bit envious, though. I've only seen one otherworldly being, back when I resided at the bookstore. It was little more than a slip of ghostly mist, an old woman browsing the shelves. Quite harmless really, but it made for interesting observing. I wouldn't have minded if she'd returned more often to talk. Fascinating creatures, spirits. They can understand the feline language, you know."

Bianca turned her nose up from where she lounged on the sofa. "Well, I've never seen such a being, and I don't ever want to see one."

Over on the rocking chair, Fern's eyes grew wide. "I've seen one! Many years ago, when I was barely more than a kitten." She dropped her voice to a whisper. "It was the ghost of a headless squirrel."

Bianca gave a huff of disbelief.

"But as I was saying earlier"—Rochester turned his gaze back to Nim—"watching is by far the most worthwhile of the three."

"Of the three?" Nim tilted her head, not sure what he meant, her heart still racing with worry.

He arched an eyebrow. "The three diversions of the cat? Surely you're well versed in them: watching, hunting, and playing."

Nim nodded. "Oh, yes. Fern taught me how to deliver the killing bite."

"I most certainly did!" Fern raised her shoulders and fixed her eyes on Rochester. "*Hunting* is the most important diversion of the three, *not* watching."

"You're both wrong," Bianca muttered with her head perched on her stretched-out front legs.

"Yes, yes." Rochester gave a casual wave of his paw. "The other diversions are certainly fine pastimes." He turned back to Nim. "But there's much more to the diversion of watching." He thrust out his white chest. "To be a true proficient, you must learn the essential subskill of observing. To quote the French poet Charles Baudelaire, 'Like those great sphinxes lounging through eternity in noble attitudes upon the desert sand, they gaze incuriously at nothing, calm and wise.'" He frowned. "Though, I do object to Baudelaire's choice of the word *incuriously*. Cats are quite curious."

"Ugh," Bianca groaned, and covered her ears with her paws. "I feel like I'm being tortured for eternity."

The rest of the evening crawled by as Nim anxiously awaited Fletcher's bedtime.

After a while, Agatha returned from her evening harvesting. She set the basket of purple-flowered stalks on the dining room table, removed her gardening boots, then rubbed her lower back. "I'll sort and bind that vervain in the morning," she muttered. As she removed her gray apron and hung it on a wall hook, she smiled sadly. "If Grimalkin were here, she'd have it all arranged into bundles, and the scissors and twine waiting on the table before I awoke."

Nim bent her ears, impressed with how helpful Grimalkin had been. Shame warmed her face. When she got home, she would make a point of helping Fletcher with his hobbies and chores.

"Good night, everyone," Agatha called as she padded into the living room in her bare feet. She made her way around to each of the cats and gave them a pat on the head. When she reached Nim, though, she held her palm out toward her as if waiting for some sort of response. After a moment, she lowered her hand and patted Nim too. Pursing her lips, she gazed at the full bowl of food. "Not eating, I see. Well, we'll try again in the morning."

Nim tingled with nervousness. Fletcher's bedtime was drawing nearer. Was he okay? Had the nightmare demon come back as Rochester said it might? What if she couldn't find him in the dream realm? She forced down the worries and ordered herself to be patient.

All around her sounded the soft breathing of the house cats. A powerful homesickness tugged at her soul. "Soon," she whispered. Soon she would tell Fletcher where she was, and he would come for her and take her home.

Longing for her green pillow bed, she settled for the next best thing. She carefully climbed up the stack of boxes, onto the nearby chair, then onto the table by the window. Remembering that Grimalkin used to sleep in the same spot, she wondered if that was why Bianca disliked her so much. Maybe she didn't want her to take Grimalkin's place, not on the table and not in anyone's heart.

Well, it didn't matter. Tomorrow she'd be gone.

Nim closed her eyes and waited. Despite her impatience, she knew sleep would come. It always did.

CHAPTER 16

Nim came to the crossroads under the purple sky and the white crescent moon. Hecate stood there in her lavender gown. A shiny black lizard rested in her hand, its skinny toes splayed against her palm while its long tail dangled through her fingers. Frowning like a little old man, it stared at Nim through its beady eyes.

"I'm going to find Fletcher!" Nim announced to the goddess. She drew her shoulders back proudly. "I'm going to tell him where I am so he can come get me."

With her free hand, Hecate motioned to the center path behind her. "You know the way."

"Thank you, Lady Hecate," she said. "Thank you for teaching me how to dream walk." Then, centering her thoughts on Fletcher, she trotted up the middle road that would take her to where others dream.

As she traveled, though, troubling thoughts swarmed her mind like an annoying cloud of gnats. What if Fletcher didn't remember the nightmare goblin and believed she was the one who'd clawed his face? What if he'd already replaced her with the silvery-striped stray cat?

"Stop being such a worrywart!" she scolded herself. She refocused her thoughts on finding Fletcher and soon came upon a scattering of crumpled papers, socks, and T-shirts lying across the path. A moment later she passed a wizard's staff sticking up out of the dirt alongside the road. At the top of the staff protruded an old gray arrowhead.

She continued into a wooded area, beams of yellow sunlight streaming down through the tree branches. The smell of pine and oak grew strong. Dry leaves crackled beneath the pads of her paws. Fletcher, wearing a tall, pointy wizard's hat, sat cross-legged on a starry bedspread lying in the middle of the trail. He was surrounded by a mound of bird feathers, piles of rocks and seashells, and stacks of his magical fantasy books. *The Hobbit* lay open on his lap, and he slowly turned its pages with a pair of pliers.

Nim stuck her tail in the air, giving it a joyful wave. "Fletcher!" she cried.

He glanced up over the tops of his round eyeglasses. "Nim?"

"Yes, it's me!" With her tail still held high, she turned in a happy circle, her paws prancing.

"Nim!" His face lit with a big smile. "I'm so glad to see you! I've been worried about you."

A wave of relief washed over her. Fletcher missed her! And he was safe! She proudly puffed out her chest. "I really did destroy the nightmare demon!"

"Aunt Caroline said you attacked me and that I only dreamed it was a monster." Fletcher shook his head. "But I knew the monster was real. You'd never hurt me." Then he scrunched his eyebrows as if suddenly realizing that he and Nim were having a conversation. "Is this actually happening or am I dreaming?"

"It's sort of both," Nim replied. "This is the dream realm, but we're really here." She gave a contented flick of her tail. "I have dream sight now, and we can talk whenever we want to!"

"Nim!" He grinned at her. "You're magic!"

She supposed that maybe she was. At least, just a little. "The goblin monster was a nightmare demon!" she said. "I scratched out its eye when I destroyed it, and now I can walk in the dream realm." She could feel her smile growing and imagined she must look a bit silly.

Fletcher peered closer at her. "Is that why one of your eyes is yellow? It looks really cool." He sat back and arched an eyebrow. "You've changed in another way too. You seem more . . . confident, I guess."

Nim beamed with pride. Nothing could ruin this moment.

"But what happened after the battle?" he asked. "When I couldn't find you this morning, I put up flyers around the neighborhood. I tried looking for you everywhere, and then I got so tired. I had to go back to bed. I think I'm coming down with a cold. Aunt Caroline's worried she might be as well."

"This is all Aunt Caroline's fault!" Nim cried. "She put me in a box, then drove me out to the country. She left me in a dump by an abandoned old mansion."

"What!" Fletcher's eyes narrowed. "Aunt Caroline said she didn't know where you were! She said you probably ran away." His face reddened with anger. "As soon as I wake up, I'm calling Dad to tell him everything. He won't let her get away with this! He'll come home right away and drive me to you!"

"But, Fletcher, there are some things I need to tell you," Nim interrupted. "I think the other jar has a nightmare demon inside it too. You have to be careful." She shuddered. "What if Aunt Caroline's dusting and accidentally knocks it off the shelf and it breaks open? If another one of the monsters comes out, I won't be there to destroy it."

Fletcher nodded. "Don't worry. I'll hide it someplace where no one can get to it. And when I tell Dad about it, he'll get rid of it. And hopefully Aunt Caroline too!" He scowled. "But, Nim, are you okay? Are you safe?"

"I'm fine," she reassured him. "Well, except for the gash from the demon."

"You're hurt?" Fletcher's voice cracked, his expression shifting from anger to concern.

"It's nothing really," Nim lied, glad her wound never appeared in the dream realm—she hated the thought of distressing him more. "I'm safe in a cottage with four strange house cats and a witch."

"A witch?" Fletcher's eyes grew round.

Nim nodded. "She's a nice witch." She nudged the open copy of *The Hobbit* balanced on his lap. "She's sort of like Gandalf, I think."

"Really?" Fletcher smiled. "That sounds amazing."

"She's taken good care of me," Nim replied, surprised that despite the annoying incidents with the sleep medicine, she really meant it. "But, Fletcher, there's something else I need to tell you." Nim's stomach dropped at the thought of the Ways of Magic keeping her at the cottage as Agatha's familiar. "I might not be able to come home."

His eyebrows shot up. "What do you mean?"

"It's just that . . . some of the cats here think I'm the

witch's familiar. I know it sounds strange, but they say being a witch's assistant is an honor. They think I'm really lucky to be one." She paused and lowered her voice. "But if it's true, then I can't leave."

"Oh." Fletcher's expression suddenly grew sad. "I guess . . . I guess I shouldn't be surprised." He gave her a small, dejected smile. "You've always been a lucky cat." He gulped and took a shuddering breath, seeming to steel himself to get the words out. "Well, if that's the case . . . if that's what you want, then maybe . . . I guess maybe it'd be best if you stayed there." He looked away, blinking hard, then wiping the corners of his eyes.

"No!" Nim shook her head. "You don't understand—"

But before she could finish, Fletcher vanished.

Nim was standing alone on the quiet, empty road.

"Fletcher?" she called out into the eerie silence. "Fletcher, where are you?"

She spun around, searching for any sign of him, or his belongings, or the woods—anything to prove that he hadn't just disappeared . . . from her.

"Fletcher!" she called again, beginning to tremble with panic. "I don't want to stay! I want to be home with you! It's the Ways of Magic that might not let me leave!" Her shoulders drooped. How could he think that was what she wanted? How could he just accept that she belonged with Agatha?

Her chest aching with grief, Nim raced away, desperate to speak to Lady Hecate.

When she reached her crossroads, she slid to a stop. "Lady Hecate!" She paused, trying to catch her breath. "I found Fletcher, but then he disappeared!"

"He must have woken up suddenly," Hecate replied as she stroked the back of the lizard now asleep in her hand. "A dream walk is severed when one of the dreamers awakes."

Nim shook her head. "I don't think that's what happened. I think . . ." She lowered her watery eyes. "I think maybe he didn't want me in his dream anymore."

"Perhaps," Hecate said, "though I'm afraid there's another possibility."

Nim glanced up as the goddess's expression turned to one of concern. "It might be that you didn't really kill the nightmare demon and it has returned."

The strength drained from Nim's legs. "What should I do?" she whispered.

"I can't tell you what to do," Hecate answered, "but I can tell you that when a nightmare demon has preyed on a dreamer, it returns to the place where nightmares dwell to feed on the emotions."

Nim cast a wary glance at the stormy road leading to

the nightmare place, a powerful dread pooling in her stomach. She did not want to go there.

"It will take much courage to travel that road," Hecate observed.

Nim swished her tail anxiously. "I have to go. Fletcher could be in trouble." She continued staring at the terrifying path. "If I find the nightmare demon there, I'll use the killing bite to destroy it once and for all."

"The task won't be easy," Hecate added. "Thousands of nightmare demons reside there. How will you find the one that attacked Fletcher?"

Nim shook her head as she thought. "I guess it'll be covered with bite marks and scratches from when we battled."

"It is more likely its injuries are not carried into this realm, as has been the case with you." Hecate tilted her head to the side. "Except, perhaps, for its missing eye. But finding this one creature out of the thousands gathered there will take a great deal of patience, focus, and careful observation."

"Observation . . . ," Nim whispered as an idea occurred to her. Maybe there was someone who could help her. "Thank you, Lady Hecate!"

As she rushed down the middle road, she turned her thoughts to finding Rochester.

CHAPTER 17

Nim raced past a tall bookcase looming in the middle of the road. A ghost lady stood before it, gazing up at the numerous volumes lining its shelves. Stacks of newspapers and magazines sat nearby. She hurried around two comfy-looking chairs, seemingly made of cardboard.

Up ahead, she spied Rochester stretched out on his stomach in the middle of the road. A pair of wire-rimmed eyeglasses were perched on his nose as he stared down at a book clutched in his front paws.

"Rochester!" she called. "I need your help! Will you come with me to the place where nightmares dwell?"

He arched a white eyebrow. "You want to willingly visit such a location?"

"Yes, I do! I'll explain everything on the way."

He shrugged. "Well, I must say you've piqued my curiosity." He closed his book and climbed to his paws. "Though, as the saying goes, curiosity did kill the cat. But let's hope it won't come to that."

They made their way back down the roadway, and by the time they reached Nim's crossroads, she had filled Rochester in on her plans. All was quiet, and Hecate was nowhere to be seen. Nim proceeded to the path that led to the nightmare place but paused before stepping onto it. In the distance the sky hung low and bruised, weighed down with angry gray clouds. Streaks of lightning leaped from them. Blankets of white fog slithered over the roadway.

She cast a glance to her side, relieved to see Rochester still there.

"Interesting destination," he observed as he gazed ahead. "Reminds me a bit of a Florida thunderstorm."

Nim took a steadying breath and they set off. She was determined that if she couldn't be home to protect Fletcher, she would do so from here in the dream realm. The swirling white mist clinging to the road made it difficult to see her feet as she walked, but she could feel grit and small pebbles poking the pads of her paws.

"Such a dreadful place." Rochester glanced all around.

The land alongside them looked charred—as if a huge fire had raced through—and the lumpy ground was dotted with strange rocks shaped like burnt cantaloupes. A white zigzag of lightning blasted down in the distance, making Nim jump. Before her skittering nerves could calm, a mechanical growl roared up the road behind them. She and Rochester whirled around, leaping out of the path of a ghostly speeding car just in time. Another one followed close after it.

Rochester pursed his lips. "One wouldn't expect to see this much automobile traffic in the place where nightmares dwell." Then, after looking both ways first, he stepped back onto the roadway.

Nim remained cowering on the shoulder. He arched an eyebrow at her, then nodded with understanding. "It appears this is the road of your own particular nightmares."

"Yes, I think so." Nim gulped. Gathering her courage, she stood and rejoined him. Thunder boomed overhead, and more lightning struck down in the distance. "Fletcher needs me," she whispered to herself.

As they continued up the road, Rochester peered over at her. "I must say, your dream-walking ability is most interesting, and extremely remarkable. We cats are generally attuned to other realms and the beings that inhabit them, but I didn't know it was possible for any of us to traverse the dream realm as freely as you do."

Nim was most definitely not enjoying her access to this particular road.

They traveled in silence, passing discarded car tires and wet, wilted cardboard boxes lying along the rocky ground. Once they passed a woman wearing sensible shoes and a cardigan sweater. Scowling, she pointed at Nim. "Don't cross my path, black cat. I don't want your bad luck to befall me!" Then she waved her hands at Nim with a shooing motion.

Worries flooded Nim's mind as she moved over the gravelly road. Was Fletcher okay? Had the nightmare demon really come back to attack him? Would she even be able to find the creature here? Or what if it hadn't been a nightmare demon at all that made Fletcher vanish? What if he no longer wanted her in his dreams? She tried to shake the thoughts away and come up with a positive reason why he'd disappeared, but she couldn't think of even one.

The farther they walked, the more overcast the sky grew, like evening fading into night. Up ahead, jagged boulders formed a spiky landscape resembling a line of giant arrowheads. Beyond them, angry shrieks like the cries of injured animals filled the air, sending goose bumps prickling down Nim's flesh.

They drew up to a first grouping of tall boulders sticking out of the ground like a giant hand reaching for the weakly glowing moon. Thunder rumbled, but the shrieks and snarls had also increased in volume.

A bolt of lightning touched down nearby, its jagged branches exploding into the scarred land and sending up showers of dirt. Crackles of blue energy sizzled and hopped along the ground like electric fingers. Nim's fur stood on end at the sights. For a moment, she was a kitten again, trapped inside a cardboard box in the midst of a thunderstorm.

When they stopped behind a second outcropping resembling the front of a sinking ship, Nim slowly poked her head around it to peer at the commotion before them.

Hundreds of nightmare demons moved all around, creeping and slinking over the potholed ground. Most of the beasts were hissing and snarling or snapping their teeth at each other. Some appeared to be entering and exiting the area by diving into the holes; every few seconds a monster would climb out of one clutching a murky, squirming form in its mouth.

Nim watched, her muscles tensing as her tail bushed, surprised and confused that they didn't resemble goblins at all.

"Ah. So that's what the fiends look like in their natural form and habitat," Rochester murmured as he peeked out beside her.

Nim couldn't pull her eyes away from them. They were like no living beast she'd ever seen, appearing more like prehistoric, mutated nightmare cats, with bony necks, hunched shoulders, and no ears or tails. Thick claws jutted from their paws. Their ashy-gray flesh was leathery and spotted with tufts of fur, as if most of it had been lost in numerous fights. The jaws of the creatures' elongated, skeletal heads were filled with jagged teeth. Their thick, impossibly long canines jutted down like knives. Nim trembled; the nightmare demons looked just like the images painted on the old clay jars. Only instead of huge empty eye sockets, tiny yellow lights glowed inside them. "I don't understand," she whispered. "They don't look like the monster that attacked Fletcher."

"That's because each demon takes on a different appearance in the physical world when it attacks a helpless sleeper," Rochester explained. He squinted at the chaotic scene before them. "I suspect those holes in the ground connect this realm to the physical world. And somewhere inside those passages on their return, the creatures morph back into their true forms, carrying a dreamer's panic and fear with them." He pointed his paw. "Look, there's one returning now."

A glowing-eyed demon crawled from a nearby hole. Clutched in its saber-fanged mouth was a writhing, limbless, and headless being made of shadow.

The devilish monster slunk away with its prey, dropping

the squirming thing to the ground beside a large boulder. Then, holding it in place with a clawed paw, it bit down, greedily chomping until not a single wisp remained.

"Rochester," Nim whispered, "can you find a demon that's missing the glow in one of its eyes?"

He rubbed his chin with his white paw. "There are too many of them. We'll be here far longer than it's safe to be unless you help me."

Nim shook her head. "But I don't know how to properly observe."

"Well, now is a good time to learn. I daresay you've had some experience with it already." He arched an eyebrow. "Surely you've watched birds through the window or a piece of string trailing across the floor."

"I guess so," Nim replied.

"Now, there's more to observing than simply growing still and looking with your eyes. It requires a healthy dose of mental discipline. You must allow your mind to empty and your breathing to slow."

"Okay." Nim nodded. She did her best to clear her mind and slow her breaths.

After a moment he asked, "Do you feel your heart rate decelerating?"

To her surprise, she did. She nodded.

"Very good. Now, exist in the moment. Listen to sounds

both near and far. Decipher scents. Feel the air around you and the surface beneath your paws. Truly examine the scene before you."

Nim grew more still and listened, detecting the rumbling phantom cars in the distance, the booming thunder overhead, the shrieks and cries of the nightmare demons all around them. She sniffed deeply, grimacing at the stench of panic and fear. The creatures reeked of it, a revolting mix of mustiness, rot, and decay. She concentrated on her sense of touch, realizing the ground's sandy gravel was pressing uncomfortably into the pads of her paws.

Rochester nodded his approval. "You'll find countless applications for this valuable skill. Proper observation is also calming for the body and soul, as well as enlightening for the mind." He frowned, his white mustache drooping. "Though in this situation, I daresay it's not so very soothing."

Nim ran her gaze over the nightmare demons as they shrieked and squabbled, attacking each other and trying to snatch the prey from those who'd not yet consumed their shadowy prizes. Her mind and body remained calm and focused. Yet she curled her lip, despising the creatures even more. They were vicious and greedy. And they had no loyalty to one another.

She and Rochester observed for a long while, and though most of the monsters were covered with bite marks and scratches they'd inflicted upon each other, none were missing the glow in their eyes.

As Nim grew more distressed, something else poked the back of her mind. The troubling thought occurred to her as she watched a returning demon bite into its spoils. The attack on Fletcher had been different. His panic and fear hadn't looked like a shadowy thing. It'd been a small, bright light. And the creature had fed on it there, rather than bringing it here. "Rochester," she whispered, "there's something I don't understand. The nightmare demon that attacked Fletcher–"

"Cats!" a slithery, gravelly voice hissed from behind them.

They whirled around, and Nim froze in terror. Rochester made a faint mewling sound like that of a kitten.

Three nightmare demons slunk side by side toward them, stopping little more than a paw's strike away. Their stench filled Nim's nostrils and tasted acrid on her tongue.

"We don't like cats," one of them snarled.

"Cats are nosy," another one sneered, "always staring, seeing things that cross over from one realm and into another."

"Mystical and elusive guardians of places and people," the other one added with a scowl.

Nim's fur shot up, but she didn't move.

"How did you acquire our dream sight, you wicked beast?" The first one took a small step closer, and the other two advanced alongside it. "You shouldn't have come here, thief."

Shoulder to shoulder, the three demons gnashed their teeth and darted their heads forward.

The thought of these monsters coming for Fletcher in his sleep filled Nim with a sudden, powerful fury. She arched her back and whipped her tail side to side. "Move away, you stinking fiends. I know how to inflict the killing bite. I've been taught by the fiercest of squirrel hunters, and I won't hesitate to use it on each one of you."

"Nimbus," Rochester whispered fearfully, "we must leave."

Folding her ears back, she stepped in front of Rochester. "We're not afraid of you," she growled at the demons. "We have no panic or fear for you to eat."

"It's not your emotions we will feed upon," the first one sneered.

"Your mystical life force is far more preferred," the middle one added.

"A rare treat to devour," hissed the third.

"Nimbus, leave this place now!" Rochester shouted, and he vanished from her side.

Lowering their heads, fixing their glowing yellow eye

sockets on Nim, the trio of demons began murmuring, speaking the same ancient words the nightmare goblin had spoken over Fletcher.

Nim's legs wobbled. Her jaw grew lax. And deep inside, a piece of her was tearing away.

Her eyelids lowered just as the beasts leaped forward.

Nim awoke with a start.

The clinking of a spoon against a ceramic bowl rang in her ears.

"Nimbus!" Rochester shook her with his paw. "Nimbus, wake up!"

"I'm awake," she murmured.

She was back in Agatha's cottage, atop the orange cushion with beams of bright morning sun streaming through the window beside her.

"Breakfast time!" Agatha called from the kitchen. "Come and get it!"

Nim shuddered with relief, never so grateful for a mealtime at Agatha's.

CHAPTER 18

Rochester stared down at Nim as the other house cats scampered to the kitchen. "Nimbus, are you okay?" His brow was furrowed with concern.

"I'm fine." She sat up slowly, feeling a bit shaky. "Agatha's breakfast announcement woke me. And just in time." She gulped.

"Thank goodness you escaped." Rochester's whiskers drooped. "Though I'm sorry we weren't able to identify the demon that attacked Fletcher."

"I am too." She placed a paw on his shoulder. "Thanks for helping me."

"You are most welcome." Rochester gave her a nod, then smacked his lips. "Our otherworldly adventure has worked up quite an appetite within me. How about you?

Come join us in the kitchen for breakfast. I'm sure Agatha would be happy to set a bowl down for you."

"No thanks." Nim wasn't hungry. Her stomach was too knotted with worry. "You go on."

He hopped down and strolled toward the kitchen.

"Thanks again, Rochester!" she called.

"I'm pleased I was able to offer some assistance," he replied over his shoulder. "It was a most interesting adventure, but not one I'm keen on repeating."

As Nim watched him go, she thumped her tail anxiously against the orange cushion. Was it possible Fletcher was angry with her and that's why he didn't want her to visit his dreams anymore? Was that the reason he disappeared? She thought on it for a moment, but it didn't feel right. He'd never be angry at her. She couldn't shake the feeling something bad had happened to him.

She rested her head on her paws, her thoughts in turmoil. Maybe she should just wait here and try to find him again tonight. But that didn't feel right either. She needed to get home. She needed to be there to defend him. Before she could rise, Agatha came out of the kitchen carrying a fresh bowl of food. She headed toward Nim, her rubber gardening boots squeaking as she went.

She set the bowl on Nim's table. "Eat this. You need your strength." Then she glanced around, looking a bit disappointed. "I don't see your rat friend this morning." She smiled at Nim. "Perhaps he'll join us for lunch. Now, let's look at your stitches." She squinted at the sutured wound and nodded. "The redness is receding. If you leave them be and get lots of rest, you'll be healed up nicely in a few days."

But Nim didn't have a few days to lounge around. She was leaving as soon as she could.

Sighing wistfully, Agatha gazed out the window. "Grimalkin used to enjoy lying here." After a moment, she looked down at Nim, studying her green and yellow eyes as though searching them for signs of her former familiar. Then she shook her head. "I'm being foolish. I must be patient. The Ways of Magic will reveal everything when it's time." With a sad smile, she patted Nim's head, took up the old food bowl, and turned away.

Nim watched as she disappeared into the kitchen and then out to work in her gardens.

The house cats strolled back into the living room looking full and content, licking the food particles from their mouths. As soon as they'd settled into their napping places, Nim stood up on the cushion. Fixing her gaze on Fern, she began, "I'm going home now. And before I leave, I just wanted to thank you, Fern, for showing me how to inflict the killing bite." She turned. "And thank you, Rochester, for teaching me the skill of observation." She cast a quick glance at Bianca and Abraxas. "Well, goodbye."

She stepped off the table and made her way down the nearby chair and stack of boxes.

"But do you think that's a good idea?" Fern's mouth drooped with worry.

"Do you still plan to attempt the journey by paw?" Rochester asked, raising his white eyebrows.

Nim nodded, remembering his earlier warning. He was probably right; it wouldn't be easy.

"The walk will be a long one." Rochester frowned. "The pads of your feet might blister."

Nim stopped. "But I have to get home."

"Stay away from the busy roads," Fern warned. "The cars might run you over."

Nim shuddered. That much she already knew from experience.

"If you haven't the skills for hunting nor the stomach for eating furred or feathered prey," Rochester continued, "you could forage in trash cans and drink from puddles."

Her stomach was already empty, and her mouth was already dry. Nim eyed her untouched bowls of food and water.

"Though, you'll no doubt become infected with worms

or other parasites," Rochester added. "If you want to avoid animal predators, travel by day. If you want to avoid humans, travel by night."

Nim nodded, her courage wilting at the seeming impossibility of it all.

"You really shouldn't leave." Fern's whiskers sagged. "We'll miss you, and Agatha will too."

"Let her go," Bianca said from her spot on the sofa. "She doesn't want to be here."

"But what if she's the one?" Fern asked.

"Well, if she is, then she'll be back," Bianca answered.

"Let her make her own decision," Abraxas growled. Then he stared down at his paws, a hint of sadness filling his eyes as he muttered to himself, "At least she knows where to find what she's looking for."

Nim took a last look at the house cats and the small living room. "Goodbye," she said.

Leaving them to argue their opinions, she walked away. She didn't belong there. She wasn't Grimalkin. She was sure of it. And though her injured side still ached, with the thick blue stitches pinching her wound, she ignored the discomfort. Fletcher needed her. The journey was going to be long and dangerous, and bad luck would probably befall her along the way, but she couldn't let that stop her.

She'd just have to do her best to make her own luck whenever she could.

She stepped into the kitchen, the air lingering with the faint aroma of cat food. She glanced around to make sure Agatha hadn't returned, running her gaze past the refrigerator, stove, and microwave oven. Her eyes came to a stop at the floor-to-ceiling shelf lined with bottles and jars in all sizes, their faded labels indicating their dried contents of smartweed, pokeroot, bladder wrack, nettles, rose hips, aconite, and elderberries.

Nim's breath caught, and her paw rose in shock and confusion. She'd never been able to read words. Her stomach clenched. Could it be the Ways of Magic at work? Was she able to read the labels of the magical herbs because she really was Agatha's familiar? Were the skills of a witch's assistant somehow waking within her?

She didn't wait for the Ways of Magic to answer. She darted away past the four empty bowls on the floor, straight to the cat flap hanging in the back door. She slowed long enough to nudge it with her paw. It easily swung outward, and she poked her head through, her whiskers assuring her the opening was wide enough. Not wasting a second longer, she climbed out.

An old blue truck, which Nim assumed belonged to

Agatha, was parked nearby, and Agatha's gardens stretched out behind it. A river of white-petaled flowers with bright yellow hearts ran down the length of the property. Rows of green herbs sprang up across from them, some tall, some short, some bushy, some sparse. Their spicy fragrances filled Nim's nose. Agatha knelt in the dirt, her long gray braid snaking out from beneath her straw gardening hat. She pushed a tiny bowl toward one of the bushy stalks, and a slosh of milk spilled over its rim. For a moment, Nim thought she saw a small, green-skinned creature gazing at the bowl. When she looked closer, it leaped away, disappearing into the leafy rows of plants.

Nim shook the image from her mind, scurrying down the steps before Agatha could see her. She rounded the corner of the cottage, glancing across the road at the deserted Victorian mansion the rats called the old Whittaker place. Dried vines climbed like tentacles up the sides of its walls; a withered flower garden grew forgotten behind it. She hurried up the dirt road, passing the mansion's huge front lawn that now served as nothing more than a stinky, cluttered dump and a territory for rats.

She set her sights on the old highway ahead, the one that would lead to the city. The thought of Fletcher rushed her steps, but the reality of the long and dangerous journey ahead sent her stomach whirling.

"Hey, Nimbus! Slow down!"

Nim glanced back as Rhett scurried up the dirt road. When he drew alongside her, he eyed her with concern. "Maybe you should wait until you've healed before you head home."

"I'll be fine!" she snapped, then regretted her harshness. Rhett had been very kind to her. "I'm sorry, Rhett, but I have to get home. I think Fletcher's in trouble."

"Oh, I'm sorry to hear it." He sighed heavily as he scuttled along. Then he cleared his throat and lifted his voice. "'When sorrows come, they come not single spies but in battalions.'" He nodded, seeming pleased with himself. "That's *Hamlet*."

"Shouldn't you be asleep now?" Nim asked, trying to ignore the painful wound in her side.

He shook his head in amazement. "You know, it's the most wondrous thing. Last night, I ate a few granules of instant espresso from a half-empty jar, and I haven't felt sleepy ever since! No, I'm not tired at all. In fact, I feel rather chatty. Hey, maybe I'll come with you!" He glanced around to make sure no one else was within hearing distance. "Lately, I've been seriously thinking about leaving the colony and heading to the city in search of stardom and fame. It's something I've always wanted to do, and maybe now is the time."

Nim kept moving. The old highway lay not far ahead, its pavement shimmering in the morning sunlight; she could smell its warm asphalt.

Rhett jabbered on about the unfair rules of the colony and their lack of appreciation for his talents, but Nim was hardly listening. When she reached the end of the dirt road, she turned left, passing a tall oak tree and a rusty green mailbox on a post. She and Rhett set off along the dusty shoulder of the long, two-lane highway.

Behind her, a rumbling rose in the distance, growing louder, drawing closer, gaining on her. Vibrations rattled beneath the pads of her paws.

Her breath caught. Panic raced through her veins. She didn't have to look back to know it was a speeding car. She remembered the sound well—she'd heard it enough times in her nightmares.

She quickened her steps, telling herself she was no longer a frightened kitten. She wouldn't run into the street. The vehicle's cruel, giant tires wouldn't crash into her.

Her heartbeats and footfalls pounded through her head. The growl of the engine swelled in her ears. She glanced back.

The big automobile was coming, roaring up the old highway. It didn't matter that it remained in its own lane and would rocket right past her. Dizzying fear overtook her. As the car drew alongside, she leaped up, twisting away and flinging herself as far from its deadly tires as she could.

The car shot past, leaving a blast of hot air in its wake as Nim crashed down on the shoulder of the road.

The tire hadn't hit her, but red-hot pain pulsed through her anyway. Dirt caked her mouth; dust filled her nose.

"Nimbus!" Rhett squeaked as he scurried over. "Nimbus! Are you okay?" He ran a circle around her as she lay motionless. Then he stood up, anxiously rubbing his paws against the front of his sock sweater, his lower lip trembling. "You're not okay. You're hurt."

Nim lifted her head and gazed at her side. The thick blue stitches hung loose, no longer holding together the edges of her wound. Blood trickled over her exposed flesh and through her dusty black coat. She rested her head back on the ground, and a flood of exhaustion washed over her, followed by a wave of humiliation.

"Stay right here!" Rhett patted her cheek. "I'll go get help!"

As she watched him go, an unwelcome thought occurred to her. Maybe Rochester and Fern were right after all. The Ways of Magic was not going to let her leave. Maybe she really was Agatha's familiar. She closed her eyes. "But I don't want to be here," she whispered. "I want to be home with Fletcher."

* * *

The next thing Nim knew, Rhett was bellowing in her ear, "Nimbus! Hey, Nimbus!" He shook her shoulder with his tiny paw.

She peeled her eyes open.

Rhett sat up on his haunches, his face etched with concern. "I brought help."

"I don't need help," she growled. She tried to climb to her feet but couldn't.

Fern leaned her colorful face into Nim's line of sight. "Don't worry, little one. I've got you." She lowered her toothy mouth and grasped Nim by the scruff of her neck.

"I don't need help," Nim growled again. What she needed was to keep moving. She needed to get home.

Fern lifted her off the ground. Nim tried to wiggle free, but it was no use. She grew as limp as a kitten. Careful to avoid Nim's injured side, Fern half carried, half dragged her down the dusty shoulder of the old highway, then down the dirt road that led to the cottage. Nim closed her eyes again.

The sweet aroma of flowers filled her nose.

"Oh, dear," she heard Agatha murmur. "Thank you, Fern. And you too, Mr. Rat."

Nim opened her eyes. She lay on the cool grassy ground next to the daisy garden. She peered at the tips of Agatha's green gardening boots, then gazed up.

Agatha peered down at her, creasing her forehead and clutching the silver owl amulet that hung from her neck. Then, with a sigh, she wiped her dirt-crusted hands on her gray apron, scooped Nim up, and carried her into the house with Fern and Rhett trotting after them. "I'll sew you up again," she muttered wearily.

CHAPTER 19

Nim had returned to the dream realm.

As she strode along the road beneath the purple sky and its white crescent moon, she knew Agatha had given her the sleep medicine again. She was probably restitching the wound at that very moment. Nim scowled. Would the woman ever stop sending her to sleep? This time when she awoke, she just might decide to pee somewhere she shouldn't, maybe in a corner of her bedroom or in one of her shoes.

She arrived at her crossroads. As usual, Hecate waited there. This time a black cat sat beside her with its tail wrapped around its front paws, its posture perfect. It gazed calmly at Nim with its light brown eyes.

Nim's mouth opened in surprise, but she quickly closed

it. She lifted her shoulders, proud that the goddess wanted to associate with black cats.

"Hello, Nimbus," Hecate said. "Did you find Fletcher or the nightmare demon?"

"No." Nim shook her head, feeling sick with anxiousness. "I'm worried he's upset that I might be Agatha's familiar and thinks I should stay at the cottage."

"What would give him such an idea?" Hecate asked.

"I told him that Fern and Rochester believe I'm Grimalkin, Agatha's old familiar who's been reborn. They said if I am, then no matter how hard I try, I won't be able to go home."

Hecate nodded. "This is true. The Ways of Magic matches the two and pulls them together. To try and escape such a connection is useless. Witch and familiar always find one another."

Nim's hopes plummeted. This was not what she wanted to hear.

"Don't despair," Hecate said. "Witch and familiar are always well matched. The Ways of Magic does not get it wrong. If you are a familiar, and if Agatha is your witch, in time, you'll adjust."

The black cat at Hecate's side stood and walked circles around her, rubbing its head and flank against the length of her long lavender gown.

Nim's shoulders slumped. How could she be expected to forget about the life that she wanted? It wasn't fair.

"It's also possible you aren't a familiar at all," Hecate added.

To Nim's surprise, the words disappointed her. She had to admit that she was a bit curious to know more about being a witch's assistant—not that she believed she was Agatha's. Her paw lifted in uncertainty. But did some small part of her hope she was? She wanted to be home with Fletcher, though. How could she want both at the same time? The only thing she knew for certain was that she wanted Fletcher to be safe.

Furrowing her brow, Nim thought for a moment until an idea occurred to her. She gazed up at Hecate. "If I travel to where my memories are gathered, could I find Grimalkin's memories there too? Then I would know for sure if I'm her or not."

Hecate shook her head. "Memories from past lives are not easy to revisit unless they are consciously activated. If you really are Grimalkin returned, you'll have to find another way to unlock your recollections of that life."

"But how can I do that?" Nim asked.

The black cat at Hecate's feet meowed up at her. The goddess held her hands out and the cat jumped into them.

Cradling it in the crook of her arm, Hecate stroked its back. "Perhaps you can talk to someone who was close to Grimalkin, maybe dream walk to a powerful memory they have of her."

Nim tilted her head to one side as she thought it over. Agatha wasn't asleep at the moment. It'd have to be one of the napping house cats. "Bianca!" she whispered. Fern had told her Bianca was close to Grimalkin. Surely Bianca would have a powerful memory of the old familiar. "Thank you, Lady Hecate! I'll give it a try."

Nim made her way up the empty middle road, passing the familiar grassy fields. She desperately wanted to search for Fletcher again but knew it would be useless since he wouldn't be asleep during the day. Setting her mind on Bianca, she padded toward the colorful shapes shifting and moving up ahead.

Soon green sofas in all shapes and sizes littered the sides of the road. The sun shone down and chirping birds swooped through the sky. Taking a few steps more, she arrived at a purple sofa in the middle of the path. Bianca lay on it, lazily flicking her tail as she watched a pair of sparrows flitting back and forth above her. At her side sat a bowl of chewy salmon-scented treats. She speared one on the tip of a claw and nibbled it.

"Bianca!" Nim called.

Bianca cast her blue eyes on Nim. "What do you want, new cat?"

"I need your help. Fern and Rochester think I might be Grimalkin and—"

Bianca frowned. "Well, you're not."

"I don't think I am either." Nim twitched her ears in annoyance. "And I don't want to be."

Bianca narrowed her icy eyes. "Why would you not want to be Grimalkin? Do you think you're better than her? With your *dream-walking ability*?"

Anger flared inside Nim, alongside a glowing ember of hurt. All she wanted was to prove to herself that she wasn't Grimalkin, that she didn't have to stay at the cottage as Agatha's familiar. Determined, she lifted her shoulders and took a step closer. "I need you to come with me."

"Go with you where?" Bianca frowned again.

"Look, neither of us want me to be Grimalkin. Take me to one of your memories of her, one that's powerful and special. If that doesn't unlock any Grimalkin memories for me, then it'll prove I'm not her."

Bianca scowled at Nim for a moment. Then she leisurely rose to her tan-colored paws. "Fine. I'll walk with you."

"This way." Nim scampered off, fixing her thoughts on

Bianca's crossroads. A moment later, they came to a place where the road stretched out in three directions. Snowflakes drifted down from a bright blue sky, the color of Fletcher's favorite blue-raspberry candy. Snow-covered fields lay all around.

As with the other crossroads she'd visited, the path to the right led to Bianca's nightmare place. Instead of stormy skies or twisted trees, though, it was an area set with a sofa, some chairs, and a TV. Toys lay scattered about as children ran around laughing and shrieking, their faces caked with dirt, their hands coated with mud.

Nim shuddered and looked away. She was certain the place where Bianca's memories were gathered was to their left. "This is your crossroads," she announced.

Bianca peered around, but at the sight of her nightmare road, she hunched her shoulders and stepped back. "Where's Grimalkin?" she squeaked.

Nim wished they could simply travel the middle road to try and locate Grimalkin in her dreams, but familiars were born into new bodies, and if Grimalkin's memories hadn't yet returned to her, she wouldn't be the same cat as before. Bianca wouldn't be able to envision the new Grimalkin at all, and they'd never find their way to her. Nim motioned to the path on the left. "This way will take us to your memories of Grimalkin." As they went, she instructed Bianca on how to find the specific time and place she wanted to visit.

They were soon strolling by scattered toys, a plush cat bed, and a carpeted scratching post.

"Those things belonged to Tiff," Bianca said with a stony voice.

"Tiff?" Nim asked.

"That's what my first human companion called me. When I briefly lived with her." Despite the coldness of Bianca's tone, her eyes grew watery. Nim quickly looked away.

The scenery changed, and they were walking along the old highway. Up ahead stood a tall oak tree and Agatha's rusty green mailbox; the dirt road lay just beyond.

It seemed like an odd place for one of Bianca's special memories. Before Nim could question her, though, a car pulled up behind them and stopped. Flinching, Nim spun around. She knew the car was only in Bianca's memories, but she still didn't like being near it. She stepped onto the road's shoulder, and Bianca joined her.

One of the car doors opened, and a younger version of Bianca was set down on the side of the road. The door closed, and the car drove off.

The Bianca next to Nim scowled. "The grabby-kid

family." She turned up her pink nose. "It was just as well. I didn't like living with them at all."

"What happened?" Nim asked.

Bianca turned her gaze on Nim. "Not that it's any of your business, but they were a family with three, maybe even four children, I don't remember. I never paid them enough notice." She frowned as though she'd just tasted something unpleasant. "They always had such grimy little hands stained with mud, or I shudder to think what else. One of them was always pulling my tail. And their parents . . ." She huffed in disgust. "They often forgot to feed me." She lifted her head proudly. "Once while I was napping, one of their grabby offspring gave my tail a painful yank, so I bit him." She glanced at the former version of herself cowering on the side of the highway. "That was the day they tossed me out." She shrugged as though it were no big deal again, but Nim noticed her shoulders had slumped ever so slightly.

They watched in silence as the younger Bianca looked around fearfully. Then, with tail tucked, she made her way past them and up the road's dusty shoulder.

"I didn't know where to go or what to do," Bianca murmured. "I was afraid."

Nim wished she could comfort Bianca, but she didn't

dare give her a sympathetic pat. She knew it would be rejected.

Up ahead, a woman walked past the oak and to the mailbox. Her hair hung in a long gray braid down her back. Tied around the front of her purple housedress was a bright yellow apron filled with numerous pockets. On her feet were a pair of green gardening boots. She opened the mailbox, reached in, and paused. She turned toward the hunkering Bianca, shook her head sadly, and strode toward her.

"Come on, sweet girl," Agatha said, scooping her up and stroking the top of her head. "You have a home now." Then, carrying the creamy-white cat beneath her arm, she retrieved a handful of mail from the mailbox before heading back toward the cottage.

"That's how I came to live with Grimalkin, Abraxas, Fern, and Rochester," the Bianca at Nim's side said.

They followed Agatha into the cottage, where she cheerfully announced to the others lounging around the living room, "This is the newest member of our family." Then she set the frightened Bianca on the green sofa.

Atop a purple pillow, on the same table where Agatha had placed Nim and the orange cushion, a white cat sat up straight and tall. Nim now had little doubt this was one of the reasons Bianca had instantly disliked her; she didn't want anyone taking Grimalkin's special place.

The white cat wrapped her tail around her paws, then blinked her green eyes at Agatha. Agatha approached with her hand held out, and Grimalkin pressed her paw to Agatha's palm.

"That was Grimalkin's special way of communicating with Agatha," the current Bianca said. She turned to Nim with a sour look. "I've never seen you do that."

Nim didn't reply. She didn't know what to say.

The younger Bianca had curled up on the end of the sofa, tears leaking from her tightly shut eyes.

Grimalkin stepped off the purple pillow. Nim could tell she was old, not only by her slow movements down from the table, but by the appearance of her fur sticking out. Her coat was not as well groomed as it could've been. The elderly white cat hopped up onto the sofa and gazed at the new cat.

The frightened Bianca curled into a tighter ball and buried her face in her chest.

"It's okay, young one," Grimalkin murmured. "You're home now." With a loud, soothing purr, she leaned down and groomed the top of Bianca's head.

The Bianca next to Nim kept her wistful gaze fixed on Grimalkin. "Over the next year, Grimalkin comforted me when I was sad." She swallowed hard and blinked her misty eyes. But when she spoke again, her voice still cracked with emotion. "And when I had a bad dream, she would let me sleep on her purple pillow with her. She'd lick my ears and tell me everything was going to be all right. She said it was okay to sometimes feel scared or sad, but not to forget to play and feel joy. Then she'd drape a paw over me, and I'd fall asleep to the sound of her purring."

"I'm sorry," Nim whispered.

Bianca shot an icy gaze at her. "I didn't bring you to this memory to feel sorry for me. I did it to prove you're not Grimalkin. If you were her, you'd remember these things."

Before Nim could agree, Bianca continued. "Do you recall any of her duties as Agatha's familiar? Do you remember fetching elder leaves from the garden or bringing dish towels from the kitchen when Agatha spilled a potion? Do you remember Agatha's favorite boline for cutting herbs or where she kept the packets of dried pokeroot stored in the darkest corner of the attic? Do you know how to identify all the plants Agatha grows? Do you even know what a moon-gazing mirror is?"

Nim shook her head.

Bianca took a shuddering breath, her voice once again breaking with emotion as she continued. "Did you know that when Agatha was twelve, the gardener's cat had kittens? Whenever Agatha visited them, a little gray one always followed her home, so Agatha named her Grimalkin. Shortly after that, Agatha discovered she was a witch, and the kitten was her familiar."

Bianca sighed, some of her anger seeming to deflate. "The first time Grimalkin died, it only took two months for her and Agatha to reunite. The way Grimalkin told us the story, there was a seed store in the nearby town where Agatha went once a month to pick up gardening supplies. One day, when she approached the store's entrance, sitting next to the door was a white kitten with her tail wrapped around her paws. She fixed her green stare up at Agatha and blinked both eyes. Agatha stopped and peered down at her, and when she reached out to the kitten, she raised her paw and touched it to Agatha's palm." Bianca smiled sadly. "Agatha scooped the kitten up, forgetting all about her gardening supplies."

"I don't remember any of those things," Nim whispered.

"No," Bianca replied, her shoulders slumping. "I didn't think you would." She gazed down at the floor, her blue eyes taking on a faraway look. "When Grimalkin was dying, she told me not to worry, that she'd return soon." Her voice dropped to a whisper. "But she was wrong. She's not coming back."

"She sounds like a special cat," Nim murmured, surprised at the lump forming in her own throat.

Bianca lifted her head and fixed her sad face on Nim. "I miss her."

Nim's heart ached for Bianca and Agatha. "If Grimalkin really is somewhere out there in the world, and there's any way that I can help get her back here, I promise I will."

Bianca's reply was interrupted by the sound of a spoon clanging against a bowl.

CHAPTER 20

Nim awoke in the physical world, once again lying on the orange cushion.

"Lunchtime!" Fern cried. She leaped off the rocking chair and scampered to the kitchen.

Midafternoon sunlight shone through the window behind Nim. She didn't have to look down to know her wound had been restitched and rebandaged. She felt the sutures, the gauze dressing, and the fire racing through her side; the smell of the greasy hawthorn ointment wafted into her nose.

Bianca hopped off the sofa. As she strode after the others, she glanced back at Nim and gave her the faintest of friendly nods.

Nim's head spun. Her dream walk with Bianca had

proved she wasn't Grimalkin. Hadn't it? But if so, why did the Ways of Magic want to keep her there? And Fletcher . . . she couldn't shake the feeling he was in trouble. She needed to get home to protect him. She had to find a way to escape these magical confines.

She tried to sit up, but her head weighed as much as a boulder. She bent her ears back in frustration. It would take too much time for the medicine to wear off, too much time that she'd have to lie there like a lump on a log. The next time Agatha came near, she was going to give her a very indignant glare. She let her head drop back onto her paws, too weary to even try pulling off the annoying bandage.

The sound of squeaky gardening boots met her ears. Agatha set down a bowl of cat food, along with a saucer containing a saltine cracker topped with a small slice of cheddar cheese.

"Now where'd your rat friend go?" Agatha glanced around. "He didn't leave your side all morning." She sighed. "Well, when he gets back, he'll have a nice little lunch waiting for him." She peered at Nim's gauze binding, gave it a slight adjustment, and shook her head. "You busted your stitches. I've done what I can, but it'll take time for this wound to heal. I hope you'll stay put long enough to recover. But that's up to you." She gave Nim a small smile, then turned away. She was halfway across the room when she stopped and looked back. "You have a home here if you want."

Nim watched her go, her emotions swirling like storm clouds. Her gaze drifted to the dining room table and the roll of gauze, tin of hawthorn ointment, and small pair of scissors lying there. Her ears burned with shame at how ungrateful she'd been for Agatha's care.

"Hey, Nimbus!" a muffled voice squeaked. Rhett scrambled up the nearby chair and onto the side table. He dropped Nim's collar and stood up proudly. "It took some scouting around, but look! I found your collar. This is it, right? I remembered you said it was green." He twitched his whiskers hopefully. "I thought it might cheer you up to have it back."

"My collar!" Nim exclaimed. It was covered with dirt and stains and the tag was gone, but it was such a comforting sight. She rested her paw on it. "Rhett, you're the best!"

He lifted his nose and sniffed, his ears perking at the sight of the saucer. "Ooh, another cracker! And a piece of cheese too!" He scuttled to the plate, then began nibbling the snacks.

An idea struck Nim. She scrambled to her feet but fell back onto the cushion.

"You still look a bit drowsy," Rhett observed as he munched. "Maybe you should try eating a few espresso granules. They'll perk you right up! I ate some more of them a few minutes ago, and I feel like I could fly. I actually ran a few laps around the dump before heading over here."

Nim wasn't sure she wanted to be quite that perky right now—or ever. "Rhett! Do you think you could find my collar tag?"

He shrugged. "I'll give it a try." He took another bite of the cracker. "What does a collar tag look like?"

"It's gold and flat. It's a disk with my name and my family's phone number engraved on it. If it was here, Agatha could call Fletcher and tell him where I am! Why didn't I think of this before?" Nim thumped her tail happily. And if she could just hear Fletcher's voice through the telephone, then she would know he was okay.

"A disk, you say?" Rhett rubbed his furry chin. "I bet I know exactly where it might have gone off to, or more specifically, *who* might have gone off with it." He shoved the rest of the cracker and the last bite of cheese into his mouth. "I'll be back soon," he said as crumbs rained onto his sweater. "You can count on me, Nimbus!" He scurried down from the table and across the floor.

Hope coursed through Nim. This plan was so simple and so sensible. It just had to work! She'd be home soon. She was sure of it. She could sense it, right down to the marrow of her bones.

When the four house cats returned, Fern stopped and stared up at Nim. "Oh, don't be so disheartened, lovey. You'll be up on your paws again soon."

"I'm not disheartened," Nim replied. For the first time in a long while, she was feeling very optimistic.

Fern strolled over to the ragged toy squirrel lying beneath the telephone side table. She grasped it in her teeth, hopped up to Nim's table, and dropped it onto Rhett's empty saucer. "Maybe practicing your killing bite will cheer you."

"Thanks, Fern." Nim smiled, though she had no interest in mauling any victims at the moment.

"What's that?" Fern motioned toward Nim's collar.

"It's my collar!" Nim beamed. "Rhett found it in the dump and brought it to me."

"He really is a darling little thing," Fern replied. Then she gave Nim a scratchy lick on top of her head, jumped down, and strode to her rocking chair. As she settled onto its cushion, something clattered to the floor in the dining room, and all heads turned toward the source of the sound.

Bianca stood on the table, swishing her tail and staring down at the small pair of scissors lying below. She turned her attention to the roll of gauze. She gave it a few pats with her paw, then slapped it off the tabletop too. Looking pleased with herself, she watched as it rolled in a small circle and came to a rest beside the scissors.

"Really, Bianca . . ." Rochester scowled from inside his box, his white mustache seeming to droop with disapproval.

Bianca stared at him, then pushed the ointment tin over the edge of the table too.

Nim wrinkled her forehead. "Why are you doing that?"

Bianca leaped down from the table, lazily waving her tail behind her. "I do it because it amuses me." She hopped onto the sofa, licked her front paw, and groomed her tan face. She cut her cool gaze toward Nim. "It's called playing."

Twitching her ears in puzzlement, Nim stared back.

Bianca rolled her eyes. "Oh, loosen up, Nimbus; have a little fun every now and then instead of always being so serious." She gave Nim a meaningful look. "As someone once told me, we should never forget to play and feel joy."

Nim gave her a small nod in reply, pleased that Bianca had actually addressed her by her name.

Fern's eyes widened with excitement. "Playing *is* one of the three diversions of the cat."

"This is true. We all must enjoy a bit of fun sometimes," Rochester said.

"Pushing something over the edge is also a great way to get attention," Bianca added, lifting her chin and sitting up straighter. "It's one of the subskills of playing, along with swatting and batting."

Without thinking, Nim shot out a paw and sent Fern's tattered squirrel shooting off the plate and bouncing across the floor.

Fern gasped.

Bianca flew from the sofa and dove for the toy. She swatted it across the room, where it spun to a stop at the base of the rocking chair. Then she lunged after it again.

A spark of happiness flickered inside Nim, and her whiskers tingled.

With a huff, Fern jumped off the rocking chair and smacked Bianca's cheek. "You naughty dingleberry!" She pushed Bianca away and plopped down on top of the squirrel, but her eyes twinkled, and the corners of her mouth twitched.

Nim rumbled a purr, and for a moment, she forgot all her troubles.

With a soft hiss and a smirk, Bianca half-heartedly bopped the top of Fern's head. Then she trotted to the dining room and swatted the roll of bandages. It tumbled across the floor to Rochester, who leaned out of his box and gave it a whack. It rolled through the dining room and came to a stop outside the kitchen just as Agatha emerged through the doorway.

"Look at you all, playing like a bunch of rambunctious kittens!" She chuckled as she stepped over the roll of gauze and made her way to Nim's table. But at the sight of the full bowl of food, she sighed. "Still refusing to eat, I see." She picked up Rhett's empty plate, then paused at the sight of Nim's collar. She peered from it to Nim and back again.

Nim twitched her ears anxiously, wishing Rhett had already returned with her address tag.

"Hmph." Agatha took the collar, stared at it for a second longer, then tucked it into one of the many pockets on her gray apron. After setting the plate back down, she turned and strode off to her bedroom.

Nim fidgeted with agitation. Why had she taken her collar? She didn't know what Agatha was going to do with it, but she wanted it back. Her strength slowly seeping back into her muscles, she managed to sit up. She fixed her eyes on the short hallway that led to Agatha's room and waited nervously, fearing she might decide to throw the collar into the trash can.

"So why do you want to leave so badly?" Bianca asked from her spot back on the sofa. "Surely it's not *that* terrible here, is it? Agatha treats us very well."

Nim turned to her. "It's not that. It's just that I need to get back to—"

"Oh, yes." Rochester nodded in agreement. "Agatha is indeed good to us, a lovely human companion and a wise and talented witch as well."

"And generous too," Fern added. "Grimalkin told us that when Agatha was a teacher, she spent endless hours sharing her knowledge with her students. She taught them how to make all sorts of magical medical remedies and other useful things, like how to find dousing rods and how to communicate with plants."

Nim's ears perked with surprise. "Agatha was a teacher?"

Fern nodded. "And she was very sad when part of her school burned. It was her home too. But that was long before any of us lived here."

"She lived in a school?" Nim tilted her head, puzzled.

"She inherited the mansion when her parents passed away," Rochester explained. "Having no family of her own to fill the large house with, and having much knowledge to share, she opened her home as a boarding school for young witches." He scratched an itch under his collar, the silver book charm softly jingling as he thought. "I think about six to eight students attended per year, but I suspect they became family for her. Then one night, a wing of the house caught fire."

Nim's whiskers shot out at attention. "The old Whittaker place!"

Rochester nodded. "Agatha, the children, and all their familiars escaped safely, but the parents of the students were worried. They'd heard that some of the nearby townspeople were whispering how witches were evil, and it was dangerous to have such a school in the vicinity." He frowned. "The parents of the students wondered if the fire might have been set by one of those narrow-minded people. They feared it was no longer safe for their children to attend the academy, even if Agatha restored the house. And so ended the Whittaker School for Young Witches."

"Fools, the whole bunch of them," Abraxas grumbled.

Nim's eyes grew enormous. "Did one of the townspeople really set the fire?"

"No, not at all," Rochester replied. "The fire was investigated and found to have been caused by a frayed electrical wire, but the children's parents didn't want to take any chances." He shrugged. "Though as Fern said, that was many years ago. I think, or at least I hope, such antiquated fears have subsided in these more modern times."

Fern's face filled with sadness. "Grimalkin said Agatha grew very disheartened after that. She didn't bother to repair the house, and she settled here in the vacant gardener's cottage instead." She gave a long sigh. "Now without her familiar, Agatha's been even more lost."

"People still come for her potions and cures, though."

Bianca scowled. "They come in the dark of night, so no one sees them. They're too embarrassed to admit they believe in magic."

Agatha's squeaky footsteps sounded from the small hallway, and she emerged with Nim's green collar clutched in her hands. She drew up to the side table and held it out to Nim. The identification tag was still missing, but in its place hung a small glass disk filled with concentric circles in black, white, and differing shades of blue.

One of Nim's paws slowly rose in confusion.

Agatha fastened the collar around Nim's neck. Then she stood back, regarding the glass disk. "It's a nazar, an all-seeing eye." She cast a troubled glance at Nim's bandaged side. "It's your protection amulet now. If something malevolent tries to harm you again, this could weaken it, or at least slow it down." She gazed directly into Nim's eyes. "The nazar is also a symbol of good luck." She rested her hand on the top of Nim's head for a moment, then turned and left, grabbing a garden basket from the wall as she passed through the dining room.

"My, my, my." Bianca smirked. "Your own amulet. I guess that makes you one of us now."

Despite the aloofness of Bianca's mannerism, Nim was sure she detected a small hint of warmth in her words.

"Oh, well done, little one!" Fern beamed. "Now you

really are part of our family!"

"Well done indeed," Rochester echoed.

Abraxas narrowed his eyes at Nim. "Remember your place in our hierarchy and see that you keep to it." Then he gave her a small nod. "Congratulations, nonetheless."

Nim opened her mouth to remind them she wasn't staying, but the words stuck in her throat. She touched her paw to the nazar. She eyed Fern's rocking chair charm, Rochester's book, Bianca's snowflake, and Abraxas's lion. Could she truly belong here?

No. She swept the thought away. She had to get home. Fletcher needed her.

Did he, though? What if he really had chosen to leave their shared dream and had already forgotten about her? Her happiness withered, and she was no longer sure hearing his voice through the phone would be such a good idea.

CHAPTER 21

"Nimbus, I'm back!" Rhett called as he clambered up to the tabletop. He stood on his hind legs, clutching her ID tag in his tiny pink paws.

Nim had been so lost in her thoughts, she hadn't seen him scuttle into the room. Despite her fears about Fletcher, the sight of the small gold disk was a relief, and she realized just how much she wanted to go home. "You found it! Thank you, Rhett."

"Wow!" he said, his black eyes shining as he gaped at the nazar on her collar. "What a beautiful piece of jewelry!" He whistled in admiration. "That's quite an accessory. I wish I could find something that nice in the dump."

Nim held her head higher to show off the nazar, proud to be wearing it. But the tag was her ticket home. And while she would miss Agatha and the house cats, this was not where she belonged.

Rhett set the disk on the table and wiped his paws against the front of his sock sweater. "It was just as I suspected," he said. "A scrounger who likes flat, round things, like coins, buttons, poker chips, even scratched-up old Mardi Gras doubloons, had it."

"What's all the commotion over there?" Rochester sat up taller inside his box, stretching his neck to see better.

"The rat's been dump digging," Bianca muttered from her spot on the sofa.

"Ooh, what'd he find this time?" Fern's eyes grew wide with interest.

"It's my ID tag," Nim said, grinning. "It's going to get me home to Fletcher."

Fern and Rochester exchanged troubled looks but made no more comments about the Ways of Magic. Nim would've ignored them if they had.

"Rhett, can you go to the garden and bring Agatha back? I need her to call home and tell Fletcher I'm here!"

"On my way!" Rhett replied. "Maybe she'll give me some more cheese too!" He dropped to his four paws and skittered off, keeping close to the baseboards as he went.

"He certainly is a helpful little fellow," Rochester said as he watched Rhett go. "Back at the bookstore, there was a family of mice living there, but they never ran errands or conversed with me. You're lucky to know him."

Rochester was right. She *was* lucky to have met Rhett. And she was lucky he'd been able to find her collar and tag in the cluttered dump. These were not things that happened to unlucky cats. Was it possible her streak of misfortune was turning good? Her paw lifted in uncertainty. Or was she creating her own good fortune through clever decisions and ideas?

Fern had been studying Nim with worried eyes. Finally, she spoke. "Must you really try to leave again? Agatha's greatly in need of her familiar."

"This is true." Rochester nodded.

"But I'm not Grimalkin," Nim said, though they seemed not to hear her.

"We've thought about trying to help Agatha by fetching items, aiding her in creating potions, and those sorts of things," Rochester continued. "It hasn't worked out, though. I suppose I could assist her with locating books on her shelves, but she already knows where to find them."

"I tried killing some of the critters in her gardens, but she didn't appreciate it," Fern added.

Bianca laid her ears back in annoyance. "Well, it's not our job to assume the duties of a familiar, now, is it? Who are we to think we could possibly take over for Grimalkin?"

"The bunch of you could help if you really wanted to," Abraxas growled. "You're just too lazy."

Fern pursed her lips. "Speak for yourself, Abraxas. I did offer my help."

"Alas"–Rochester shrugged–"we simply don't possess the supernatural senses to know when Agatha needs a familiar's assistance."

Before Nim could remind them again she wasn't Grimalkin, the back door opened and shut. Squeaky boots sounded through the house. Rhett scurried into the living room with Agatha following. She stopped and ran her gaze all around, as though looking for something that had gone wrong. "Hmph. Is it another cracker you want? Is that why you brought me here?"

Rhett skittered up the boxes and chair and onto Nim's table. He crouched beside the gold tag, squealing and twitching his whiskers.

"What's this?" Agatha approached, wiping her hands on the front of her gray apron. She took the disk in her dirt-stained fingers and peered at the writing engraved on it. She arched an eyebrow at Nim. "Nimbus? Is that your name?"

Nim thumped her tail against the orange cushion.

Agatha gazed at the tag again. "I suppose it's worth a try." She went to the telephone on the other side table.

Nim's heart raced like a wild rabbit. Rhett hunkered nearby, both keeping their eyes glued to Agatha.

Squinting at the gold disk, Agatha dialed the number printed on it.

Nim heard the phone ringing back home. She grew still, every muscle tensing as she waited to hear if Fletcher would answer the call.

A click sounded. The ringing ended.

"Hello?" a woman's voice asked.

It was Aunt Caroline.

Nim's hopes plummeted. She barely heard Agatha's words, but Aunt Caroline's came through quite clearly. "Nimbus? Yes, we did have a cat by that name, but it ran away after it attacked my nephew. He's afraid of it now and doesn't want it to return. Perhaps you can find a new home for it? No need to call back. Goodbye." There was a click as she hung up.

Fletcher didn't want her to come home? A buzzing like a thousand mosquitoes filled Nim's ears, and tears prickled her eyes.

She didn't understand.

Last night he'd said he didn't believe Aunt Caroline's lies. Had the woman made him think otherwise after the dream walk? Maybe she'd gone into his room to check his injured cheek and she'd awoken him, pulling him out of the dream realm. Then somehow, she'd convinced him it was his cat that attacked him. Nim gulped. That's why he was blocking her in the dream realm. Not because he believed she was Agatha's familiar, but because he was afraid of her.

Grief squeezed her heart, threatening to crush it.

Scowling, Agatha hung up the phone, but when she glanced at Nim, her expression softened. "I'm sorry, Nimbus. It seems like it's just not meant for you to return to your old home." She paused, wrinkling her forehead. "Is it possible?" she whispered. "Could you really be my Grimalkin?" She rubbed her chin, studying Nim, carefully watching her eyes.

But Nim didn't blink at her.

Agatha crossed to the table and held her hand out. Nim didn't press her paw against the offered palm either.

"No." Agatha's shoulders slumped. "I guess not." With a sad sigh, she turned away and left the room.

CHAPTER 22

Nim struggled up to her feet.

"Nimbus? Are you okay?" Rhett asked, his whiskers drooping.

She wobbled down the nearby chair and onto the floor.

From inside his box, Rochester shook his head sadly. "I'm very sorry about the phone call."

"Oh, lovey . . ." Fern's calico face filled with compassion. "Try not to be sad. Things will work out. You'll see."

Even the usually cold gazes of Bianca and Abraxas were sympathetic.

Despite the pain in her side, and the uncomfortable bandage wrapped around her middle, Nim stumbled to the kitchen and slipped through the cat flap. Tucking her tail, she scurried away. She didn't know where she was headed, only that she needed to be alone.

Before she realized it, she was skulking through the overgrown tangles of the Whittaker mansion's old garden. Weaving her way between elders and oaks, she hurried past herb beds grown wild, detecting the aromas of chamomile, mint, fennel, and lemon balm.

A dilapidated wooden shed sat in the distance. The faint scents of lilac, honeysuckle, and peppermint wafted from it. She'd never been able to identify so many plant smells by name, and the realization unsettled her. She hurried on, passing a toppled birdbath, its moldy bowl brimming with murky water. On the ground next to it, the word *RATS* had been spelled out with pebbles. Except the letters *R* and *S* had been formed backward. Nim didn't care about the rats' silly territory rules or their poor writing skills. She skulked up a set of mossy steps, onto a leaning back porch, and stole through a broken window.

The room she entered was a crumbling ghost of its former self. Collapsed ceiling beams lay like blackened tree trunks. Vines clung to the mildewy drapes. Ferns sprouted from the warped floorboards.

She gazed at the other items scattered throughout. A dented old birdcage sat in a corner. Strewn nearby were an assortment of flash cards with illustrations of plants on one side and their identifications listed on the other, names like fleabane, toadflax, and mandrake. Nim could easily read them, and her stomach tightened with anxiousness. One of the cards had been propped against the wall. The plant's species had been smudged over with soot, and the word ЯATƧ had been scrawled underneath it.

As Nim ran her eyes around the rest of the room's contents, she guessed she was standing in one of Agatha's former classrooms. Moldy, water-stained books lay everywhere; some of them still lined the warped wooden shelves. Small tables with rat-gnawed legs stood near sofas and chairs with their stuffing spilling out. A few of the tables held old microscopes, weather thermometers, and magnifying glasses on brass stands.

She padded to the middle of the room and plopped down behind a tattered sofa. An age-spotted mirror leaned against it. Its round wooden frame had been carved with shapes depicting the lunar phases. She knew it was a moon-gazing mirror, like the one Bianca mentioned in their dream walk, and this realization troubled her too. Something was happening to her. Knowledge was blooming inside her.

With a heavy heart, she understood what it was.

There could be no other explanation for the strange occurrences. She could no longer deny the truth.

She really must be Grimalkin, and these were her memories finally returning.

There was no point in fighting it.

The Ways of Magic had won.

This would be her life from now on.

Lowering her head to her side, she gnawed at the bandage. Having removed it twice before, she had no trouble freeing herself again. Then she curled into a ball, draped her tail around her, and lay brooding. The only thought bringing her any comfort was that Aunt Caroline had confirmed Fletcher was safe. She lay for a long while, wondering about the future that awaited her. Eventually, she fell into a long, dreamless sleep, not wanting to go to her crossroads or talk to Hecate, not wanting to talk to anyone.

"There you are!"

Nim lifted her head with a start. Beyond the smudgy windows, it had grown dark outside.

Rhett sat up in the room's doorway, his hands on his hips. "I've been looking all over for you, Nimbus! What in the world are you doing here?"

She set her head back on her paws. "Please go away, Rhett. I want to be alone."

He dropped down on all fours and scuttled over. "I'm sorry you're feeling sad. Maybe you need a friend right now." He lay down beside her, his eyes filled with sorrow. "I'll just stay here with you. I'll even try not to talk."

A few seconds of silence passed.

"This not talking thing is kind of hard," he whispered.

"It's still talking, even if you're whispering," Nim replied.

"Oh. Yeah. Right." He nodded.

A few more seconds of silence passed.

Rhett twitched his whiskers. "So . . . do *you* want to talk? I can just listen."

"No. Not really." Nim flicked the tip of her tail indecisively. "Well, maybe just a little."

Rhett waited quietly.

"The Ways of Magic is too strong." She sighed heavily. "No matter how hard I tried, I couldn't escape it."

"The Ways of Magic?" Rhett asked.

"It's a power that brings things together. It leads you where you need to be."

"Ah. I see." Rhett stroked his chin.

"Fern and Rochester were right. I'm meant to stay here because I'm Agatha's familiar." She glanced down at her paws and whispered miserably, "My life with Fletcher is over."

"Are you sure about all that?" Rhett asked.

"There are other signs that prove it." Nim sniffled. "I can read so many words now. And I can identify things that are used for magical purposes, like moon-gazing mirrors."

Rhett frowned. "Why do you care so much about this

Fletcher kid anyway? What's so special about him?"

"What's so special about Fletcher?" Nim gaped at him, hardly knowing where to start. She told him how Fletcher had rescued her as a kitten after she'd been hit by a car. Then how he took care of her as she healed, reading to her from his favorite book, *The Hobbit.*

She sat up, her tail swishing and stirring up small clouds of dust and old ash. She told Rhett about the interesting rocks and shells Fletcher collected and how he once found a very old arrowhead in the woods. That he liked making arrows with his own hands and shooting them from a bow like the elves of Middle-earth did. "I would watch him through the window when he practiced in the backyard." She smiled proudly. "He didn't think he was very good at it, but he could always hit something." Nim's memories filled her with warmth, like a roaring fire on a cold day. "On Saturday nights we'd sit on the sofa and watch his father's TV show."

"What?" Rhett sprang up on his paws, his eyes bulging. "Fletcher's father is on TV?"

Nim nodded. "He's a weatherman during the weekdays, but on Saturday nights he turns into a horror host."

"A horror host?" Rhett's eyes sparkled. "I don't even know what that is, but it's amazing!"

"It's sort of an actor." Nim grinned. "He paints dark circles under his eyes and wears a messy wig and an old-fashioned butler's uniform. He walks around inside the attic of a haunted house. Fletcher says it's just a set, that it's—"

"An actor?" Rhett's ears went floppy, and he swayed on his paws as though he might pass out. He gazed at Nim in wonder. "You know an actor," he whispered in awe.

Nim's smile dropped. That was the life she used to live. But Agatha's cottage would be her home from now on.

Rhett shook his head sadly. "I can see why you want to go back."

"I wish I could return one more time." Nim sighed. "Even if it was only to tell Fletcher goodbye." She narrowed her eyes. "And while I was there, I'd destroy any other nightmare demon that might be lurking inside the old jar."

"Going back for a visit sounds like a reasonable idea," Rhett replied.

Nim paused, staring off into the distance. "I wonder . . . ," she murmured. "Now that I've accepted my role as Agatha's familiar, would the Ways of Magic let me go home for just a short visit?" She thought on the idea a moment more. The journey there would be long and difficult, but she had no doubt the Ways of Magic would provide her a way back to Agatha again.

"Well then," Rhett said, sitting up and wiping his paws together as if he'd just completed a difficult task, "that's what you need to do. You have to go home, tell Fletcher goodbye, and get rid of the other nightmare demon."

Nim nodded. "You're right, Rhett."

He smoothed his whiskers with one paw. "'Jesters do oft prove prophets.'" Then he added, "That's a line from *King Lear.*"

"I have to head home right now." Nim climbed to her feet. Then, catching a glimpse of herself in the moon-gazing mirror, she scowled at the red wound and blue stitches. "I'll never really make it back, will I?"

Rhett flapped his paw to dismiss the notion. "It's self-confidence that counts!" He pointed a finger at her reflection. "*That* is a cat who can do great things." He turned his head side to side, studying his profile. "And next to that magnificent cat, I see her brilliant rat friend who'll one day become a famous star, bathed in the spotlight and deluged with bags of fan mail."

"I don't know." Nim frowned. "The journey to the city won't be easy."

"You'll be fine," he replied. "Just be more ratlike. If there's an obstacle in your path, find a way around it. Do what you're called to do no matter what gets in your way." He wrinkled his forehead. "That's actually good advice for myself."

"But the journey by paw will be a long one." Nim's

shoulders slouched. "And full of dangers."

Rhett flapped his pink hand again. "Oh, you don't have to walk back to the city. I know how you can catch a ride."

"You do?"

"Sure! There's a big flower shop truck coming to the old woman's cottage tomorrow morning. While the driver's off in the garden gathering bundles of daisies, all you have to do is climb in and hide. When the man returns, he'll drive back to his shop in the city. Then you can walk to Fletcher's house from there."

"Oh!" Nim's eyes grew round with surprise. "Thanks," she replied, realizing that if she hadn't been so determined to leave immediately, he might have mentioned the truck before. "But, Rhett, I—"

A faint skittering sounded in the dark hallway outside the room.

"What was that?" The fur rose on the back of Nim's neck as she peered into the empty shadows.

Rhett shrugged. "Probably just a large cockroach, or maybe a lizard."

Her fur settled, and the heat of embarrassment crept up in its place. She lowered her eyes and stared down at her paws. "Rhett, about hitching a ride on that truck . . . I don't think I can do it."

He furrowed his brow. "Why not?"

Nim gave her lips a nervous lick. "It's just that . . . I'm afraid of cars." She dropped her voice to nearly a whisper. "I won't be able to get anywhere near that big truck."

Without a word, Rhett scuttled over to the wall and grasped the flash card with the word *ЯAT2* scrawled across it in soot. Carrying it between his teeth, he scurried back to Nim and held the card up in his paws as he faced the mirror. "You need to think more like the determined rodents whose name is spelled out on this sign: rats! We rats—" His jaw dropped, his black eyes bugged out, and he stood motionless.

"Rhett?" Nim's ears twitched nervously. "Are you okay?"

"Nimbus," he whispered, never taking his gaze from his reflection. "Look! It's . . . it's a sign!"

She peered into the mirror. With the letters *S* and *R* written backward, the word *RATS* reflected as the word *STAR*.

"I really am a star!" He pointed. "It says so right there." He shook his head, beaming with disbelief. "It must be the Ways of Magic directing me! It's telling me I'm going to become a star!" His voice filled with awe. "I know what I need to do now."

Nim smiled, surprised at the hope flaring inside her, and she wondered if Rhett's confidence might be contagious.

Tomorrow morning, she would not let a loud truck or its terrible tires frighten her. She would think of her fear as nothing more than an obstacle in her path, and as Rhett had suggested, she'd find a way around it. Then she sighed, feeling strangely older and a bit wiser. Maybe it was time she went back to the cottage and started her new life. She turned toward the broken pane of glass but stopped and stared up at another nearby window.

At the top of its dry-rotted drapes rested a brilliant blue feather striped with bars of black. She easily recognized it as a blue jay's tail plume. Its brightness looked so out of place in the dreary, charred room. "I wonder how that got there," she murmured.

Rhett gazed up alongside her and shrugged. "Probably blew in through one of the broken windows."

"I wish I could climb up and get it." Nim shook her head. "But those moldy old curtains would never hold together. I'd fall for sure and bust my stitches again."

Rhett studied her. "What do you want that old thing for?"

"A blue jay's feather symbolizes loyalty and good fortune. It's also a sign of protection. Don't ask me how I know, I just suddenly do." The discomfort she'd felt with her fast-growing knowledge was slowly transforming into pride. She leaned her head to one side. "I'd like to bring it to Agatha as a gift since she was kind enough to give me this nazar." She pressed a paw to the glass disk hanging from her collar. "I guess it'd also be a way of showing my loyalty as her familiar. Maybe she could use it to create a protection amulet." She sighed. "I might as well start proving myself useful to her."

"Well, that's very nice of you, Nimbus." Rhett gave her a nod. "You're a good friend to everyone." Then he skittered toward the curtain, calling over his shoulder, "Don't worry. Rats are great climbers and very lightweight." He scrambled up the fragile fabric, grabbed the feather with his mouth, then scurried back down and offered it to her.

Nim smiled. "Thanks, Rhett." She took the feather with her teeth. "You're a good friend too."

"This is so exciting." Rhett rubbed his paws together. "The two of us stowing away on that truck to the city tomorrow is going to be such an adventure!"

Nim's mouth fell open, and the feather dropped to the floor. *The two of us?*

A scurrying of small feet sounded behind them, and they wheeled around.

Rhett gasped. Nim rumbled a soft growl.

Five huge rats hunched in the room's doorway, their beady eyes glaring unblinkingly. Nim recognized some of them from when she'd first arrived at the dump. There was Thorn, the one Rhett had identified as the sovereign's second-in-command. The others were probably Cinder, Bristle, and Raider, part of the sovereign's guard, as Rhett had also explained. But the rat in the center, the biggest rodent she'd ever seen, she did not recognize.

The pack slowly advanced, then drew to a stop before them. The hulking rat in the middle rose on his hind legs, sweeping his fat pink tail back and forth behind him.

"Sovereign!" Rhett squeaked. He fell onto his paws and bowed his head.

CHAPTER 23

The sovereign's four guards crouched at his side as he loomed over Rhett. "You have broken the law, Rhett."

"Who? Me?" Rhett lifted his head.

"Your crimes are many," Thorn added.

"I don't know what you're talking about." Rhett sat up, anxiously twitching his whiskers. "I haven't broken any laws. Well, at least not *that many*."

Thorn pointed at Nim. "You have befriended this predator and brought it back into our territory. You have crossed the neutral road and entered the old lady's cottage, eaten her food, and associated with the cats living there."

Rhett's lip trembled. "I was just being friendly."

"It's against colony law to be friendly to predators!" Thorn snapped. "Your reckless behavior has put the colony at risk. What if those other cats come over too? They'll feed upon us!"

"Oh, no. You're wrong." Rhett shook his head. "The old lady's house cats are much too well-fed to eat rats." He gave Thorn a sideways glance. "And besides, are you sure I've really done all those things?"

Thorn scowled. "We know what you've been up to. Bristle was assigned the job of following and observing you to discover if you were the thief."

Rhett's ears stood up straight. "I haven't stolen anything!"

The sovereign fixed his cold gaze on Rhett. "We've just caught you in the act of stealing an item from rat territory and giving it to the cat." He indicated the blue jay feather lying on the floor before Nim. "Now there's no doubt you're the thief." He frowned. "And it appears the two of you were in on it together, conspiring to run away and take our stolen belongings with you."

"In on what together?" Rhett scratched his head, appearing truly puzzled.

"An unforgivable theft." The sovereign shook his head sadly. "It vanished the morning this cat arrived in our territory. During all the commotion, and while I was away attending to other duties, someone took it from the burrow's treasure room."

Thorn pointed at Nim again. "She created a distraction." He turned his finger toward Rhett. "And then you stole it. You can't deny it. The two of you were seen leaving the dump together yesterday morning. No doubt you've hidden it somewhere in cat territory."

"What theft?" Rhett furrowed his brow. "I still don't know what you're talking about."

"Don't bother trying to use your bad acting skills to get out of this," Bristle chimed in.

Rhett gave him a scowl.

"The theft is being kept secret until the culprit has been discovered," the sovereign said. "We don't want the colony to believe misfortune will befall us without our lucky heirloom."

Rhett gasped and clapped his paws to the sides of his face. "Dragon's Eye has been stolen?"

"As soon as we realized it'd been taken, we searched your burrow room while you were away. We didn't find it there, but I know it was you." Thorn sneered. "Were you planning to take it with you on your search for stardom? We all heard about your scheme to run away to the city."

"I most certainly did not steal Dragon's Eye!" Rhett placed his hands on the sides of his sock sweater. "That is ridiculous!"

The rat king turned his attention to Nim.

She shrank low, tucking her tail.

"You must leave this place and never return," he ordered. "If you encroach on rat territory again, you will be attacked by my guards." He turned his steely gaze on Rhett. "You have disrespected our ways and endangered the colony, Rhett, and you must be punished. All your belongings shall be confiscated, chewed up, and used for bedding material. You will be imprisoned until Dragon's Eye has been returned. Then when an assembly of your peers is satisfied you have repented, you'll be released."

Rhett's shoulders sagged in defeat, and the king's guards drew around him.

"No!" Nim cried. "Rhett didn't take your heirloom."

With his ears drooping, Rhett slowly wiggled out of his sock sweater. One of the rats grasped it in his long yellow teeth and scurried away, disappearing into the shadows of the old house.

A sick feeling churned inside Nim. Rhett's accessories and magazines meant everything to him. She pushed the blue jay feather toward the king. "Here, you can have your feather. Just don't punish Rhett."

Thorn pointed at the old birdcage.

Rhett gulped. "Couldn't I just be sent to my room in the burrow? I promise to stay there and not come out."

"Criminals are not allowed in the burrow," Thorn

growled. "The sovereign has spoken his will."

Rhett hung his head, and the remaining guards escorted him to the old birdcage. He slunk into it, and the creaky door was slammed shut behind him. He hunkered down, his whiskers drooping along with his ears. The rats positioned themselves around his prison to make sure he didn't escape.

The rat king sighed. "Rhett, I don't want to do this, but it's for the best. As sovereign, I'm tasked with taking care of the colony." He shook his head sadly. "Black Tail himself, the first sovereign of our ten-year-old colony, would be so disappointed that I allowed such a treasure to be taken."

Nim's heart melted at the sight of Rhett with his small paws wrapped around the cage's rusty spindles. He looked like an ordinary rat now, except much sadder.

"Go," the sovereign ordered Nim. "And never return."

She remained rooted to the spot, though. She couldn't leave Rhett like that. She knew he'd never steal a valuable heirloom from the colony.

Thorn darted forward, thrashing his tail and snapping his long teeth at her.

With a half-hearted hiss, she took a step back, her thoughts racing. Surely there was someone who could help, someone who could at least tell her what to do . . . *Lady Hecate!*

Bristling his fur, Thorn crept closer.

"Wait!" Nim held out a paw as an idea occurred to her. She glanced at the sovereign. "I can prove it wasn't Rhett who took the heirloom that morning! And I can help you find it."

Thorn continued advancing, sweeping his tail over the dusty floor and snapping his teeth.

"Halt!" the sovereign commanded, and Thorn obeyed, crouching with his watchful eyes fixed on Nim. "How could you know the heirloom's location?" The sovereign glared. "So, you do have Dragon's Eye."

"No!" Nim shook her head. "I don't even know what a Dragon's Eye is. But I can use my magic cat powers to find it." Though if she'd been completely honest, she would've clarified it was actually the goddess Hecate who would help her find it.

The sovereign silently studied her.

"It's true!" Rhett nodded inside the cage. "Nimbus has magic powers!"

"All cats possess mystical abilities," Thorn replied. His expression grew suspicious. "But why would this cat assist us?"

Nim straightened her shoulders. "If I help you, you have to release Rhett. And you have to give back his sock sweater and promise not to destroy his other belongings."

The sovereign twitched his whiskers, continuing to study Nim. He thought on the proposal for what seemed like hours as Nim's heart thudded and Rhett's grip tightened on the bars of the cage.

Finally, the king spoke. "What is your name?"

"Uh . . . Nimbus."

"Nimbus," he said with a nod, "I accept your offer. If you return Dragon's Eye and reveal the true thief, then Rhett shall immediately be released, and all his things returned to him intact."

Nim replied with a nod of her own, doing her best to appear confident despite the trembling of her legs. "So . . . what exactly is Dragon's Eye?"

The king sighed softly. "It's a most beautiful object, the only item from Black Tail's stash of treasures that he managed to save from the burning house. He believed it held a lucky power, enabling him to escape with nothing more than a tail singed black."

Seeming to have forgotten his unfortunate predicament, Rhett sat up and his whiskers perked with enthusiasm. "It was right after that when humans started dumping an endless supply of food, magazines, and gnawable items onto the front lawn."

"And with those boxes and bags of unwanted items,"

the sovereign added, "more rats arrived, and the colony grew and prospered."

Nim didn't want to be rude, but they still hadn't answered her question. "What exactly is Dragon's Eye, though?"

The sovereign cupped his pink paws as though he were cradling an invisible object in them. "Dragon's Eye is a mystical glass orb sheltering a jade swath within its heart."

"A glass orb? A jade swath?" Nim frowned.

"It's a marble," Rhett called from the cage. "A cat's-eye marble." He glanced at the sovereign, then lowered his eyes. "Uh . . . sorry, sire, but that's what they're known as. I saw someone on a TV show call them that."

"Oh!" Nim knew what marbles looked like. Fletcher kept some in a box of valuables underneath his bed.

"Black Tail named it after a cat in a book," Rhett added. "He used to hide under a sofa and listen to the kids when they read stories aloud, back when this place was a school. It was his favorite because it was about a bunch of really smart rats. And I'm sorry to say, a really bad cat."

The sovereign's face grew stern as he stared at Nim. "Go now. If you can discover what happened to Dragon's Eye, come back to this room no earlier than three in the morning—once I have completed colony business—and reveal its location to me. Do not delay. I won't wait past sunrise." Then he dropped onto his four paws, strode out of the room, and disappeared into the dark hallway beyond it.

Thorn remained crouched with his eyes fixed on Nim, his tail swiping back and forth over the ash-covered floor.

"Don't worry, Rhett. I'll be back." Nim turned, and as she headed out through the broken window, her stomach pinched with worry.

She didn't really know if returning to the dream realm would help her find the lost marble, but Lady Hecate was wise. Surely she would help her discover its whereabouts.

CHAPTER 24

The sky was dark and the stars were out as Nim scurried away from the old, abandoned mansion. The lights were still on inside the cottage as she hurried past Agatha's garden and the boxes of fresh-cut daisies sitting nearby. She pushed her way through the cat flap and into the kitchen.

Agatha stood barefoot at the sink, scrubbing dishes. Her green gardening boots stood near the door. At the sound of the cat flap swinging shut, she turned to Nim. "Glad you came back, Nimbus." She motioned her head toward the living room. "I left some fresh food and water on your table. Don't worry. I didn't add anything else." She gave a half-weary sigh. "I've given up on trying to force you to rest."

Nim's empty stomach gave a nervous twist at the

realization that Agatha would soon be calling her Grimalkin instead. It wasn't an unpleasant name; she just preferred the one Fletcher had given her. Trying not to dwell on how much she missed him, she reminded herself the other house cats had gotten used to their new names. Surely in time she would too.

She was making her way across the kitchen when another realization stopped her. It wasn't Agatha's fault things had turned out the way they had. If anything, it was the Ways of Magic that had messed it all up. She glanced back at the old witch, and her heart softened. Agatha had been kind, not only to her, but to all the cats in the house, and even to Rhett. Nim strolled over, bumped her head against her ankle, then rubbed a circle around her feet. It was the best way she knew to show her thanks, not just for the food and water, but for everything Agatha had done to help her and the others.

Understanding Nim's meaning, Agatha smiled down at her. "You're welcome," she said.

Nim padded to the living room, her insides swirling with emotions. She glanced at Fern on the rocking chair, Rochester in his cardboard box, Bianca on the sofa, and Abraxas lying in a spot of lamplight on the floor, all of them looking pleased and content as they tended to their nightly grooming. Should she tell them she'd finally come to accept she was Grimalkin, even if she still didn't remember having been her? *No.* She would wait and let them know after she'd talked to Fletcher and told him goodbye.

"Where have you been?" Rochester sat up and arched his eyebrows.

Fern gazed down at her. "You gave us a scare, little one. We thought you'd run off again."

"It's none of your business where she's been," Abraxas growled. Then he lowered his head onto his large paws, muttering his annoyance with their constant nosiness.

"Oh hush, you ginger-striped crab," Fern scolded, though she didn't pry any further into Nim's disappearance.

Nim was grateful Abraxas had spoken up. She really wasn't in the mood to explain that Rhett had been jailed by the other rats and that it was now up to her to free him. Or that it was her fault he'd been imprisoned. Her shoulders drooped. She shouldn't have asked for the feather. And if Rhett hadn't helped her at the dump when she'd first arrived there, he wouldn't be in this situation. She climbed up the boxes and chair and onto the table by the window.

The mouthwatering aroma of chicken and beef in rich, hearty gravy met her nose, momentarily erasing her worries. She was so hungry and thirsty. She lowered her head and dug in.

"Ugh. Slow down!" Bianca frowned at her. "Or it'll

come right back up again."

But Nim kept eating and drinking, and when she'd had her fill, she lifted her head and licked the delicious morsels from her mouth. With her belly feeling as if it were bulging, she settled down on the orange cushion. She rested her head on her paws, anxious to return to the dream realm and ask Hecate where the marble had been taken so she could free her friend from prison. She tried not to imagine what would happen if she failed.

"Going to sleep already?" Fern asked.

Nim yawned, hoping it would make her feel drowsier. "I need to find something," she murmured. "Something that's been lost."

"Not everything that's been lost can be found," Abraxas grumbled.

Nim peered down at him, surprised by the sadness filling his usually gruff face.

"Oh!" Fern exclaimed. "Are you going dream walking again? I hope it's a happy memory like the one you led me to."

"My dream walk made me sad," Bianca said from her place on the sofa. But a faint smile stretched across her face. "Though I was glad to see someone I miss very much."

"Well"—Rochester arched a white eyebrow at Nim— "while I appreciate your extraordinary dream-walking ability, I wouldn't want to repeat our particular other-worldly adventure."

Abraxas, who'd been sulkily observing each of them, huffed in annoyance.

Fern nodded enthusiastically at him. "Abraxas, you should ask Nimbus to take you dream walking too. It's great fun."

Before he could grumble a reply, the light in the kitchen snapped off. "Good night, everyone," Agatha called as she made her way to the living room. She went around and patted each house cat on the head. Then she stopped at Nim's table. "Good night, Nimbus." When she reached out to pat her, Nim raised her paw and pressed it against Agatha's palm.

Agatha's eyebrows shot up. She leaned forward, squinting as she peered at Nim. Then she stood and smiled, but it was a smile tinged with sadness. "Good night, Nimbus." She walked away, turning off the floor lamp as she went, then disappeared into the small hallway leading to her bedroom.

Fern and Rochester exchanged hopeful glances.

"Why did you do that?" Bianca asked with narrowed eyes.

Nim shrugged. She wasn't sure if she was disappointed or relieved that the motion hadn't triggered any memories of her former life as Grimalkin. She sighed. Though in time, it probably would.

Fern stretched her mouth into a wide yawn. She glanced at Nim, then pulled the scruffy squirrel close. "Good night, little one," she murmured. She laid her head on her paws and closed her eyes.

The other cats curled up or stretched out in their places and shut their eyes too.

Nim settled back down on the cushion. Despite the anxiousness gnawing away at her, she tried to convince herself everything was going to be okay. Soon she would discover the location of Dragon's Eye, tomorrow morning she would climb onto that flower truck without fear, and when she arrived home, she would see Fletcher once again.

Focusing her thoughts on the crossroads beneath the purple sky, she waited for sleep to come, but it didn't. She stretched out her back legs. She pulled them in again. She stood up and turned in a circle, trying to find the most comfortable spot. She lay down again and curled up.

By then, the other cats' breathing had slowed, sounding with the soft, relaxing rhythms of peaceful sleep.

Nim tucked her tail alongside her, impatient to drift away, wondering why time always moved so slowly when you were waiting for something to arrive. She wished Agatha had put some sleep medicine in her food and water after all. Then she sighed. Maybe she shouldn't have drunk so much water because now she needed to visit the litter box. She climbed down from the table and padded toward the bathroom where the box was located.

"Nimbus!" Abraxas whispered, and waved one of his big paws at her. "Come here."

Nim stopped. Hesitantly, she went to where he lay in a pool of moonlight.

"Are you truly ready to go out into the world again?" he asked in his gruff, raspy voice.

She paused, unsure how to reply. "I have to get home to Fletcher," she murmured. It was the truth, though she neglected to add she would be returning to the cottage.

"Your loyalty is admirable." He fixed his orange eyes on her. "It's good that you've learned the three diversions, but there's one more lesson you need before you leave."

"There is?" She lifted a paw, puzzled.

He nodded, the slow and self-assured response of an elder who'd experienced many things in life. "You must learn to walk with confidence. Not a subtle confidence, but with the dignity and bearing of a big jungle cat. Allow an unwavering belief in yourself to overtake you. Do this not only during the three diversions, but in everything you pursue."

While Nim appreciated his wise advice, she wasn't sure

she'd ever be able to do anything with such a level of certainty.

He raised his head, straightening his posture as he lay like a sphinx in the white moonlight. "Keep your shoulders up at all times. Move as though you are a mystery. Allow your belief to erase your doubts. Walking with confidence is the key to any locked door that stands between you and what you want. Will you remember these things?"

She nodded. "I will."

"Good luck to you, then. It appears I misjudged you." Then he rested his head on his large paws and shut his eyes.

"Thanks, Abraxas," she whispered, and she strolled off to the bathroom.

When she returned to the dark living room a few moments later, Abraxas was sound asleep.

She made her way up to her cushion bed and waited for sleep to come for her as well.

CHAPTER 25

Nim scampered up the roadway, wondering if she'd ever fall asleep. Then she noticed the purple sky and the crescent moon and realized she already had.

Hecate stood waiting at the crossroads with a crow perched on her shoulder, its black feathers gleaming blue and purple in the pale moonlight. It tilted its head, studying Nim, the cleverness clear in its black eyes.

When Nim came to a stop, she gazed up at the bird, wondering why the goddess always appeared with a different animal.

"I prefer the company of misunderstood creatures," Hecate answered, even though Nim hadn't asked the question out loud. "I see something is troubling you again."

Nim nodded. "I need to find an old marble so that my

friend Rhett can be released from a birdcage." She paused, realizing how nonsensical that sounded. She continued, "Someone stole the marble the morning I arrived at the dump." She fixed her pleading eyes on the goddess. "Can you tell me where to find it?"

"No," Hecate replied.

"Please, I need to find that heirloom. I have to help Rhett!" Nim's stomach twisted at the thought of Rhett locked in the rusty old cage while all his treasured belongings were gnawed to shreds.

"I can only offer you direction and inspiration," Hecate replied. She motioned to the dream roads stretching out around her. "Perhaps you can find the missing heirloom by traveling one of these paths."

Nim glanced at the stormy nightmare place and shuddered, thankful she couldn't think of a reason to search for the marble there. She peered at the road ahead that led to where others dream. But since she didn't know who'd taken Dragon's Eye, it'd be useless to head in that direction and ask where it was.

As she stared at the faraway blurry images to her left, she remembered Hecate's earlier words: *All the pieces of your past reside there, even the smallest details you might not recall when you're awake.*

An idea flickered, then grew brighter in Nim's mind.

What if somehow, in all the heaps of rotting food and broken things, she'd seen Dragon's Eye yesterday morning? Since the rats believed it disappeared when she arrived, maybe she'd witnessed the thief taking it away!

Swishing her tail hopefully, she returned her gaze to the goddess. "Thank you, Lady Hecate!" Then she dashed up the road toward the moment when she awoke at the dump.

As she made her way along the empty path surrounded by grassy fields, she soon traveled by random odds and ends from her past: a faded green sofa, an old wooden rocking chair, and an orange cushion. She walked across Fletcher's starry bedspread, over her green pillow bed, winding her way through scatterings of his books and the arrows he'd made by hand.

Finally, she arrived at the dump in the dark, pre-morning hour. The old Whittaker place loomed in the distance. Heaps of junk rose from the mansion's former front lawn. Rats scuttled everywhere, chewing and foraging among the trash bags overflowing with rotting produce and half-empty yogurt cups. How would she ever find a tiny marble in all this?

She licked her lips nervously as she glanced around, willing herself to remain calm, commanding herself to focus. What the situation required was strong mental discipline. What it really required was the skill of observing.

Whispering her thanks to Rochester for his teachings, she grew still, clearing her mind and slowing her breathing. Existing in the moment, she listened to the scritchings and scratchings and squeakings of the rats. She sniffed the tangy, overripe stink of spoiled food. The coolness of the morning air pressed in all around her. Then she examined the scene before her.

Up ahead, she spied the shallow cardboard box Aunt Caroline had put her in. She stepped over to get a closer look. Rhett sat up inside it, clutching a puffy Cheez Doodle. "Hey, are you alive?" he asked. A moment later, he cried out, "Oh! You are alive!" He shoved the rest of the Cheez Doodle into his mouth.

Nim's heart ached at the sight of her former self cowering in the box, remembering all too well how hurt and discouraged she'd been at that moment.

The rising sun was lightening the sky to a blue gray. Nim ran her gaze over mangled lawn chairs, busted televisions, and rusting appliances, past broken furniture, torn mattresses, and dented paint cans. But there was no sign of the tiny marble. What if she hadn't actually seen Dragon's Eye when she'd been at the dump? If she couldn't find out where it went, what would become of Rhett?

She shook the thoughts away. Refocusing on the lessons

Rochester taught her, she studied her surroundings again.

As she let her senses and instincts lead the way, her eyes drifted to the entrance of the main burrow, where a gathering of young rats played nearby. One chewed on a pencil gripped in its tiny pink paws. Two others played a game of tug-of-war with a piece of twine. A fourth one poked his pointy nose out of the burrow's entrance, sniffing and wiggling his whiskers. He glanced around at the others, as though checking to make sure none were watching. Then he ducked back into the hole.

Nim's ears perked at the sight of the suspicious behavior. She stared hard at the burrow's entrance, her muscles tensing, her heart hoping.

A few seconds later, the small rat reappeared, exiting backward. His white-spotted hind end emerged first as he tugged something forward with his front paws.

Nim held her breath, not daring to blink.

When the tiny rodent had backed all the way out, he turned and nudged a round object over the ground—a small, clear glass ball with a swirl of bright green set inside it.

"Dragon's Eye!" Nim whispered, her whiskers jutting at attention.

She watched as the young rat rolled the scuffed and scratched marble away. All that fuss and upset for such a small, ragged thing? She shook her head. It certainly didn't look like much of a treasure, but then again, not everyone saw things the same way.

The little rat came to a stop at an old, rusted washing machine. He reached underneath and pried open the lid of a tin can that was wedged there. A trove of round items had been stashed inside it: a golf ball, a tiny Christmas ornament, a handful of wooden beads. The rat rolled the cat's-eye marble into the can, nudged the lid closed with its nose, then darted off.

Nim leaped to her paws and raced back toward her crossroads, amazed that her idea had actually worked. It took only a moment to realize her shoulders were held high as she ran. She might even have been moving with the dignity and bearing of a big jungle cat. She grinned, imagining how proud Abraxas would be, and she wished she could offer him something in return for his confidence-inspiring advice.

When she arrived at her crossroads, Hecate and her crow were gone. Nim's thoughts still lingered on the big ginger cat, remembering his sad face when he'd mumbled about lost things and not finding them.

She came to a stop, her ears swiveling as she wondered. Had Abraxas lost an important item she could help him find? Would he even let her into his dream to see if she could?

She took a step toward the road that would take her to him. There was still plenty of time before the sovereign was due to return to the mansion. It wouldn't take long to lead Abraxas to his memories so he could see where he'd misplaced the item. If he found it again in the physical world, maybe he wouldn't be so grumpy all the time.

Nim set off along the middle road, determined to put her abilities to good use and accomplish one more helpful deed before she awoke. Though knowing Abraxas, she suspected he'd just kick her out of his dream again.

CHAPTER 26

A s Nim walked, she grew lighter at the thought of Rhett soon being released from his prison.

Suddenly, Rhett appeared up ahead, and she knew her thoughts had brought her to him. She stopped and stared as he stood on a stage, still dressed in his sock sweater and taking alternating bites from the cracker and piece of cheese clutched in each paw. A bright spotlight shone down on him. From all around came the sounds of cheers and applause.

"Hello, Nimbus!" he called to her.

"Rhett," she called back, "I know where Dragon's Eye is! You'll be free soon!"

He took another bite of the cracker. "Thanks, Nimbus," he said as crumbs rained onto the stage. Then he took a big bite of cheese. "The food here is really good!"

Smiling, she refocused her thoughts on finding Abraxas.

She hadn't walked long when the road turned grassy beneath her paws. A chain-link fence sprang up around her, and she realized she was in a backyard. A garden hose lay coiled nearby. Half-gnawed rawhide bones were strewn everywhere. A barbecue grill stood on a cement patio behind a white stucco house, and the sun shone bright overhead.

Growls met her ears, and she whirled around, confused for a moment by the strange sight. Then she remembered she was still in the dream realm where anything was possible.

On the lawn, Abraxas was wrestling a huge rust-colored bear that was wearing a dog collar and tag. Nim couldn't see the name engraved on it, only that it began with the letter *S*.

She watched hesitantly for a moment, not sure if Abraxas would be angry to see her intruding on his dreams again. Then, recalling his advice, she lifted her shoulders, allowing her confidence to erase her doubts, and she moved toward them.

The snarling cat and bear tumbled and rolled. Abraxas ended up standing upon the bear's back, his tail swishing victoriously and the silver lion charm gleaming from his collar. "Beg for mercy!" he shouted.

"Never!" the bear cried, his voice sounding muffled due to his snout being pressed into the ground.

At the sight of Nim, Abraxas froze and bent his ears back.

"Hi, Abraxas," she called cheerfully, despite her growing nervousness.

He stared at her for a moment, as though trying to decide how to respond. Then he gave her a small nod. "Hello, Nimbus."

"I don't have much time," she said, "but I think I can help you find the thing you lost."

He narrowed his eyes. "What makes you think I lost something?"

She shifted her feet uneasily. "I heard you mention it tonight at the cottage."

Beneath Abraxas, the huge bear turned his face to the side and spat out a blade of grass. "Can we get on with the battle?"

Abraxas gave the bear a small swat to the back of its head.

"I can lead you to a place where you might find that thing," Nim said. "You just have to trust me."

Abraxas scowled at her.

"Fern and Bianca were pleased with their dream walks."

Nim hesitated. "Well, Rochester's wasn't so great. But I wouldn't lead you to the nightmare place."

Abraxas continued studying her, his frown slowly fading. He looked down at the bear, who was now yawning and drumming his claws against the ground. Sadness filled his eyes, then he sighed. "Why not?" He hopped off the bear and strolled toward Nim. "Where are we going?"

"This way." Motioning for him to follow, she turned her thoughts to finding his crossroads. "All we have to do is revisit your memories and see if you can find the thing you misplaced."

"I didn't misplace it," he said as the backyard faded behind them. "It was taken away from me by the parents of my previous human family."

"I'm sorry," Nim said, and she truly was. "What did they take?"

"Striker."

She turned to him, tilting her head to one side. "What's a striker?"

"Not a what. A who. Striker was the family's dog, and he was my best friend."

"A dog?" Nim gaped at him, then snapped her mouth shut. If her best friend was a boy, there was no reason why his couldn't have been a dog.

The big tabby's eyes grew watery. She offered him a

half smile, desperate to say something comforting. "I bet he was a great dog."

"Yes, he was." Abraxas gazed into the distance, as though he could see Striker there.

"Tell me about him," she said, still hoping to cheer him.

"He was big. Not very furry." Abraxas wrinkled his forehead. "I think he was brown. Or maybe reddish brown. I can hardly remember now." He lowered his eyes, staring down at the road they were traveling. "But he was my friend. That much, I will always remember."

Sadness lapped at Nim's heart. She knew how it felt to be separated from your one true friend. "Why did they take him away?" she asked.

"The family was moving from a house in the country to a small apartment in the city, and they couldn't keep Striker anymore. The parents took him to live with another family where he could run and play in their big yard, and be much happier than in the city." Abraxas's shoulders slumped. "Over the next week, while they finished packing their belongings, I grew despondent. I didn't want to play anymore, and I might have peed in the corner a few times . . . a day. So, right before they moved to the city, the parents took me to the dump and drove away."

A lump rose in Nim's throat. Their stories were so very similar.

"Agatha, of course, took me in and gave me a new home," he continued. "That was five years ago." He gave a sad sigh. "But as the months passed, I started forgetting what Striker looked like. Sometimes I couldn't even remember his name." Abraxas's whiskers drooped. "Soon I'll have completely forgotten my friend."

"Abraxas, I'm sorry," Nim murmured. She couldn't think of anything to cheer him, so they walked on in silence.

When they arrived at the place where the road split into three directions, a glowing forest of sunbeams shone down from the sky. All around them lay fields of tall, rust-colored grass wagging in the breeze like dog tails. Countless mice and lizard carcasses lay scattered about.

Off to the right, bags of garbage and heaps of junk rose like misshapen mountains. The red taillights of a car receded in the distance.

Taking Abraxas to the left to visit one of his Striker memories would certainly help him remember his friend, but Nim had a better idea. Maybe she could take him to the real Striker, or at least the dream version of him. Then they could talk to each other just as she and Fletcher had.

"Is this the magical place you promised to lead me to?" Abraxas asked, glancing around curiously.

Nim nodded. She motioned to the middle road. "This path will lead you to where others dream."

He gave her a skeptical look but didn't argue.

"All you have to do is picture Striker as best as you can."

He bent his ears with concentration as they strode up the roadway and past more fields of waving, rust-colored grass.

Nim desperately hoped he could remember enough of Striker to lead him to his old friend, and she hoped Striker was asleep in the physical world. Otherwise, her plan wouldn't work and Abraxas would not be pleased. But a moment later, they strolled past an old shoe that'd been chewed nearly to shreds. The road turned to grass beneath their feet, and they wove their way through a series of holes that'd been dug in the ground, mounds of fresh soil sitting beside them.

Abraxas cast her a questioning look as they came to a car parked in front of an older brick house. They crept beneath the car and peered out at a wide front yard dotted with statues of deer, squirrels, and garden gnomes. The smell of dog filled Nim's nose, and her eyes widened at the sight of a huge, reddish-brown pit bull.

They watched as the dog chased a fat white rabbit, but as soon as he caught it, it turned into a thick stick. He gave it a few chews before dropping it from his mouth, then turned and lapped water from a bowl the size of a child's wading pool. When he was done, he looked up and small, crunchy treats smelling like turkey and gravy rained down. He raced around the lawn, flinging strings of drool and gulping up the tasty morsels.

"Striker?" Abraxas whispered, his eyes shining.

The dog froze and spun toward them. "Who's there?" he asked in a voice that boomed like thunder.

Abraxas stepped out from under the car, his tail swishing cautiously. "It's me."

Nim remained motionless, watching, hoping.

The dog's ears perked as he fixed his brown eyes on the cat. "Bo?"

"Oh, no," Nim whispered, her heart sinking. Striker had forgotten Abraxas and was now mistaking him for someone else.

To her confusion, though, Abraxas replied, "Yes! It's me!"

"Bo!" the dog boomed.

Nim tilted her head, puzzled for a moment until she realized Bo must have been Abraxas's former name. A grin spread across her face. *Bo* sounded nice, but in her opinion, Abraxas was a far more fitting name for the surly ginger tabby.

Striker dropped to his front paws, his hind end jutting up as he swept his tail side to side.

"Striker, my friend!" Abraxas sauntered over with his tail held high. He strolled back and forth, rubbing his yellow-and-orange-striped side against Striker's rust-colored one. Then he butted his head against the dog's giant face.

Striker gave him a slobbery lick with his wide pink tongue, and Abraxas purred loudly and happily.

From her hiding place beneath the car, Nim thumped her tail against the ground in amusement, wishing Fern, Rochester, and Bianca could see this transformation.

Striker's ears suddenly perked, and he peered in her direction. His face wrinkled with suspicion. "Who's under the car?" he growled.

Nim froze.

"It's just a cat from the house where I live now." Abraxas gave a casual wave of his yellow paw. "She's all right."

Striker's face relaxed, and the smile spread across it again.

Still too afraid to move, Nim crouched with her muscles tensed, yet she couldn't help but feel pleased Abraxas had described her as *all right.*

"Striker," Abraxas said, "I've missed you since they took you to live with your new family."

Striker tipped his head to the side, puzzled. "But they didn't bring me to a new family. They left me outside of a big old burned house, all alone, except for a bunch of unfriendly rats."

"But . . ." Abraxas gaped at him. "The parents told their

children they took you to a nice home, somewhere with a big yard."

Striker shook his head, though he didn't seem sad. "I did find a nice home. Later that day, a lady came by and brought me to her house not far away." He motioned around. "This is where I live now. With two other dogs she took in; this is our front yard." He thrust out his chest. "The lady calls me Thor." Then he licked the top of Abraxas's head. "But you can always call me Striker."

Nim's whiskers tingled with excitement. Striker's description of the burned house sounded just like the old Whittaker mansion. If his new home wasn't far from the dump, then maybe he and Abraxas had been living near one another all this time. She scampered out from under the car and to the edge of the front yard. The old highway ran right in front of it. She looked to one side and saw nothing she recognized. But when she looked the other way, her stomach fluttered at the sight of the old oak and Agatha's rusty green mailbox in the distance.

She turned and hurried back, taking shelter beneath the car again. "Abraxas!" she called, and waved at him.

He trotted over. "Nimbus," he began. He shook his head. "I don't know how to thank you for this."

"Abraxas," she said, her eyes widening with anticipation, "you and Striker are neighbors! Come and see!" She led him to the edge of the yard and motioned to the oak and the mailbox. "Agatha's cottage is right down that dirt road. You can walk here in the physical world and visit Striker anytime."

Abraxas remained quiet, but his eyes grew shiny. Nim wasn't sure if the gleam was happiness or tears. She supposed maybe it was both. "Nimbus," he whispered, "you are indeed a very special cat." He bumped his forehead against her cheek. "Thank you," he said, and this time his voice wasn't a growl—it was soft and kind. "Thank you for helping me find what I thought I had lost forever." Then he galloped back to his friend.

"Striker!" he cried, rubbing circles around the big dog. "I will find you when I wake up, and I will visit you every day!"

Striker gave a happy *woof* and wagged his tail back and forth. The two friends tumbled to the ground, rolling around as Abraxas spat half-hearted hisses and pawed at Striker's snout.

Nim watched them play for a moment, then headed back down the road, eager to return to the physical world. As soon as she told the rat king where to find Dragon's Eye, Rhett would be freed. Things were working out so well! She lifted her shoulders and raised her head. And with a smile, she realized she was indeed walking with confidence.

CHAPTER 27

A loud pounding sounded on the front door, startling Nim awake. The four house cats sprang up, gazing around with eyes wide and ears perked.

More knocks sounded, and Nim scrambled down from her cushion. She scampered after the others as they dove for shelter beneath the sofa.

"Hello?" a woman's voice called from the other side of the door. "I need your help."

Agatha emerged from her bedroom, wearing her slippers and frowning as she drew her housecoat closed. "It's four in the morning, why do they have to show up at all hours of the night?" she grumbled. "I'm getting too old for this nonsense. If they want their cures, they're going to have to start coming to me during the light of day."

The pounding continued as Agatha switched on the floor lamp and pulled open the front door.

A woman in a misbuttoned cardigan sweater, with muddy pants and shoes, stood there. A flowery headscarf was tied beneath her chin, large black sunglasses shielded her eyes, a silk scarf lay wrapped around her neck, and brown leather gloves covered her hands. Except for her forehead, nose, and the lower half of her face, every inch of her remained hidden.

Agatha's frown deepened. "Ridiculous," she muttered, "feeling the need to hide one's identity at this time of the night."

Despite the stranger's unusual choice of clothing, Nim still recognized her. It was Aunt Caroline. Though Nim didn't know why she was dressed that way.

As Agatha stood scowling, Aunt Caroline stepped into the house. She gazed around the dimly lit room, then turned her sunglass-covered eyes on Agatha. "Have you spotted a little black cat? I just took a walk through that dumpy old lawn across the way and didn't see it there. I wondered if maybe it had wandered over here."

In the shadows beneath the sofa, Nim hunkered lower, afraid the woman had come to dispose of her someplace even worse than the dump.

Wincing and rubbing her forehead with the fingertips of

her leather glove, Aunt Caroline went to the old television and peered behind it. "The cat used to belong to a boy, but it attacked him and frightened him terribly." She scratched her cheeks and her chin; then, wincing again, she pushed the nearby floor lamp away. She turned around, and patches of pinkish-white bumps had sprouted against her skin like mosquito bites. She scratched again, and the welts grew redder.

Agatha pursed her lips. "There are four cats that have lived here for years, a ginger tabby, a gray tuxedo, a calico, and a Birman mix. Not a black cat among them. It appears you've wasted your time. Goodbye."

Ignoring her, Aunt Caroline stepped over to the side table, scratching the bridge of her nose as she peered down through her dark sunglasses at Nim's cushion. She poked it with one of her leather-gloved fingers. "Hmmm, black cat hair."

Agatha's eyes narrowed, and her voice grew cold. "There's nothing here for you." She drew out her owl amulet and let it drop against the front of her housecoat.

"I think the boy might be missing the cat now." Aunt Caroline rubbed the back of her glove against her mouth, and when she pulled her hand away, her lips had puffed up. "I'd like to bring it back to him." Smiling tightly, she turned to Agatha. But at the sight of the silver amulet, her smile fell.

"Nimbus," Abraxas whispered, "you must get out of here. You can't let that woman take you."

"There's something not right about her," Bianca growled.

"I concur," Rochester added, twitching the tip of his tail. "Whatever she wants with you, it can't be good."

Keeping her eyes glued on the two women, Nim slowly nodded. She didn't trust Aunt Caroline at all.

"We'll distract her," Fern said. "Then you must run, little one, out the back door and far away."

"Thanks," Nim whispered.

One by one, the four house cats slunk out from beneath the sofa and spread across the floor.

Rochester circled the room, yowling. Bianca leaped up to the bookshelf and struck out a paw. She knocked a metal votive candleholder over the edge, sending it bouncing and clanking against the floor.

Aunt Caroline whirled toward the sound, and Nim scurried out from under the sofa. She slipped into the dark kitchen, where she stopped and peered around the edge of the doorframe.

Aunt Caroline turned to Agatha again, only to find Fern sitting at her mud-crusted feet. The calico bared her fangs and gave a loud hiss. "Shoo!" The woman waved her hand. "Go away, cat."

Fern quickly skittered off.

Aunt Caroline returned her attention to Agatha. "About that black cat, I know it's here." She gave her splotched face another scratch.

A snarl sounded from across the room, and Abraxas launched through the air as though he'd been shot from a cannon. He landed on the leg of Aunt Caroline's pants and drove his claws in. She screeched and flailed her gloved hands, desperate to knock him away, but he leaped down and rocketed across the room before she could lay a finger upon him.

"Leave my house." Agatha's eyes flashed with anger. She pulled the front door fully open and stepped away to allow the woman a wide passage.

Aunt Caroline took a reluctant step forward, then stopped. "The boy, Fletcher, is not feeling well and seeing the cat again will cheer him. Surely you can't be that selfish. Think of the poor little boy and help me return his pet to him."

Nim's heart dropped. She didn't like hearing Fletcher was sick. Though in their dream walk, he did say he thought he was coming down with something, and that Aunt Caroline might be too. Nim furrowed her brow. Maybe Aunt Caroline had a cold and that's why she was dressed so strangely. Nonetheless, she didn't trust the woman. She turned and slipped out through the cat door.

CHAPTER 28

Though it was morning, it was still dark outside. Stars twinkled in the black sky. Coolness hung in the air, and dewdrops draped the ground.

As Nim rushed down the back steps and past Agatha's gardens, she couldn't stop thinking about the strange way Aunt Caroline had been dressed. It was as if she'd been too preoccupied with something else. But what could be so important? Nim's heart gave a painful thump as she rounded the corner of the cottage. *Was Fletcher sicker than Aunt Caroline had let on?*

Parked next to the dump, Aunt Caroline's car sat with the driver's door hanging open, as though she'd leaped from the vehicle in a hurry. But Aunt Caroline wasn't the hurrying kind.

Nim tensed with dread. Aunt Caroline must've believed Fletcher was extremely ill. Why else would she come all the way out here at this time of the morning to bring her back home? Now certain that something was very wrong with Fletcher, Nim came to a halt.

Maybe she shouldn't wait for the truck. She didn't know how long it would take her to walk home from the flower shop; she might not reach Fletcher until much too late tonight.

She twitched her ears with indecision. Maybe it'd be better if she returned with Aunt Caroline after all. She'd just have to do it without the woman seeing her. She could hide in the car, then sneak into the house when they arrived. It would be risky, but Nim's instincts were insisting she get back to Fletcher as soon as possible.

She hurried to the car, noticing it was muddy and covered with scratches and dents. Aunt Caroline was definitely not herself. She went to the driver's door and peered in. Aunt Caroline's purse lay open on the seat with the car key sitting inside it, as if in her haste, she'd left them behind. This had to be even more proof the woman was panicking and fearful for Fletcher.

Nim's breath caught. Was Fletcher so sick he might be in danger of dying? She shook her head. "Oh, Fletcher, I should've been there with you!" Her shoulders sagged under the weight of her shame and sorrow. She knew the Ways of Magic still wouldn't let her remain with him, but if Fletcher wanted to see her again, she would go to him and comfort him. She would do anything she could to help him. She crouched, about to leap into the car when she remembered her task.

"Rhett!" She couldn't leave him in jail. The sovereign had allowed her only until daybreak to reveal the location of Dragon's Eye. Nim lifted her paw, never having felt so unsure in her life.

She glanced at the Whittaker place. She glanced back at the car.

Sighing heavily, she shook her head. She had to free Rhett, and she had to do it now. If she ran to the old house as fast as she could, she might be able to tell the king where to find his marble before Aunt Caroline drove away.

She bolted toward the mansion. Her old leg injury ached, and the demon wound in her side stung with pain, but she didn't slow down. Fletcher and Rhett needed her.

When she arrived at the burned-out room, the sovereign was waiting with Thorn and Bristle at his side. The other two guards remained hunkered around the birdcage. Rhett lay sound asleep on the floor of his jail, smacking his lips and dreamily murmuring, "Very tasty cracker . . . this cheese is so delicious."

"Rhett! I'm back!" Nim exclaimed breathlessly.

His eyes flew open and he scrambled up to his hind legs, wiping imaginary crumbs from his whiskers. "Nimbus! I knew you could do it!"

"Then I assume you've discovered the location of Dragon's Eye," the sovereign said.

"Yes!" She nodded, still trying to catch her breath. "A young rat with a white spot on its rear took it from the burrow. You can find it under the rusty old washing machine and inside a can with some other round things."

"A scrounger." The sovereign scowled. "I should have known."

"Ah!" Rhett wrapped his pink fingers around the jail's spindly bars and poked his nose through them. "That makes sense."

"Cinder, go." The sovereign motioned to one of the guards at the cage. The rat skittered away, disappearing into the dark hallway outside the room.

The king then turned to one of the guards at his side. "Bristle, bring back Rhett's shirt."

"It's a sweater," Rhett said.

Bristle scurried out of the room.

"You're free now, Rhett!" Nim turned to leave, but Thorn's words stopped her.

"The prisoner cannot be released until Dragon's Eye

has been safely returned. It's the law."

The sovereign nodded. "Thorn is correct."

"Please!" Nim shifted from paw to paw. "Can't you just free him now?"

"Nimbus, what's wrong?" Rhett's whiskers quivered with concern.

"I have to catch a ride with Aunt Caroline to get home to Fletcher right away. I have to get to her car before she leaves!"

Rhett's eyes widened. "Right now? And with the awful aunt who dumped you here in the first place?"

"Fletcher's very sick. Aunt Caroline's so worried that she's not thinking clearly. She even forgot her car key on the front seat and left the door hanging open." Nim swallowed down the lump in her throat. "I'm afraid Fletcher might be dying." Tears filled her eyes at the thought of a world without Fletcher in it.

Rhett's whiskers sagged. "Gee. I'm sorry to hear that."

"Raider," the king ordered the remaining guard at the cage, "hurry to this car and take the key. Keep it away from the woman until Nimbus has climbed on board."

"Yes, sire." Raider dashed off.

Rhett nodded enthusiastically. "Oh, that's a good idea. You're very clever, sire!"

"You would do that for me?" Nim gaped at the sovereign.

He nodded. "I hope you make it back to the city." He stared at her pointedly. "And I hope you will stay there."

"Thank you," she whispered. She didn't bother telling him the Ways of Magic would not allow that.

Inside the cage, Rhett scrunched his brow. "Sire, are you sure Raider's the best one for the job?" He cupped a hand to the side of his mouth and whispered, "You know how he has that unfortunate pooping problem when he gets nervous."

"What will you do to the thief?" Nim asked the sovereign, hoping she hadn't gotten the small rat into trouble. "He's just a little thing. Please don't put him in a cage."

"We don't imprison our young," the king replied. "We're not that heartless. The juvenile scrounger will be punished appropriately, though. He must learn there are some items that may not be taken for oneself."

Rhett nodded, further explaining to Nim, "It's fair game to collect anything you find in the dump, but it's forbidden to take heirlooms from the treasure room."

"It's also forbidden to take property from rat territory and give it to predators," Thorn snarled.

Rhett scowled and stuck his tongue out at him.

With Rhett's sock sweater clutched in his teeth, Bristle skittered back into the room and dropped it beside the cage. Then Cinder returned, carrying a cat's-eye marble in his mouth. He hurried to the sovereign and set it at his feet.

The sovereign turned the scuffed orb over and over, studying the wave of green inside it. Seeming pleased with the condition of the heirloom, he motioned to Cinder. "Release the captive and allow him the return of his shirt."

"It's a sweater," Rhett corrected him again.

Cinder opened the cage door and Rhett darted out, snatching his sweater. He pulled the garment over his head, then smoothed it down over his belly. His eyes brightened, his whiskers perked, and he looked like himself again.

Still clutching Dragon's Eye in his paws, the sovereign declared, "As per our agreement, Rhett's other belongings will remain unharmed."

"Thanks, but I don't need them." Rhett flapped his paw at the king. "You can have all of it gnawed up if you want to. I'm leaving the colony for the bright lights of the big city. Setting off to seek stardom and fame."

The king nodded. "Perhaps that is for the best."

Rhett gave him a bow. "Goodbye, sire." He dropped onto his four paws, then slipped out through the broken window.

Nim gave the king a polite nod. "Thanks for your help." She hurried after Rhett, calling over her shoulder, "Good luck with your marble!"

Under the dark morning sky, she scampered through the mansion's tangled backyard and caught up to Rhett. "Are you sure about this?" she asked. "Do you really want to leave your home and your family?"

He stopped beside the toppled birdbath. All around them the garden hummed and chirped with the singing of night insects. He gave a dramatic sigh and gazed off in the direction where the dump lay, as though he could see it through the walls of the old mansion. "All the world's a stage, Nimbus. And all the men, women, and rats are merely players: they have their exits and their entrances."

"More Shakespeare?" she asked.

He nodded. "Except for the part about rats. I added that." He gave a satisfied smile, then hurried off.

Nim followed him, surprised by how pleased she was that she wouldn't be making the journey alone.

As they drew near the car, they caught sight of Aunt Caroline hunched and tromping through the dump, peering at the ground through her dark sunglasses. "I will find you, you vile, key-thieving vermin," she growled. "If I had my way, every one of your kind would be exterminated."

A powerful uneasiness enveloped Nim. While Aunt

Caroline had never been the nicest of people, Nim had never seen her lose control of her anger like that.

With a loud squeal, and clutching the car key in his teeth, Raider leaped from an old tire and zipped past the woman's feet.

"There you are!" she screeched, and she set off after him.

Nim and Rhett jumped into the car. The contents of Aunt Caroline's purse lay spilled across the front seat. Among the coins, tissues, and tubes of lipstick were a sprinkling of tiny dark pellets that looked and smelled very much like rat droppings.

"Rhett, this is dangerous." Nim's heart was pounding hard. "You heard what Aunt Caroline said about rats. If she finds you, she might hurt you . . . or do something worse."

Rhett shrugged. "We rats are pretty good at avoiding danger. And besides, I can't let you do this alone. You might need my help."

"Thanks, Rhett." Nim gave him a grateful smile. "Just please make sure she doesn't see you." She peered over her shoulder.

Raider was winding his way through the dump with the key still clutched in his mouth; Aunt Caroline chased after him, calling him names. He scrambled to the top of a rickety wire shelving unit, then glanced over at Nim.

She gave him a nod, and he dropped the key onto

Aunt Caroline's upturned face.

"Ow!" she cried, rubbing her rash-covered nose and muttering more insults. She snatched up a moldy old boot and threw it, missing the rat as he skittered away.

With Rhett right behind her, Nim was scrambling toward the back floorboard when she spotted Aunt Caroline's picnic basket on the back seat. She and Rhett slipped in, letting the hinged lid drop shut behind them.

Rhett snuggled down in a corner of the empty hamper and wrapped his long pink tail around him.

"I'm glad you're here with me, Rhett," Nim whispered.

"I'm glad to be here with you, Nimbus," he replied.

Filled with worry, Nim curled into a ball, comforting herself with the possibility that Fletcher might get better. And when he did, she would dream walk with him again to explain the demon attack and why she wouldn't be able to stay with him. She clenched her jaw. And before she left the house, she would destroy any other monster that might be hiding inside the second old jar.

The sounds of muttering and stomping feet approached the car.

The back door opened.

With spaghetti noodles clinging to her sweater sleeves and coffee grounds encrusting her gloves, Aunt Caroline lifted the basket and gave it a shake, sending Nim and

Rhett jostling inside it. "Got you!" she cried. Then she dropped the basket back onto the seat and glanced around nervously. "We can't stay here, though," she muttered to herself. "The old witch might stop me."

She stared off toward the cottage. "They're all the same," she sneered. "Witches, warlocks, whatever it is they call themselves. They're nosy and tricky." Her sneer turned to a scowl as she looked up at the dark blue twilight of the early morning sky, twisting her fingers in agitation. "Too much time has passed anyway, too much time wasted crashing this car into things and getting it stuck in the mud. I must hurry back."

Nim's heart hammered. What was it that Aunt Caroline didn't want anyone to stop her from doing? Something was very wrong with her, something far worse than any concern for Fletcher's health.

Aunt Caroline leaned into the rear seat again. As she latched the basket, a cold, ancient mustiness wafted off her. The odor was laced with the smells of panic and fear—the stench of a nightmare demon.

Nim's stomach twisted. Had the foolish woman been handling the other jar? Had she somehow opened it?

Aunt Caroline climbed into the front seat, then paused and sniffed the air. She looked down at the spilled contents of her purse and lifted a small black pellet. "Rat poop." She frowned in disgust as she wiped her hand on the front of her sweater. "Stinking key thief! The next rat I see, I will stomp it."

Inside the basket, Nim and Rhett gazed at one another, their eyes wide and frightened.

Aunt Caroline peered into the rearview mirror, scowling as she poked at her swollen lips. "A horrible old woman," she grumbled, "with a horrible, repulsive lamp." She scratched furiously at the red bumps on her face and snarled with anger.

Within the confines of the car, the sour smells of the dump were quickly overpowered by the evil, ancient odor. The demonic stench seemed to soak through Nim's fur, intensifying her own panic and fear.

"Now that I finally have you, little black cat, I'm going to take back what you stole from me the night we battled," the woman said.

Nim began to tremble. She'd never stolen anything from Aunt Caroline, and they'd certainly never battled. The only being she ever fought was the nightmare demon from the old jar Fletcher opened. Cold, heavy dread settled onto her shoulders as she remembered Lady Hecate's words: *Blinding the creature granted you its dream sight.*

Nim peered through the side of the picnic basket, and she had a terrible realization. The woman sitting there wasn't Aunt Caroline. Nim didn't understand what was happening, only that it had something to do with the night-mare demon.

But she had destroyed it. Hadn't she?

"All I wanted was to return home to the place where nightmares dwell," the fake Aunt Caroline continued, "to just seep through a shadowy hole in the floor into the infinitely branching tunnels between this world and mine." Her voice turned stony. "But I no longer possessed enough dream sight to guide me through the tunnels anymore. Because of you, I was stuck here in this world."

Nim's insides iced over, and her trembling grew more intense. She hadn't really destroyed the nightmare demon.

She hadn't protected Fletcher at all.

CHAPTER 29

The creature pretending to be Aunt Caroline rammed the key into the ignition. After turning the car around in the middle of the dirt road, it backed into the grassy field, then forward into the dump, then back again before zooming off. It took a sharp turn onto the old highway, swerving across lanes, veering on and off the shoulders of the road.

Nim's fur prickled and her breath quickened as she dug her claws into the bottom of the basket.

The Aunt Caroline impostor tipped its head back and inhaled through its nose. "Ah . . . the intoxicating aromas of panic and fear." It chuckled, but there was no merriment in the sound. "It's your own fault, you know. If you hadn't attacked me, you wouldn't be in this situation." Its voice grew colder. "And neither would I." The phony Aunt

Caroline tightened its grip on the steering wheel as they raced along the old highway.

The car veered to the side of the road, then back to the center, slowing and speeding, lurching its way through the early morning darkness. The impostor drove in silence for a moment, then spoke again. "You've made things very difficult for me," it snarled. "After you attacked me, I had to hide in the little shed in the backyard, burrowed into a bag of potting soil. I only had the terror of the roaches scuttling around in there to tide me over during the daylight hours."

A shiver rippled through Nim, and Rhett grimaced as if the thought of eating roach emotions were too unappetizing to contemplate.

"All I wanted was to grow strong and go home," the fake aunt said petulantly. "But I needed to regain my missing dream sight for that. So when the lights went out in the house the next night, I drifted back inside but couldn't find you. I returned to the boy's room instead; fortunately, I heard the two of you talking in the dream realm as I prepared to pull him into a nightmare." The demon sighed contentedly, as though recalling a fond memory. "Once I learned his aunt had taken you away, of course, I fed again. The boy's life force is so tempting, after all. And nearly gone too. Such a shame there are only three portions to consume."

Fletcher's life force! Nim's eyes widened. The tiny flickering light the goblin demon had eaten wasn't Fletcher's night terrors. It was a part of his very life! And it was the demon who'd pulled him from their dream walk last night. A surge of rage rushed through her, and she thumped her tail furiously.

The fake Aunt Caroline sniffed the air again. "Is that anger I smell? Not as fulfilling as panic or fear, though still a tasty morsel." It tapped its gloved fingers against the steering wheel. "But if anyone should be angry, it's me! The boy's foolish aunt had taken too much cold medicine and wouldn't wake that night. I was forced to wait another day to find you."

Nim was hardly listening; she didn't care that the creature had gotten furious and poured the cold medicine down the sink. The only thing that mattered was that Fletcher was very near death.

The fake Aunt Caroline, or the *demon aunt*, as Nim now thought of the horrible being, released a heavy sigh. "Listen to me, just babbling on. It's your intense emotions that have me so keyed up." The demon sniffed again. "Your scents are odd, though. There's a mingled quality to them, as if they're emanating from two different sources." It gave an angry hiss. "It's probably because you possess half my dream sight." It gripped the steering wheel tighter. "I really despise you, cat."

It sped up the car, swerved, and hit a pothole, sending

the picnic basket bouncing up and down. Nim had no doubt it'd done it on purpose.

The demon aunt muttered to itself for a while before returning its attention to Nim. "Finally, tonight, I was able to settle inside the woman's head as soon as she fell asleep. Human minds are quite easy to manipulate, you know. I made her lead me to you."

The car swerved again as the demonic Aunt Caroline peered through the window and up at the sky. "No need to worry," it murmured to itself. Though it sounded very worried. "There's still enough time."

Enough time for what? Nim wondered. The sides of the basket seemed to close in on her. She desperately wanted to climb out and run far away from the creature. Rhett appeared to want the same thing as he gazed at Nim with fearful, rounded eyes.

"I confess, I'm pleased to have finally retrieved you," the demon aunt continued, relief now filling its voice. "I was most anxious to get you back as soon as possible. I didn't even stop to feed tonight. What if you ran away, or got run over, or were killed by another animal? Then I'd be trapped in this wretched world forever."

A half hour before daybreak, the car skidded to a stop, sending the basket crashing to the floorboard. A moment later, the demon aunt hauled it into the house.

Rhett rested a warm paw on one of Nim's. As she stared at him, her courage began to return. She didn't know how she was going to help Fletcher, only that somehow, she had to.

Without switching on any lamps or overhead lights, the demon strode through the dark house. It paused in front of the tall wall mirror, scowling and staring into it through its dark sunglasses. "I'll be glad to leave this body now that it has served me well." It turned Aunt Caroline's face side to side. "At least those horrid bumps have stopped itching."

It made its way to Fletcher's father's office, easily maneuvering through the darkness. There, it dropped the basket onto the huge desk with a thump.

Frowning in disgust, it used a pencil to push Fletcher's favorite arrow over the side. It clattered to the floor, and the demon aunt kicked it away before removing the scarves from its head and neck. While spaghetti noodles and rat poop still clung to its sweater, the faint smell of the dump was overpowered by the demon's strong, ancient stench.

Nim bared her teeth as she crouched inside the basket.

Staring through the lenses of its dark sunglasses, the demon pointed up at the tall shelf and the ancient clay jar sitting alongside the figurines of the Mummy, Dracula, the Creature from the Black Lagoon, and the Wolf Man.

"Do you see that vessel," it sneered, "that *prison* that still holds one of my sisters? I was locked in mine for thousands of years too."

Nim bent her ears back, uninterested in any more of the creature's ramblings, wanting only to escape and rush upstairs to Fletcher.

"And all due to a tricky old sorceress who used her magic to travel to the place where nightmares dwell and lure us away."

Keeping its gaze fixed upward, the fake aunt shook its head in disappointment as it spoke to the jar. "It was hard for us to ignore such a special life force, my sister. Wasn't it? We all wanted to consume it and become more powerful. But that sorceress was too clever, speaking her terrible incantation that bound us in clay prisons, ensuring that only those of her ilk could release us." The demon aunt pursed its lips disapprovingly. "So despicable of her to do the same thing night after night, capturing legions of us to do her bidding."

Nim thumped her tail, glad to hear it. The evil nightmare demons deserved it.

"Wicked, wicked old woman," the phony Aunt Caroline muttered in disgust. Then it sighed. "I'm sorry, my sister," it said, keeping its eyes on the jar, "but you must wait a bit longer. I don't plan to leave the boy around to release you as well. You'll just have to stay in there until someone else comes along to free you."

Desperate to get to Fletcher, Nim attacked the basket, ferociously clawing and tearing at its sides.

The demon picked up the basket and lugged it toward the kitchen, swinging it widely, banging it into the walls as it went. "Once I've regained my dream sight, I will consume the third and final portion of the boy's life force." Then it added, "Three is quite the mystical number, isn't it? Birth, life, and death. Past, present, and future. Breakfast, lunch, and dinner. The list goes on."

Nim hissed, yearning to scratch and bite the monstrous being that was controlling Aunt Caroline, anything to keep it away from Fletcher.

"Well, we need to eat too." The demon huffed. "I don't see why you should begrudge me a few meals."

It set the basket on the kitchen table, pulled off its sunglasses, then leaned close. It glared at Nim through one of Aunt Caroline's hazel eyes and one electric-yellow eye.

Nim hissed again, readying herself to leap out and race upstairs to Fletcher to protect him however she could.

The monster unlatched the basket. Moving quicker than Nim had expected, it lifted the lid and yanked her out by her scruff.

As Nim twisted and spat, the fake Aunt Caroline gasped and reared back with a grimace. "A protection amulet!" It slammed Nim onto the tabletop, sending a hot flare of pain through her wounded side and leaving her too dazed to move.

"Hateful things!" The creature snatched a pair of tongs from a nearby canister, clamped them onto Nim's collar, and yanked it off over her head. Swaying, and with eyes squeezed shut, it flung the collar and tongs through the kitchen doorway and into the hall. "Oh," it moaned, "I don't feel so well." It gulped and took a shaky breath. "Disgusting amulets," it hissed. Holding Nim down with one hand, it pulled off the brown leather glove from the other with its teeth.

Glaring, the demon woman pressed the tip of its index finger to Nim's forehead, just as it had with Fletcher when it had appeared as the small goblin creature.

The strength drained from Nim's muscles. Her body grew heavy, her head grew light, and a numbing paralysis spread throughout her. She wanted to fight, to free herself, but she couldn't move.

The demon whispered a string of menacing words, different from the ones it'd spoken over Fletcher but sounding just as ancient and malevolent. Nim's head throbbed and hummed, and as she closed her eyes, the nightmare demon took a deep inhale.

A part of Nim's mind seemed to slip away. And with a

pang of sorrow, she knew it was the dream sight leaving. She'd never be able to walk in the dream realm or talk with Fletcher there again.

From somewhere beside her, a squeal pierced the air, and a gray streak flew from the open basket.

It landed on the demon aunt's arm, and with a yelp of surprise, it released its hold on Nim. "A rat!" it screeched. "Vile vermin!" Growling in fury, the creature yanked off the other glove and struck Rhett as he sank his teeth into its sweater sleeve.

No longer under the creature's power, Nim felt the strength begin to seep back into her body. She struggled up to her feet as the demon woman wrenched Rhett from its sleeve, flung him into the basket, and latched the lid. "Vile! Disgusting! Rat!"

Nim tried to limp away, but the monster's cold hands seized her. It pressed her down and touched her forehead again.

Nim managed a small hiss before her limbs grew heavy and she grew still.

The nightmare demon repeated the ominous words, and this time, Nim's consciousness slipped away.

CHAPTER 30

Nim stood at the crossroads beneath the purple sky and the white crescent moon.

"Hello, Nimbus," Hecate said. A line of black, spindly-legged spiders crept around her neck, circling it over and over like a living necklace.

"Lady Hecate! Fletcher's in trouble, and so am I!" Nim's whiskers bristled with agitation as she shifted from paw to paw. "The nightmare demon came back like you said it might, and it's taking the dream sight from me. Then it's going to steal the rest of Fletcher's life force! How can I stop it?"

Hecate shook her head sadly. "It's not my purpose to tell you what to do. You must choose your own path, as you have done in your previous dream walks."

"Just this once, can't you tell me?" A flash of white lit the sky like lightning, and Nim jumped.

"Sometimes one must discover a truth, rather than having it told to them," Hecate said.

Nim lifted a paw in confusion. "Please! How can I destroy the nightmare demon?"

"You must figure it out on your own. Only then will you realize who you are."

The sky flashed white again. Hecate cast a glance up. "Your time here is growing short. You need to hurry, Nimbus."

Nim peered around in panic. Cracks were spreading across the ground at the entrances to each path.

With her pulse racing, she turned left. Her memories had helped her before; maybe she could find answers there again. Thunder boomed overhead, vibrating the ground. The smell of stormy weather filled her nose. She glanced behind her, tucking her tail at the sight of the roiling, lightning-streaked clouds racing from the nightmare place and toward the crossroads. She turned and ran, galloping as fast as she could.

Maybe taking a closer look at her memory of the possessed Aunt Caroline would show her how to destroy the demon once and for all. Nim focused on returning to the cottage, to the time when the demon aunt had arrived.

Up ahead on the side of the road, Aunt Caroline's scarves lay twisting and writhing. As Nim drew closer, they transformed into venomous, hissing snakes and struck out at her. She leaped away and continued onward, coming upon the demon aunt's brown gloves lying in the middle of the path. They stood up, as if their fingers were legs, and chased her as she ran, soon falling behind. Overhead, the clouds grew dark purple. A jagged white flash struck the sky. Holes opened on the road before her, and she hopped over them, not understanding what was happening.

Thunder boomed louder. The stormy weather was catching up to her. She ran on. A car suddenly zoomed past. She leaped out of the way, and a loud, rumbling truck sped after it.

Nim thought of the cottage and the demon aunt's arrival there with all her might.

Hurry, Nim! a voice whispered behind her.

The road dipped and rolled beneath her paws as she ran. Then it crumbled and fell away before her. She skidded to a halt, staring down into the bottomless depths below. She scrambled away, dashing into the grassy field alongside the road. A dirt path appeared between the tall blades of grass, and she took it. Soon the back of the cottage rose ahead.

She dove through the cat door, scampered across the

tilting floor, and came to a stop in the living room. Breathlessly, she studied the impostor in its dark sunglasses, misbuttoned sweater, and muddy shoes, searching for something she might've overlooked, any hint at a way to defeat the demon.

As Agatha and the monster woman argued, the house cats crept from beneath the sofa and fanned out around the room. Bianca jumped to the top of the bookcase, knocked the candleholder off the shelf, and it thumped to the floor. She fixed her bright blue eyes on Nim. "Pushing something over the edge is a great way to get someone's attention."

When Nim looked down at the candleholder, though, it had become Fletcher's flashlight. It spun in a lazy circle and stopped with its beam directed on the books lining the bottom shelf. But Agatha's copies of *Jane Eyre* and *Charlotte's Web* weren't there. In their place stood *The Hobbit*.

This memory wasn't right. Nim furrowed her brow. This wasn't the way these things had really happened.

Rochester sat up straight and tall beside her. "You'll find countless applications for the valuable skill of observation." He pointed a white-gloved paw at the flashlight's beam. Then he rose and strolled away.

Nim's heart jolted as understanding flared. She hadn't arrived at the place where her memories dwelled; she was now in a dream of her own making, one that her mind had stitched together from pieces of her memories and fears.

As Rochester began yowling and circling the room, Abraxas strode toward her, his huge ginger paws padding silently across the floor. He drew up next to her. "You must allow an unwavering belief in yourself to overtake you and erase your doubts," he said.

Fern scampered over, a serene smile filling her calico face. She came to a stop on Nim's other side. "Grasp your prey by the back of the neck, little one!" She swished her tail cheerfully. "Be mindful to position your mouth where the skull meets the backbone. Then drive your teeth in and sever the spine!" She licked the top of Nim's head. Then, purring loudly, she trotted off.

Abraxas fixed his orange eyes on Nim, staring at her intently. "Will you remember these things?" he asked.

Nim nodded and gulped. "I will."

Outside the cottage window, streaks of white zigzagged down from the dark purple clouds overhead. Thunder rumbled, shaking the glass panes. The front door blew open. A gust of wind roared in and swept up Nim, spinning her around, blurring colors and scenery. It whisked her outside, whirling her through the lightning-cracked sky and dropping her with a hard thump at her crossroads.

She climbed to her wobbly legs, the purple world fading to lavender as if morning light were racing up the horizon.

"Goodbye, Nimbus." Hecate gave her a sad smile.

The goddess stood gazing down at her, but the spiders no longer circled her neck. This time, a shiny black snake lay wrapped around her wrist like a thick, scaly bracelet. It lifted its head and licked the air with its forked tongue, then bit down on its own tail.

Nim reached out a paw, hoping to somehow anchor herself to the dream realm, at least long enough to ask the goddess what the nonsensical dream images meant.

A blast of white light obscured her vision. Hecate's voice floated through her head: *You're far cleverer and more courageous than you think you are. You only need to believe it.*

Nim awoke at home on the kitchen table. Her eyesight was bleary, her thoughts were jumbled, and she couldn't identify the strange scraping and chewing sounds coming from nearby. She tried to leap up, but she'd grown as heavy as a sack of bricks.

The Aunt Caroline demon hovered over her with eyes squeezed shut in relief. "My dream sight is mine again," it whispered.

Nim wanted to snarl ferociously, but the best she could manage was a tiny growl.

The creature opened its eyes, both now glowing yellow in the darkness. A murky membrane slid from one corner to the next, then back again, just like the nictitating eyelids of a reptile. It hadn't seemed to notice that the scraping and chewing had stopped. Nor did it see Rhett wiggle out from a small hole in the side of the basket. With a squeal of attack, he leaped from the table and onto the impostor's sweater sleeve once again.

Screeching and stumbling back, the demon flailed its arm, trying to fling him away.

"Rhett!" Nim cried with worry. She struggled up to her shaky legs.

"Run, Nimbus!" he shouted, jumping from the monster woman's arm and onto the tabletop. He rocketed past Nim and sprang onto the kitchen counter. "Run, Nimbus!" he shouted again as he zoomed back and forth, knocking an empty bottle of nighttime cold medicine into the sink.

Nim hopped off the table as the fake Aunt Caroline lobbed an oven mitt at Rhett. Staggering to the door, Nim glanced back as the monster woman stomped to the counter. With a snarl of rage, it snatched up the mitt and smacked it down, over and over, missing the racing rat every time.

"Rhett, come on!" Nim called. She had nearly reached the doorway when a loud *clang* stopped her in her tracks, and she whirled around.

The glowing-eyed demon woman stood panting with

a frying pan clutched in its hands. Atop the counter, Rhett lay curled on his side.

"Rhett!" Nim took a step toward him.

"No, Nimbus!" he ordered, stopping her in her tracks. "It's too late for me."

"Rhett, get up!" Nim cried.

With a great deal of effort, he lifted his head and fixed his bleary black eyes on her. "'Ay, there's the rub; for in that sleep of death what dreams may come when we have shuffled off this mortal coil.'" He took a deep, wheezing breath, then whispered, *"Hamlet."*

"Rhett!" Nim stepped toward him.

"Run, Nimbus," he murmured. He closed his eyes, and his whiskers wilted. "Save Fletcher." His head fell back, and with his tongue protruding from his half-opened mouth, he lay still.

The scowling nightmare demon poked him with its finger. And when he didn't move, it smiled.

Nim turned and ran.

CHAPTER 31

Nim scooped up her collar as she passed it in the hall and clutched it between her teeth. She cast a glance at her image in the wall mirror; a pair of green eyes gazed out from her reflection, but their brightness no longer filled her with pride. Her yellow eye had vanished, and with it, her ability to walk in the dream realm. That wasn't the only thing she'd lost, though.

She made her way to the dark staircase, her heart heavy as she climbed each step. Rhett was gone too. He'd been a great friend. She'd never thought it possible to have another friend as special as Fletcher, but losing Rhett felt as if a part of her had been broken off and left behind. She swallowed down her sadness. She would grieve later. Right now, Fletcher needed her help, and this time she wouldn't fail him.

When she reached the top of the stairs, she scurried into his dark, quiet room.

Everything smelled the same. Everything appeared the same too: books on the shelf, desk with drawers hanging half-open, overflowing wastepaper basket, jar of arrows sitting on one of the bedside tables. She leaped onto the big bed, her stitches pulling painfully.

Fletcher lay asleep on his back, looking small beneath the huge blanket. He looked thinner, dark circles ringed his eyes, and the fiery-red scratches still marked his face—so different from the way he'd appeared in their dream walk. She laid her collar on his chest as it slowly rose and fell, his breath rattling. The nazar probably wouldn't keep the nightmare demon away, though it might slow it down. Nim licked Fletcher's forehead and rubbed her cheek against his, but he didn't stir.

"Be clever like Gandalf and courageous like Bilbo," she murmured to herself. She lifted her shoulders, just as Abraxas had instructed her. She would fight the nightmare demon with everything she had, and she would destroy it once and for all.

If she could just figure out how to do that.

Footsteps sounded on the staircase.

Nim hopped off the bed. She scrambled to the wastepaper basket next to Fletcher's desk and took shelter behind it. Crouching among the crumpled papers on the floor, she tried to decipher the puzzling images she'd seen in her last dream walk.

The footsteps climbing the staircase drew closer. "Here, kitty kitty," the demon aunt sang.

Remembering Rochester's suggestion that proper observation was calming for the body and soul, Nim tried to relax. Focusing her senses on the doorway, she grew still and observed. Maybe she could learn what she hadn't been able to understand in her dream walk.

The monster woman stepped through the doorway and paused, running its glowing eyes around the room.

Nim remained still as a stone. As she observed the demon, she realized the true Aunt Caroline wouldn't have covered herself with scarves and leather gloves on a warm spring night. She wouldn't have worn sunglasses inside the house either and certainly not while driving in the early morning darkness. Those were choices the nightmare demon had made.

Fixing its yellow gaze on the sleeping Fletcher, the creature moved toward him. Then it suddenly drew back, curling its lip and hissing. It grabbed the pliers from Fletcher's bedside table, then used them to snatch Nim's collar off Fletcher's chest and toss it into the hallway again.

Dropping the pliers to the floor, the demon aunt spoke

to the room. "Protection amulets can keep certain beings away." It smiled wickedly. "But they'll never be able to prevent nightmares. The mind will always invent frightening dreams on its own."

To Nim's satisfaction, the demon still looked a bit ill. The nazar had at least offered a small amount of protection.

The creature took an unsteady step forward. "I know you're in here, cat."

Nim folded her ears back and opened her mouth in a silent hiss.

"Trying to protect the boy, are you? Well, I suppose that's understandable, considering how special he is compared to most dreamers."

Special? Nim's ears slowly rose, then twitched with confusion. Fletcher had always been special to her, but why would the nightmare demon think he was different from any other dreamer?

Seeming to have recovered from the nazar's effects, the demon widened its smile. "Energy such as his has tempted my kind for thousands of years. We covet it because it makes us grow larger and stronger."

Nim's fur bristled. If the creature lunged toward Fletcher, she wouldn't hesitate this time. She would leap out and attack it.

"I have waited patiently for this third and final portion."

The demon woman licked its lips. "With a powerful life force such as his, to consume more than one fragment at a time would have destroyed me. Now my waiting is over."

Nim bared her fangs. She would not let the monster take the last of Fletcher's life force.

"Now, where are you?" the creature murmured. "Are you like me, little cat? Do you admire the night?" It took another step forward. "Do you appreciate how its darkness provides us with so many places to hide?"

Though Nim despised the demon, they did have that in common. The dark was indeed a great place to hide, and yes, she admired the night. When it was dark, sleeping cats didn't have to cover their eyes with their paws to block out the brightness. And only when the sky was black could you gaze in wonder at the stars and the moon. It was the time when night-blooming jasmine shared its fragrant aroma and when beautiful ghostly-green luna moths made their appearance. The night was good.

Nightmare demons were not.

Nim continued studying the Aunt Caroline impostor, thinking again about its strange choice of clothing, remembering how its lips had puffed up and how itchy bumps had erupted on its face. The demon seemed allergic to Agatha's lamp. Or more specifically . . . to its light. That was why it had covered itself with gloves, sunglasses, and scarves. It didn't want any light to touch it.

Nim gazed up at the window blinds. They were drawn tightly shut, preventing any streetlight from coming in. There were no lamps or overhead lights on inside the house either.

"Do you think you have the advantage by hiding from me? Or, are you afraid of me?" The monster woman chuckled. "Oh, if you're afraid of this pathetic human shell, just wait until you see my form specifically summoned by the boy." It leaned down and peered at the lower shelf of the bookcase, as if Nim might be hiding there. Then it stood up again.

Nim remained silent, thinking and observing.

"Did you know we assume the appearance of our victim's worst fear?" The demon prodded Nim's green pillow bed with the toe of its muddy shoe. "Just in case they escape the clutches of our nightmare, we can terrify them in real life. It's delightful how endlessly inventive the human mind can be, especially when it comes to frightening itself."

The monster woman came to a stop. "Would you like to be reacquainted with my chosen form, little thief, the thing that your boy fears the most?" It tilted its head as though waiting for Nim to reply. "Not going to answer?" It chuckled a low, cold laugh. "Then I will show you."

Closing its glowing eyes, it tipped its head back and

spoke in a voice that had grown deep and jagged. "We are riders of the night winds, leapers and crushers, bringers of nightmares. We are those who feast upon panic and fear."

The creature collapsed like a marionette whose strings had been cut, and the temperature in the room plunged. As Aunt Caroline lay motionless on the floor, a sooty smoke spiraled up from her body.

Nim leaped to her trembling legs and arched her back.

A figure was taking shape within the gritty haze, growing taller, its limbs stretching as the smoke slowly dissolved around it.

Tail bushing, Nim stared at the monstrosity standing as tall as Fletcher's father and draped in tattered clothing. It was the same goblin-like creature she'd battled before, only it'd grown much bigger. As she peered closer at the shadowy, musty-smelling form, though, she saw it wasn't wearing torn clothing at all. Its body was actually covered in bandages, and they dangled from its torso in long, dirty ribbons. With a jolt, she realized she'd seen the ragged strips before, though on a much smaller creature, one that was made of plastic and stood on the shelf in Fletcher's father's office. "Bandages like the Mummy's!" she whispered.

Snapping her tail, she studied the two upper fangs protruding from its mouth like Dracula's. She ran her gaze over the rest of the beast. Its hands were webbed and clawed like the Creature from the Black Lagoon. Its ears were pointy, and dark hair sprouted from its arms, legs, and feet like the Wolf Man's.

The Mummy, Dracula, the Creature from the Black Lagoon, and the Wolf Man. Fletcher's greatest fear was a goblin-like jumble of classic movie monsters.

She laid her ears back. But how could it be killed?

Seeming to have forgotten about Nim, the nightmare demon turned away. It took a lumbering step past Fletcher's bookshelf, the ends of its grimy bandages trailing along the floor behind it.

Nim's gaze lingered on the shelves that housed Fletcher's magical fantasy books, and her eyes fixed on *The Hobbit*, the book she'd just seen in her dream walk.

Lady Hecate had told her solutions to problems could be found in the dream realm, but Nim still didn't understand how that book was the answer. She certainly knew its story well enough, recalling even now how the courageous Bilbo had faced down a fearsome dragon and how the clever Gandalf had outsmarted a band of trolls by keeping them arguing until daybreak arrived and turned them to stone.

Across the room, the creature rumbled a deep growl

and fixed its yellow eyes on the sleeping Fletcher.

There was no more time for figuring out dreams. The moment had come to fight. Nim tensed her muscles and unsheathed her claws, readying herself to attack. But when her gaze darted back to the book, an idea sparked inside her mind.

CHAPTER 32

Nim crept out from behind the wastepaper basket, but she didn't head toward the monster. She climbed up the desk's half-opened drawers instead, and she made her way to the window that was tightly covered by the set of closed blinds. She pushed down one of the wooden slats. Outside, the sky had faded to grayish blue.

A whimper sounded behind her, and she glanced back. The nightmare demon had stopped midstride and thrown its hairy arms up, shielding its face from the world beyond the window.

Nim's whiskers tingled with excitement. Just like the trolls in *The Hobbit*, the nightmare demon feared the morning sun. That's why it was so worried about getting home in time. It wanted to make sure it'd taken back its dream sight and consumed Fletcher's life force before the sun rose. If something as small as lamplight could cause it to break out in a rash, what would the sun's powerful light do to it?

The creature spun away from the sight of the pale sky and sprang onto the foot of the bed. It crouched on its webbed hands and hairy feet, staring at Fletcher.

A fierce anger grew up in place of Nim's earlier fears. She released her hold on the blinds, plunging the room into darkness again. The sun would rise soon and destroy the nightmare demon; she was sure of it. But until then, she had to keep the monster from taking the last of Fletcher's life force. Growling and thrashing her tail, she jumped from the desk to the bed. Her wounded side stung, but she didn't stop. With a loud snarl, she leaped onto the crouching demon, sinking her claws into its loose bandages. She scrambled up to the beast's shoulders, remembering Fern's teaching: *Be mindful to position your mouth where the skull meets the backbone. Then drive your teeth in and sever the spine!*

Nim drove her fangs in, and the creature reared its pointy-eared head back in a howl. The musty odors of panic and fear flooded Nim's nose as she sawed her teeth back and forth. Her mouth filled with a terrible, venomous taste. She knew that each bite she inflicted would sicken her, maybe even kill her. Lady Hecate had told her so, but it didn't matter. She would keep Fletcher safe no matter what.

Slinging its head side to side, the nightmare goblin screeched as it swung its hairy arms, frantic to dislodge Nim. More poison seeped into her mouth and raced through her body. Her stitches strained against the wound on her side, but she held on. The demon twisted around and swiped a clawed hand over its shoulder, raking gashes across her neck. She bit harder, and the beast squealed. A wave of sickness crashed over her, and the room spun. Her jaws loosened. Her claws slipped from the monster's flesh.

The creature struck her again with its webbed hands, this time knocking her away. She tumbled over the side of the bed and onto the floor, landing with a painful thump.

A thread of warm blood trickled from her stitched side, mingling with the fresh gashes the demon had inflicted. Her head whirled. Her stomach heaved. She gazed blearily up at the beast. She had to keep it away from Fletcher for only a little longer and then somehow open the blinds. She tried to stand, but her legs folded like soggy cardboard.

Crouching at Fletcher's feet, the monster again fixed its yellow eyes on his sleeping face. Then it lunged.

"No!" Nim cried, struggling to climb to her paws.

The creature fell back. Shrieking in frustration, it jerked its head around. It narrowed its eyes at one of its trailing bandages that lay pinned to the bed by a handmade arrow.

Confusion spun in Nim's brain. How had one of

Fletcher's arrows come to be there? For a second, she wondered if she might be seeing things. Then she spied movement on the other side of the monster's big feet. A small gray rodent dressed in a piece of dirty sock skittered out with three more of the arrows clutched in his teeth. He dropped them onto the bedspread, then rose on his haunches. Gripping one of the weapons with his paws, he rammed it into another of the goblin's hanging bandages, just as he'd rammed the rats' garden-stake boundary marker into the ground a few days ago.

"Rhett?" Nim's heart swelled with elation.

The enraged monster swiped out its webbed hand as Rhett ducked and drove an arrow into one of its long, hairy feet, eliciting a howl of pain from the creature.

"Stay back, thou rankest compound of villainous smell that ever offended nostril!" Rhett commanded. "I'm not going to let you hurt Nimbus's friend!" He plunged another arrow into its other foot, and the demon shrieked. It swung its hairy arms, slashing out with its clawed hands. But Rhett had already shot off to gather more arrows from the jar on the bedside table.

"Rhett! You're alive!" Nim climbed to her wobbly legs, hope reenergizing her. "I thought you were dead!"

"The angry nightmare lady thought so too," he muttered

around a mouthful of arrows. He dropped them clattering to the bed. "It was just part of my plan to launch a surprise attack, and my best death scene performance ever, if I do say so myself." Then he leaped away, dodging another swoop of the snarling beast's paw.

Nim crouched low, trying to gather enough strength to jump up and assist Rhett, but she paused, unsure what she was seeing.

The upper half of the demon's body flickered; its colors faded to gray, then dissolved into a sooty, smoky shape. Its lower half remained in its goblin-like form, though, as if it couldn't free itself from the arrows holding its feet in place. Its smoky upper half tried to pull away, but it remained bound to the lower part of its body.

Rhett wove around the half-mist, half-solid beast, snatching up arrows and plunging them into its loose bandages and furry feet. Then he scampered off to gather more weapons.

The frantic monster's hazy portion solidified again, and it howled in pain and fear. It tried to lunge away, but it was pinned firmly in place, and it toppled forward instead. Not wasting a moment, Rhett thrust an arrow into the webbing of one of its hands, then into its other, resulting in more demonic shrieks.

Deciding Rhett needed no help, Nim stood. Her wounds throbbed, her stomach churned, and her head pounded, but she forced herself onward. She scrambled up Fletcher's desk and limped to the window. She rose on her hind legs, swaying as the room seemed to tilt around her. Then she touched a paw to the slats of the blinds and looked back at the bed.

The trapped and screeching demon peered over its shoulder at her, its monstrous face pinched with fear.

Nim pushed her paw down, forcing the blinds apart.

Outside, the gray sky had grown lighter, now streaked with swaths of light blue and pink.

The nightmare goblin's eyes bulged at the sight. Its fanged mouth dropped open.

Stretching and yawning, Aunt Caroline sat up. She gazed down at herself, blinking in puzzlement. "Why am I on the floor?" She glanced up, and her eyes fell on Rhett zipping back and forth atop Fletcher's bed. "A rat!" she shrieked. Then she caught sight of the crouching nightmare demon. "No, no, no, no," she whimpered. She scrambled away, crawling across the room and snatching up Nim's green pillow bed, then holding it before her like a shield.

But the monster wasn't interested in Aunt Caroline. Bucking like a bull and shrieking like a banshee, it fought to escape its bonds as Rhett scurried around, forcing down any arrows that jiggled loose.

Nim's strength was fading, and her limbs trembled with effort, but she refused to release her hold on the blinds.

The world outside grew steadily brighter, and finally, a beam of sunlight broke through the grayness. It rushed through the window and pierced the creature like a spear made of gold.

The nightmare demon uttered one last screech, then burst into a spray of ash.

A cloud of gritty particles lingered in the air for a moment before silently drifting down like burnt snowflakes. As soon as they touched the bedspread, they vanished.

Two flickering beads of light remained hovering. Then they glided toward Fletcher and disappeared into his slightly opened mouth.

CHAPTER 33

Nim released the window blinds. She crouched on the desk, panting and trying to regain her strength.

"Nim?"

Fletcher sat up in bed, peering at her. The color had returned to his face. The dark circles had faded from under his eyes. Each breath he took was less rattled. Except for the red scratches on his cheek, there was little indication he'd been so close to death.

Nim gave a contented thump of her tail.

"Nim!" he cried, sitting up straighter and pulling his eyeglasses on. "It's really you!" He tried to climb from the bed, then slumped back against the headboard. He took a few gasps of air. "I'm so glad to see you!"

Still huddled in the corner, Aunt Caroline lowered the

pillow-bed shield. "Nim," she whispered, her eyes wide and glassy. "You saved us. You and . . ." She pointed a shaky finger at Rhett sitting up on the foot of Fletcher's bed. "You and that rat." She frowned. "Is it wearing . . . a sock?"

Nim wanted to go to Fletcher, to rub her cheek against his and groom the hair sticking up on his head, but she had more work to do. She jumped off the desk.

"Nim?" he said.

She didn't turn back as she limped through the doorway. Who knew how long the Ways of Magic would let her stay before returning her to Agatha's. Now might be her only chance to keep him safe.

"Hey, Nimbus?" Rhett asked as he caught up to her hobbling down the staircase. "Where are we going?"

"We have to destroy the other nightmare demon."

"Oh." He shook his head with awe and disbelief. "I have to say, we never had this much excitement in the dump."

In the downstairs office, they stepped over Fletcher's prized arrow that had been knocked to the floor by the demon. Then they stopped before the tall shelf. As Nim stared up at the ancient clay jar, a snarl escaped her throat. She motioned toward the window. "Rhett, can you make an opening in the blinds when the demon appears?"

He nodded and scurried off.

Blood seeped from Nim's wounds; pain and sickness

weighed her down. "You can rest soon," she whispered to herself as she climbed to the top of the shelf.

Across the room, Rhett sat up on the windowsill, watching her with his bright eyes.

She drew to a stop before the ancient sand-colored jar, gazing at the image of the skull-like, saber-toothed nightmare demon painted upon it, and a clever idea occurred to her. Hoping her plan would work, she allowed herself a tremble of fear, recalling the three demons that had attempted to steal her life force in the place where nightmares dwell.

With her heart pounding, she pressed her front paws against the jar, and a lonely coldness seeped through the pads of her feet. A musty, malevolent odor filled her nose.

She glanced at Rhett, and he gave her another nod.

Nim shoved the old clay jar as far as her limbs would stretch. It came to a stop at the lip of the shelf.

She inched closer. Recalling Bianca's amusement for pushing things over the edge, she shoved the jar again and it tumbled down to the tile floor, crashing in an explosion of clay shards.

The room grew cold. An ancient, malicious stench mushroomed in the air. A shiver rippled the fur bristling on Nim's back.

A shadowy column of fog rose from the debris, twisting and curling like a wisp of gritty smoke. It climbed higher, gliding to the top shelf, then swirled around her head. She squeezed her eyes shut, envisioning the horrible nightmare demons with their elongated heads, daggerlike teeth and claws, and greedy gazes. Ghostly fingers seemed to seep into her head, prodding and searching her mind.

With her pulse thundering in her ears, Nim scrambled away as the smoky form followed her to the floor. It circled around to face her; the shadowy mass twisted and churned, thickening and solidifying, growing into the shape of the thing she feared most when she had released the demon.

Rhett's mouth hung open as he stood motionless on the windowsill.

"Get ready," Nim whispered to him.

The last tendril of smoke vanished, and an earless, tailless, leathery-skinned creature stood facing her—as if straight from the nightmare realm. It crouched on its thick-clawed paws, the glowing yellow eyes in its elongated head glaring at her—just as she'd planned.

"What the heck is that thing?" Rhett muttered, his face twisting with confusion.

Nim gave him the signal.

He scuttled up the blinds and leaped onto one of the dangling cords. But nothing happened.

Growling and hunching its shoulders, the monster crept toward Nim.

"Rhett?" Nim said as she took a step backward.

"They're not opening! I need a moment to figure—" Nim missed the rest of his words as the creature lunged at her. She snarled and struck at its face with her clawed paw, but the beast slung its head to the side. Before she could take another swing, it struck out its own large paw and knocked her to the floor.

Nim cried out as more of her stitches popped free, sending a stream of blood seeping from her wound. Suddenly, the beast was upon her, holding her down with its paw.

Nim growled as the nightmare demon hissed into her ear, "Ah, a familiar. Lucky for me another liberator arrived so quickly." It crouched lower and pressed a thick claw to Nim's forehead. The last of her strength drained away as the monster whispered the ancient, menacing words that had been spoken over Fletcher.

Panic raced through Nim. This had not been part of her plan. She willed herself to get up, but her jaw dropped open instead. Something inside her gave a sharp tug, then tore away, leaving behind a cold, empty space. A tiny droplet of light drifted out of her mouth and hovered in the air.

With its toothy maw stretched wide, the nightmare demon leaned forward, eager to gulp down the flickering bead of life force. But instead of biting down, it screeched and whirled around.

Fletcher stood behind it, his hands gripping the end of the stone-tipped arrow he'd retrieved from the floor and plunged into the demon's leathery side.

Snapping its jagged teeth, the creature released its hold on Nim. It stumbled as it slunk toward Fletcher. The tiny sphere of light floated back into Nim, returning her warmth and renewing her strength. She struggled to her feet.

As Fletcher slowly backed away, the monster fixed its furious gaze on him. With the arrow still protruding from its abdomen, and with its legs wobbling, it prepared to pounce. Nim leaped in front of it, arching her back and bristling her black fur. She slashed out with her clawed paw, raking it across the side of the demon's face and through one of its glowing yellow eyes.

The creature howled in anger, and a flash of light flared in her head, blurring her vision for a moment.

"Oh! Wrong string!" Rhett cried. He leaped onto the adjacent cord and wrapped his paws around it, and as his weight pulled him downward, the slats of the blinds flipped open.

Bright morning sunlight flooded the room and washed over the demon. The monster managed to emit a brief, high-pitched shriek like a boiling teakettle. Then it burst into a cloud of tiny pieces.

The grainy particles floated to the floor and faded into nothingness.

Trembling with relief and exhaustion, Nim dropped onto her belly and rested her heavy head on her paws.

"Nim!" Fletcher crouched beside her. His hair stood out at all angles, and his wizard pajamas were rumpled.

Aunt Caroline leaned against the doorway, her face blanching with horror.

Fletcher stroked Nim's nose. "Nim, you smart, brave cat!"

Unable to lift her head, she answered with a thump of her tail.

He peered at her face. "Your eye! It's yellow. Just like in our dream!"

Her plan to regain the dream sight had worked, but she had no strength left for a reply.

"Nim?" he whispered. "Are you okay?"

Rhett skittered across the floor to them.

With shaking hands, Aunt Caroline switched on the overhead light, illuminating the rest of the room. Taking a deep breath, she ran her troubled gaze over Fletcher, Nim, Rhett, the handmade arrow, and the ancient jar's broken shards.

As Nim rested her eyes on Fletcher and Rhett, contentment settled upon her. She was pleased to have the two of them with her and relieved that Fletcher was safe. Her vision began to dim, though, and her breaths grew shallow. With a sinking heart, she realized the nightmare demon's poison was doing its work. She smiled sadly as her eyelids lowered half-shut. She would miss her two friends.

Rhett lay down beside her and rested his head against her ragged fur.

"Nim?" Fear overtook Fletcher's voice. He leaned closer, observing her many wounds. "We have to get her some help!" he called to Aunt Caroline. "We have to get her to Dr. Glass!"

"It's too early. Dr. Glass won't be in yet." Aunt Caroline held her hand out, motioning for him to stay put. "Wait there. I'll make some quick phone calls. I'll find someone who can see her right now."

Nim grew lighter, feeling as though she were drifting away. But there was no purple sky and white crescent moon where she was headed.

She was going somewhere beyond the dream realm.

CHAPTER 34

The doorbell chimed, loud and startling in the silence.

"Who in the world can that be at this time of the morning?" Aunt Caroline frowned. "Don't worry," she said to Fletcher. "I'll get rid of them. Then we'll get Nim to someone who can help her." She hurried from the room.

"You're going to be okay, girl." Fletcher stroked Nim's nose again.

Nim closed her eyes. In the distance, she heard Aunt Caroline open the front door. Angry words passed between her and another woman. The woman declared that she didn't give a darn what Aunt Caroline would or would not allow. She was coming inside.

A moment later, the visitor entered the room. Nim's nose twitched at the smell of parsley, cilantro, mint, and catnip. As if by magic, the aromas tugged her back toward the physical world. She opened her eyes, pleased to see Agatha's wrinkled, tanned face and silver owl amulet peering down at her. Agatha swept her gaze to Rhett on the floor next to Nim. "I see you're still sticking close to your friend." She gave him a small nod of approval.

"Um," was all Fletcher seemed to be able to say.

Agatha turned her eyes on him, taking in his wizard pajamas, round eyeglasses, and messy hair. She studied his face for a second, and her eyebrows shot up with surprise. "Well," she muttered. "That certainly explains things." She motioned to his father's large desk. "Clear those items away."

Fletcher hopped up. "Who are you?" he asked as he swept his father's books, lamp, and pencil cup from the desktop. They clattered to the floor, eliciting a gasp from Aunt Caroline in the doorway.

Agatha set a worn and cracked leather medical bag on the desk and returned her attention to Fletcher. "My name's Agatha."

Fletcher cleared his throat nervously. "I'm Fletcher."

"A maker of arrows," she muttered as she unlatched the black medical bag.

He furrowed his brow. "How'd you know I make arrows?"

"I didn't." She glanced up. "It's the meaning of your name."

"Oh," he whispered. "That's an amazing coincidence."

Agatha shook her head. "It's no coincidence. It's the Ways of Magic."

"The Ways of Magic?" He furrowed his brow again.

"A power that steers objects and living beings to where they need to be, or who they need to be." She shrugged. "It's also an energy that can be drawn from, and one that'll impart guidance when requested." She rummaged inside the medical bag, then took out a few small brown bottles and set them on the desk. "When I couldn't find Nimbus, I suspected that awful woman had taken her and might try to hurt her or make her sick again." She glowered at Aunt Caroline.

Aunt Caroline's mouth dropped open. "I never! I never tried to hurt Nim or make her sick!"

"Hmph." Agatha held her glare on the woman a little longer, then dug around in the medical bag again and pulled out a small pair of scissors, a tin of hawthorn ointment, a roll of gauze, a curved needle, and a spool of thick blue thread. "After a bit of research, I was able to find an address that was linked to the phone number on Nimbus's ID tag," she said.

Fletcher's eyes filled with sudden understanding. "You're the witch Nim mentioned in our dream walk!"

"Witch?" Aunt Caroline's hand flew to her chest, and a horrified expression filled her face. She took a step back, out of the doorway and into the hall.

"Dream walk, huh?" Agatha pursed her lips. "Well, that's interesting." She pointed at the desk. "Set Nimbus here."

Fletcher carefully lifted Nim off the floor.

Nim's wounds pulsed with pain, but she didn't cry out. Rhett watched, his whiskers drooping with worry while Fletcher carried her to the desk and gently set her down.

As Nim lay stretched on her side, Agatha examined her eyes, mouth, and limbs. "Poison," she muttered bitterly, "*again*." She cast another glare at Aunt Caroline.

"I didn't poison Nim. I swear!" Aunt Caroline anxiously twisted her fingers. "And it wasn't really me who drove to your house early this morning and argued with you. I only remember bits of it really, as if it were a horrible nightmare." She looked at them pleadingly. "It was as though I couldn't control what I was doing."

"Hmph." Agatha scowled as she pulled the dropper from one of the small bottles.

Rhett had quietly climbed to the top of the desk and crouched down, keeping a worried watch over Nim.

Fletcher stroked Nim's nose. "Can you help her?" he asked Agatha.

"Yes, I can. I did it before, and I'll do it again." Agatha peered down at Nim. "Take this, Nimbus. It'll counteract the poison's effects. You'll be feeling better soon."

Nim didn't fight or resist as Agatha lifted her chin and squeezed a cold dribble of liquid into her mouth. A minty sort of flavor coated her tongue, and trusting Agatha, she swallowed it down.

"It *was* me who took Nim away," Aunt Caroline blurted from where she stood in the doorway. She hung her head. "And I left her at the dump." Her lip trembled. "But now I know Nim would never hurt you."

Fletcher's face clouded over. "I don't understand why you would do such a terrible thing."

"I thought it was for your own good," she mumbled. "Please forgive me."

"I don't know if I can," he replied.

"I'll make it up to you." Aunt Caroline sniffled. "And to Nim too." With shoulders drooping, she slowly approached the desk. As Rhett skittered away to a far corner, keeping his shiny eyes on her, she gazed down at Nim. "I'm sorry, Nim. Truly sorry." She gave her fingers another anxious twist.

"Hmph," Agatha muttered again.

Aunt Caroline turned to Fletcher. "I'll give Nim lots of treats and gourmet food, and I'll buy her toys." She nodded.

"Yes, lots of toys. And catnip too! Anything you think she might want."

Fletcher's only reply was to cross his arms and scowl at her.

Nim knew the woman regretted what she had done. Nim could see, hear, and even smell her remorse. But her cruel actions didn't matter anymore. Fletcher was safe. That was the *only* thing that mattered.

"I'm sorry, Nim," Aunt Caroline repeated.

Nim gave a small thump of her tail to indicate her forgiveness.

"That's very generous of you, Nim." Fletcher petted her head and scowled at his aunt again.

Aunt Caroline offered him a hopeful smile. Then she pointed at Rhett. "I'll even give her rat friend some cheese, and a new sock too if he wants."

Agatha narrowed her eyes at Aunt Caroline. "You stink."

"What?" Aunt Caroline's eyes widened.

"You smell like the dump."

Aunt Caroline sniffed her collar and wrinkled her nose. Then she glanced down, whimpering at the sight of dark smudges and dried spaghetti noodles clinging to her sweater. With her cheeks burning pink, she backed away to her place near the door.

As Agatha pulled the dropper from another one of the brown bottles, she scrutinized Fletcher again. "Yes, it makes sense now," she mumbled.

"What makes sense?" he asked.

Nim didn't understand the meaning of her words either.

Agatha held the full dropper to Nim's lips and looked into her eyes. "This will dull the pain of your injuries, but it won't make you sleep. I think you need to hear what I have to say."

Nim swallowed the medicine. It wasn't as pleasant as the minty-tasting drops, but not as bad as what Agatha gave her the first time she tended to her wounds.

"Nimbus is a familiar," Agatha said. "A witch's protector and assistant."

Nim's stomach tightened with dread. And while the medicine was already dulling the pain of her injuries, it couldn't dull her disappointment and distress. She liked Agatha very much, she'd even grown quite comfortable around her, but she didn't want to be taken back to the cottage to live there as her familiar. All she wanted was to stay here with Fletcher.

"Yeah, Nim told me she was a familiar." Fletcher's shoulders slumped. "I guess that means she has to live with you." He exhaled a long, dejected sigh. "But . . . could I at least come visit her sometimes?"

"That won't be necessary," Agatha said. "It's the reason she kept trying so hard to get home."

Fletcher scrunched his eyebrows in confusion, but Nim's heart jumped with hope. She held her breath, eager to hear more yet dreading what words might come next.

"The Ways of Magic draws the witch and the familiar together," Agatha explained.

Fletcher shook his head. "I don't understand."

"What's to understand? Witch and familiar always find one another." Agatha pressed her lips together. "Nimbus was trying to get home to her witch."

"What?" Aunt Caroline exclaimed from the doorway. She shook her head vigorously. "I'm not a witch!"

Agatha rolled her eyes. "Not you, you empty-headed harpy." She jutted her chin toward Fletcher. "Him. He's the witch. Or warlock if you prefer that term. Both names are applicable for such magical beings."

Nim could hardly believe Agatha's words. A joyous grin filled her face. She was a familiar, and Fletcher was her witch! If she'd had the strength, she would've leaped up and rubbed her cheek against Fletcher's, and maybe against Agatha's too.

"I'm a witch?" Fletcher's eyes grew round with wonder

behind the lenses of his glasses. "I can do magic?" Then he shook his head doubtfully. "But how? No one else in my family is a witch."

Agatha shrugged. "Who are we to question the Ways of Magic? What I can tell you, though, is you are a witch, and Nimbus is your familiar. And that is that."

Fletcher ran a shaky hand through his messy hair. "Are you sure?"

Agatha drew her shoulders up. "I'm quite capable of recognizing magical children. I taught a school of young witches for many years." She pointed a finger at him. "*You* are a green witch."

"I think I'll just go. . . ." Aunt Caroline frowned down at her clothing, gave her collar another sniff, and grimaced. "I'll just go get cleaned up."

Agatha cut her eyes toward her. "That would be for the best."

Aunt Caroline turned and shuffled away.

"What's a green witch?" Fletcher asked.

"Green witches draw their powers from the elements of nature, like plants, animals, stones, and even the celestial bodies." She snipped off a piece of gauze, doused it with liquid from one of the brown bottles, and set to work cleaning Nim's wounds. "Perhaps you find yourself drawn to such things or have experienced a few unusual occurrences with them?"

Fletcher shrugged. "Well, I like to collect rocks and fossils and old stone arrowheads." His gazed drifted down to the clay shards on the floor, and he wrinkled his forehead as he thought. "Actually . . . I think maybe something unusual did happen." His eyes widened as he returned his attention to Agatha. "No matter how hard I tried, I couldn't get the stopper out of a magical old jar like that one." He pointed at the shattered remains. "But when I tapped it with a rock, it suddenly came right out. Almost as though the rock had acted as some sort of key that unlocked it." He sighed unhappily. "Though, it would've been better if I'd left the thing sealed."

And as Agatha tended to Nim's wounds, Fletcher told her about the nightmare demons and how Nim and her rat friend had defeated them, and how Nim could talk to him in his dreams. Agatha listened, sometimes raising her eyebrows in surprise. When he finished, she squinted at him. "Where's your protection amulet?"

He shrugged. "I don't think I have one."

"Of course you do. Every witch has an amulet with the power to weaken evil, and they always keep it nearby, even those who don't yet know they're witches. You'd have encountered your amulet as soon as your powers began to manifest, so that creatures like these nightmare demons wouldn't be drawn to your life force. It'd be something of great importance to you, something that feels valuable. Perhaps it's an item that was handed down from an older family member, maybe it was a gift from a friend, or something that you found."

"Oh!" He dashed over and retrieved the arrow from the floor. "I stabbed the nightmare demon with this, but I normally keep it hanging on the wall in my room." He pointed to the old arrowhead on the end of it. "I found it in the woods. Do you think it could be my protection amulet?"

"I most certainly do." Agatha nodded. "But you should keep it on you, not on that stick. An amulet works best when it's worn near the heart." She wiped her hands on the front of her long gray apron, then fixed her gaze on Nim. "I won't bother bandaging you." She shook a finger at her. "But you have to promise not to pull out the stitches."

Nim flicked her tail in reply.

"One last thing," Agatha said to Fletcher. "Where's Nimbus's collar?"

"It's right here." He reached into the top pocket of his wizard pajamas and pulled out the green collar with the nazar still attached to it. "I found it upstairs." He clicked it into place around Nim's neck, and Nim smiled happily. "I guess you gave her the nazar?" he asked Agatha.

Agatha sighed. "It was my attempt to provide her with

a protection amulet." She frowned down at all Nim's injuries. "I'm not sure it worked very well, though. You might want to replace it with something else."

"But I think it did work," Fletcher said. "Nim's going to be okay." He grew quiet, thinking for a moment. "Don't nazars also draw good luck?"

"Yes. That's another one of their attributes."

Fletcher grinned. "Well, Nim found her way home, brought a rat friend with her, defeated two monsters, and then we learned that I'm a witch and she's my familiar. I think maybe the lucky part of her protection amulet's working very well."

Nim thought that maybe he was right. She began to purr loud and rumbly, never having felt so happy and hopeful in her life.

"Or maybe the nazar had nothing to do with those things." Agatha petted the top of Nim's head. "Maybe you've just been lucky all along, Nimbus." Then she reached into her medical bag and withdrew Nim's small gold ID tag. She attached it to the collar, alongside the nazar. "You're home now," she murmured.

Nim replied her thanks with a slow blink, and the sound of her purring grew even louder.

Agatha gave a sad sigh as she packed up her medical bag. "I wish some of your luck would rub off on me and help reunite me with my—" She sighed again and picked up her bag. "It was nice meeting you, Fletcher. And you too, Nimbus, as well as you, Mr. Rat," she said to Rhett. She turned to go but paused and looked back at Fletcher. "If you and your familiar would like a bit of magical training, have your parents give me a call." She pulled a green business card from one of the pockets on her apron and handed it to him. "Goodbye," she said. Then she left.

Nim stretched her paws out before her on top of the desk. Rhett skittered over and huddled next to her. Fletcher stood on her other side, stroking the top of her head. They watched through the window as Agatha left the house and headed down the sidewalk. She'd made it halfway there when the silvery-gray tabby emerged from the hedges and stopped in front of her.

Agatha halted and stared down at the cat. The cat stared up at her.

Agatha crouched, and the cat stepped closer.

"Hey, look at that! The stray cat's not afraid of Agatha," Fletcher said. "I wonder what she's saying to it."

But Nim's feline hearing was keen enough to make out her words perfectly.

"Grimalkin?" Agatha asked. "Is it really you?"

The cat sat, wrapped her tail around her feet, and blinked her green eyes at Agatha.

Agatha held her hand out, and the cat lifted her paw and pressed it to Agatha's palm.

With a cry of happiness, Agatha dropped her bag and scooped her up. She rose to her feet, hugging the cat to her chest, resting her cheek against the top of her head. Then she turned toward the window, seeming to know Nim, Rhett, and Fletcher were watching. Her eyes shimmered with tears, and she smiled.

Nim smiled back. Maybe her good luck had rubbed off on Agatha after all.

As Fletcher watched the reunion of the witch and her familiar, he wrinkled his forehead. "It almost seems like they know each other." He turned to Nim with a questioning look, and Nim gave him a slight nod. She would tell him all about Grimalkin in their next dream walk. She would tell him about many things. They had much to discuss.

With a crooked smile lighting his face, Fletcher leaned down and scratched her ear. She rubbed her cheek against the side of his face, mingling her scent with his, creating the reassuring smell that always comforted her. Then she rested her head on her paws, purring softly as contentment settled over her. All was right in her world.

EPILOGUE
NEARLY SEVEN MONTHS LATER

The October morning sun shone down on Nim as she trotted through the back garden of the renovated Whittaker mansion, the big house that now served as a school for a new generation of young green witches.

Gone were the overgrown tangles. Bird and bat houses stood in their place. The toppled birdbath had been set upright and filled with clean water. The rats' boundary markers had also been removed, but Agatha hadn't neglected them. When the front-lawn dump was cleaned up, she had a special habitat created for the colony, and her seven students enjoyed bringing the rodents fresh apples, carrots, and other healthy foods, as well as rawhide for them to gnaw on and soft fleece for them to use as bedding material.

The gold tag and nazar softly jingled on Nim's collar as she headed toward the newly constructed herb-drying shed. Across the way, Abraxas and Striker chased one another around the trunk of an elder tree. Nearby, Fern stared up at a squirrel, licking her lips hungrily as it scolded her from the branch of an old oak.

"Hello, Fern!" Nim called.

"Hello, Nimbus," Fern replied, her eyes never losing sight of the squirrel.

To Nim, this morning felt like part of a happy dream, but it wasn't. Now that Fletcher was attending school at the Whittaker mansion, this had become her new life.

She smiled as she passed the lush beds of chamomile, mint, fennel, and lemon balm—some of the herbs the students were using to create healing teas. Agatha's green magic had enabled the plants to grow faster and thicker. Fletcher didn't care much for tea making, claiming he wasn't very good at it. Nim thought the ones he'd brewed yesterday smelled wonderful, though, despite him saying they looked more like mud-puddle water.

What Fletcher really liked was working with rocks, minerals, and shells. It was his specialty. He enjoyed glimpsing supernatural creatures through the holes in fairy stones, drawing energy from crystals, and listening to the wisdom of the ocean whispered inside of seashells. He'd even grown very good at casting and reading rune stones.

Nim pushed open the door of the herb-drying shed. The aromas of viburnum, lilac, honeysuckle, and peppermint swelled inside her nose. She leaped onto the worktable and grasped a small bundle of toadflax, careful to carry it by the thick bands of twine wrapped around the stalks. Agatha had sent her to fetch it for that morning's lesson on the preparation of foot-rash ointments. Nim swished her tail proudly. Retrieving small items was one of her many duties as a familiar-in-training.

Clutching the bundle between her teeth, she scampered away, through the garden, up the steps, and through the cat flap set in one of the back doors.

She emerged inside the library, the wood-paneled room that was furnished floor to ceiling with mahogany shelves brimming with books old and new. She wound her way around the assortment of floor lamps and comfortable sofas and chairs and toward Fletcher, who'd also been sent on an errand by Agatha.

On a shelf just above Fletcher's head, Rochester strolled along the Divination section, past the copies of *Aeromancy for the Beginner*, *Austromancy in North America*, and *Ophiomancy Through the Ages*. He stopped at the Infections and Allergies section and nudged a thick book with the tip of his nose.

Fletcher reached up, his arrowhead amulet swaying from a cord around his neck as he withdrew the heavy volume. "Thanks, Rochester." He grinned and ruffled the top of the cat's gray head. Rochester squeezed his eyes shut, apparently pleased.

Nim grinned too. Rochester was enjoying his life at the new school as the official library cat. The students often asked for his assistance when they couldn't locate a particular book. And they always rewarded him with generous amounts of pets and praise.

With the small bunch of toadflax still clutched in her mouth, Nim trotted out of the library, and Fletcher followed with *The Encyclopedia of Pimples, Rashes, and Assorted Fungal Infections* tucked beneath his arm. He hummed happily as they made their way through the mansion and into the glass-ceilinged conservatory, where they rejoined Agatha, Grimalkin, and the other six student witches and their familiars.

He handed the book to Agatha, who stood at the head of a long wooden table. She still wore her green gardening boots, but her dress was now purple instead of mauve, and she'd replaced her old gray apron with a bright yellow one. The silvery-striped Grimalkin sat straight and tall beside her on the tabletop. "Thank you, Fletcher," Agatha said as he returned to his spot among his witch friends gathered around the table.

Nim hopped up and dropped the bundle of yellow-flowered stalks before her. "Well done, Nimbus." Agatha gave her a smile. Nim bumped a nose greeting with Grimalkin, then returned to take her seat on the tall wooden stool next to Fletcher, just as all the other familiars were doing, sitting straight and tall beside their witch.

She ran her eyes over the variety of protection amulets dangling from the cats' collars as well as the ones worn by the young witches. Agatha had helped them discover each unique amulet.

In front of every student sat a small iron cauldron hanging over a tiny burner. Alongside those lay assorted dried herbs, leaves, and stems; mortars and pestles; pitchers of water; and a selection of mixing and measuring spoons.

"Before we begin," Agatha announced, but she was interrupted by Bianca leaping onto the table. Swishing her tail and wearing a mischievous grin, she scampered past the students, batting leaves, stems, and mixing spoons to the floor. Despite the students' half-hearted cries of protest, Nim smiled. Bianca was so much more pleasant now, and often even friendly. Nim had no doubt the return of Grimalkin was responsible for thawing the cat's icy attitude.

Agatha shooed Bianca away. "Before we begin," she repeated, "please take a moment to make sure you have all your tools and supplies on hand." She arched an eyebrow at Fletcher and a few of the other students.

"Oops," Fletcher muttered. "I forgot one of my measuring spoons."

Nim rose to her paws.

"It's the teaspoon," he said. "Do you know where it is?"

She bumped her head against his arm as a reply, and before she could leap down from the stool, he scratched her beneath the chin. "Thanks, Nim. You're the best familiar a witch could ever hope for."

She gave him a wink, knowing without a doubt he was the smartest and most talented witch a familiar could ever hope for. Then she scampered off, hurrying up the grand staircase to the student rooms on the second floor.

Inside Fletcher's bedroom, she passed the basket of cat toys Aunt Caroline had given her. The woman had been trying very hard to make things up to her and Fletcher and to earn their forgiveness. She'd also taken to sewing little costumes for Rhett—much to his delight—as well as driving him back to the city every Saturday for his appearances on Fletcher's father's horror host show. Ever since he began his costarring role, the program's ratings had soared. Rhett had truly become a star.

"Hi, Nimbus!" Rhett waved at her from atop Fletcher's desk.

She hopped up and joined him. "Hi, Rhett," she replied as she stepped over the scattering of crystals, runes, tweezers, tongs, and assorted spoons. She grinned as she glanced down at the latest edition of *Rat Fancy Magazine* lying there. It had arrived yesterday, and on its cover appeared a photo of Rhett dressed as a tiny mad scientist, one of the costumes Aunt Caroline had made for him.

"Which one do you think I should wear on the next show?" He held up a tiny black hat and a tiny gray one. "The Phantom of the Opera's fedora, or the Invisible Man's fedora?"

Nim shrugged. "I don't know. They both look pretty good to me."

He furrowed his brow. "The Phantom ensemble would require a black cloak," he mumbled to himself, "but I wore a black cloak a few episodes ago when I dressed as a vampire."

Smiling, Nim left him to his deliberations. With the teaspoon grasped between her teeth, she jumped off the desk. On her way out of the room, she padded past Fletcher's assortment of cauldrons and potted plants, then past the moon-gazing mirror leaning against the wall. Pausing, she peered into its reflective surface, pleased at the sight of her green and yellow eyes staring back. She knew she was lucky to possess such a rare ability as dream walking.

She turned to leave but stopped again, this time eyeing her comfy green bed. Maybe she would take a nice long nap after lunch. Lately, she'd been sleeping so soundly and trouble-free that she seldom ended up at her crossroads to seek Hecate's guidance. Maybe during that nap, she'd travel there just to have a chat with the goddess and tell her about all the good things that had been happening.

Still clutching the teaspoon in her mouth, Nim hurried out of the room and back down the grand staircase.

As she descended the last step, she cast her gaze at the mansion's front door. It'd been a while since she'd been afraid of the world outside. She knew it was still filled with bad things, but she'd learned there was good in the world too and that sometimes you had to embrace the adventure that was life.

With shoulders held high, she walked with confidence back to the conservatory and back to her witch, knowing she was indeed one very lucky black cat.

ACKNOWLEDGMENTS

It takes the support of many friends and family members to get a story written. It takes the support of many professionals to get that story published and out into the world. My deepest thanks to all of them.

To my husband, Charlie Eldredge, thank you for your love and encouragement and for taking care of absolutely everything while I was trying to find my way through Nim's worlds. To my kids, Jamie Eldredge, Chase Eldredge, and Savannah Eldredge, and to my brother and brother-in-law, Tym (Tibby) Holley-Byrd and Richard (Ricket) Holley-Byrd, thank you for your love and enthusiasm.

Heartfelt thanks to my magnificent literary agent, Elena Giovinazzo, and to all the Pips at Pippin Properties: Holly McGhee, Sara Crowe, Ashley Valentine, Morgan Hughes, and Marissa Brown.

My sincerest gratitude to my most magical editors, Alessandra Balzer and Caitlin Johnson; to Devin Elle Kurtz for her gorgeous, otherworldly art; and to the rest of the dream team who worked on this book: Andrea Vandergrift, Amy Ryan, Robby Imfeld, Katie Boni, Sona Vogel, Lindsay Wagner, Mark Rifkin, Kerry Moynagh, Kathy Faber, Patty Rosati, Mimi Rankin, and Almeda Beynon.

To my writing family—the Inkies, the Croctopies, the OWLS, the Shredders, and others—thank you for your critiques, your cheerleading, and especially your friendship. I'm lucky to know you, Amy Paulshock, Taryn Souders, Leslie Santamaria, Ruth Owen, Marcea Ustler, Charlotte Hunter, Zebo Ludvicek, Jennye Kamin, Brian Truitt, Marlana Antifit, Rina Heisel, Peggy Jackson, Vivi Barnes, Dennis Cooper, Stephanie Spier, Mimi Powell, Lisa Iriarte, Joe Iriarte, Lynne Ryder, Alina Blanco, Mark Chick, Usman Malik, Evergreen Lee, Gary Lee, Ann Meier, Brian Crawford, Kimberly Lekman, Deepa Pailoor, Lara James, Barb Nefer, Charles Waters, Jonathan Rosen, Ed Masessa, and Linda Rodriguez Bernfeld.

And last, but certainly not least, warmest, cuddliest thanks to my feline inspirations over the years: Sinbad, Sparky, Mandy, Girlie, Jonesy, Buffy, Neo, Bingley, and Biddy.